Palette of the Soul

Palette of the Soul

MADDIE EVANS

Philangelus Press
Boston, MA

ISBN: 978-1-942133-57-5
Cover design by Once Upon a Cover
Editing by Charity Horniek
Section art by HailMarii Art

CHAPTER ONE

Lilah lived in a world of colors. She saw them, knew how they should sound, and understood how they would taste. She couldn't smell them because she was wearing a respirator mask to keep them from killing her.

Colors were reality, and acid dye powder was dangerous. That, in one sentence, was Lilah's world.

Beneath the high rafters of her barn, she worked at a plastic-lined table surrounded by floor lamps, adding powder into graduated beakers with a measuring spoon. Her hands were gloved, her eyes behind protective goggles. Across the table, water roiled in her electric kettle while more water heated to boiling in her six-quart pot. Above, thunder rumbled.

Beauty required a touch of peril.

Her phone rang on the table, and she side-eyed it. The number came up as Austin Young, manager of the Fruits de Mer restaurant, and, well, he could talk to her voicemail. Or he could hang up and text the way he should have in the first place. Not that Lilah had her hands free to reply to a text right now, either.

Instead she measured hot water into a clean beaker,

then began adding water to the dye powder a bit at a time. Stir. Add. Stir. Add. Blend the acid dye, then add more. At the end, with nearly all of the water in the dye beaker, she used a funnel to pour the dye into a squirt bottle, then swished the last of the clear water around the beaker to clear any remaining drops of dye. She poured that into the bottle as well.

She peeled off the proper label (*"1% Cerulean Blue"*) and measured out water for the next.

A text popped up. Austin. "We need to discuss the Crafters Guild exhibit."

She ignored it again because Austin had exactly one reason to talk to her in the first place, so this message gave her no additional information. She had so much to do. Not just mixing dyes for tonight's yarn-dyeing session, but also preparing for the Brighthead economic planning board meeting next week and handling more paperwork for the Brighthead Crafters Guild.

Fruits de Mer was wicked generous to exhibit the guild members' artwork in their waiting area. Tourist season was poised to start, and with it, the restaurant's busiest season. By featuring the BCG's artists on their walls—and making those pieces available for sale—Brighthead's only high-end restaurant could give a few local artists invaluable exposure at no cost to anyone.

Granted, they might be generous right now because the owner was madly in love with Lilah's friend Natalie, but generosity was generosity.

Thunder rolled again, even though Lilah hadn't seen any lightning.

While Lilah added water to the red dye, two more texts popped up. "I've gotten an insurance rider for the exhibit, so that's covered." Very good. No one would be arguing about priceless artwork if something got stolen. "Also, Emerson Charles doesn't want his slot any longer, so we'll need a new artist."

Lilah's brow furrowed. Emerson, backing out?

Emerson's paintings were brilliant. Someone must have

encountered his website and purchased every last one of them—and if so, good for him. What a wonderful world that would be, populated with patrons so overburdened by cash that they hunted down young artists and attempted to part them from their office jobs with bushels of twenties.

Come to think of it, that *would* be a wonderful world. Emerson could quit his job with the National Parks Service and paint full-time, decorating every home in Maine with object studies and visages of lakes and evening skies. People would see the natural world with new eyes, and, dazzled with wonder, they'd approach their everyday activities with a greater respect for their resources and one another.

Which was art at its finest, and the entire reasoning behind the BCG to begin with.

Still, though... What was up with Emerson?

Emerson's art was a natural pairing with Fruits de Mer. His high-end paintings would draw the attention of the restaurant's high-end tourists. During an hour-long wait for a table, surely some of those flatlanders' expensive taste would lead them to admire his work, take his business card, and maybe inquire about making a purchase.

Even more, Emerson deserved that kind of attention. He deserved name recognition and patronage. Though she'd only met him twice, she'd been struck both times by his perception, his sense of humor, and his ability to banter. His looks, too. He was a tall Black man with his hair in short dreadlocks, his eyes bright and his smile broad. Online, he was persuasive and always cut to the core of an argument. But most fascinating was the way he saw the world—or rather, the way he framed it. Emerson gave off an aura of vision. He saw reality, but he also saw potential.

Why would he back out now?

Did the BCG have other artists who could take his slot? Absolutely, but before calling them in, Lilah needed to talk to Emerson.

Before she could talk to Emerson, though, she needed her hands free and the respirator off her face. Which meant, in effect, not now.

Now was a time for colors, for mixing one percent solutions of the half-dozen dyes she'd need for tonight's yarn, and then for mixing and blending them in a way to enchant the spirits of knitters, crocheters, and weavers who would see her yarn and envision its fulfillment.

The barn door rolled open, and a moment later, Brooke wheeled her bicycle inside. Across the wide room, her voice echoed. "Is it safe?"

"Nope!" Mid-mixture, Lilah hoped her voice was audible through the respirator. Brooke knew the dyeing process, though, and wouldn't come over unless she heard an all-clear.

More thunder. The light flickered, and Lilah hoped she'd at least get the first skeins into the pot if the power went out. Maybe she should start those without waiting longer.

After unbuckling her bicycle helmet, Brooke settled against the wall on the far side of the barn and pulled a book from her backpack. That was Brooke, armed with either a book or knitting, or both. Lilah finished up the purple dye and moved on to the bronze she'd have to make by combining the powders herself. She checked her notes and began measuring.

Emerson. It was a great opportunity. He needed to take it.

When she'd mixed the last of the dyes, Lilah capped the powders and returned them to their cabinet, then removed the respirator. "We're safe," she called as she tugged the gloves off her manicured hands. She was getting tired of the orange and red and would probably change them tonight or tomorrow.

Brooke didn't look up. "I'll be there in a minute."

Lilah pulled her undyed skeins from the basin where they'd been soaking in tap water, and she wrung them out. The large pot was simmering, so she measured out the correct dye combination and added all six skeins.

Lilah's converted barn was the perfect home for an independent yarn-dyer. Behind a wall at the back end were a cluster of rooms that formed an apartment of sorts: her kitchen, a bathroom, a bedroom, and something that could have been a bedroom but was more of a storage room. And then this, the open space that could have housed six horses but instead served as her laboratory. In the hay loft, she could read or knit. At the opposite end were the rolling barn doors, open to a world that smelled of impending rain and electricity, plus the occasional breeze that felt like a kiss from the cosmos.

Lilah had strung the barn's interior with white lights, and she'd hung decorations from more than half of the wooden beams. Wind chimes, sun-catchers, and airborne sculptures twisted overhead whenever the wind beckoned. LED candles turned themselves on every night at six and turned off at eleven, filling the room with even more glittery light. During the daytime, the barn welcomed the world, and at night, it became a cathedral in honor of infinity.

Lilah added white vinegar to the dye vat, lowered the heat, and set a timer for twenty minutes. Then, finally, she had a chance to text Emerson. "What's going on with Fruits de Mer? I thought you were all set."

What if it was something awful? What if he was moving back to Boston? What if he was hurt or someone had stolen all his paintings?

Unnerved, Lilah sent a second text. "Are you okay? Do you need help? We can still make this happen, whatever it is that's going on."

Brooke closed her book and headed over. Peeking in the pot, she said, "Forest green?"

Hands shaking as she replaced her phone in her pocket, Lilah said, "Emerald. I got an order this morning for a sweater quantity of worsted—at least, I assume it's a sweater quantity—and I wanted to get that knocked out tonight so I could mail it by the weekend. Then while that's going on, I thought maybe I could play with some one-of-a-kind skeins." Lilah tried to flush the assorted images of Emerson out of her head— Emerson sick, or Emerson giving up painting. "What's up?"

Brooke pulled a box out of her backpack. Per usual, she was wearing fingerless gloves even though it was early May. "My mother mailed me a birthday gift, and now it's a gift for you."

Chocolate-covered cherries. Lilah angled the box in her hands. "Haven't you told her you don't like these?"

Brooke shrugged. "Only every year. 'No, Mom, I don't like them. I gave the box to Lilah. Again. Like I did last year when we had exactly this same conversation.' I'm at the point where I don't even want to thank her for them anymore."

Lilah frowned. "Why does she keep sending these?"

"It's my own fault for being picky. Everyone else can gag them down without the texture making them choke." Brooke shuddered. "It's still light out, and I figured I might as well rid my apartment of the box because every time I looked at it, I got frustrated."

Lilah said, "Next year, maybe you should have an online wish list."

"Already have one, with gift ideas at price points from two dollars to seventy-five, plus links, order of importance, and notes about why I like what I like." Brooke shrugged. "At least you can eat these."

"But you should get something that makes you feel special." Lilah looked at her dye. The yarn was picking up the color well, and she tested the water with her spoon. "What do you want to do for your birthday?"

"I feel like I should say going to Fruits de Mer because we'd get something comped." Brooke laughed, her eyes lighting up. "But in reality, I'd like pizza and a movie. Maybe we can re-watch the *Pride and Prejudice* mini-series."

Lilah said, "Sounds great! You, me, Natalie—who else?"

"Three people is enough of a party. Just, no chocolate-covered cherries." She looked into the dye pot. "Could we do something fun, too, like ice-dyeing the yarn or hand-painting some skeins?"

Lilah beamed. "We could try solar dyeing if you come over in the morning. Make a whole day of it. But we should invite more people."

Brooke shrugged. "I like things low-key."

Lilah had been trying since fifth grade to get Brooke more high-key, and it had never stuck. "At least this year, we don't have to invite Hal."

Brooke sniffed. "Although it would be fitting to torture my ex by making him solar-dye yarn. Could he have been more obvious last year how much he disliked being with us?"

"No." Lilah huffed. "He couldn't have. But now that he's gone, we could invite some of the BCG members, maybe try to fix you up with someone."

Brooke studied her. "Am I being unclear that three people is a perfectly good party? Also, I'm fine being single for now."

About to say, "We need to fix that," Lilah was interrupted by her phone ringing in her pocket.

"Hey!" she exclaimed. "Emerson Charles, my good sir! You're on speaker phone with me and Brooke."

The phone diminished the rich quality of his voice, but not the laughter. "Were you calling together a search party to hunt me down?"

Brooke said, "I was about to turn on the headlight on my bicycle and search the highways and byways. Either that, or I didn't know you were missing."

He chuckled. "Lilah's texts made her sound terrified. Nothing's wrong."

"Something's wrong," Lilah said, "or you wouldn't be pulling out of your exhibit slot."

Brooke said, "You're what? Why?"

The note in Brooke's voice drew Lilah up short.

Emerson sighed. "My artwork isn't a good fit for the restaurant. Someone else should have that slot."

Before Lilah even had time to draw breath, Brooke said,

"Absolutely not. Under no circumstance are you to pull out of that. It's an amazing opportunity, and we all agree you should have it."

Lilah added, "Brooke knows because she polled everyone on earth. Now you have no choice."

Brooke said, "You're a smart guy, but you're wrong. Your art will go amazing there."

Emerson said, "If the early exhibits don't get the good word out, we're not going to be able to get other restaurants and coffee shops to do the same kind of thing. I'm too much of a risk."

How could Emerson be a risk? Lilah decided to parry rather than argue. "Art is supposed to be risky. Beauty is risky. Sharing your heart is risky."

Emerson said, "I'm not willing to risk the guild's future."

Lilah said, "How about, as acting president of the guild, I personally am willing to stake the guild's future on your artwork?"

Emerson sighed. "I didn't decide this lightly."

Brooke said, "Don't you think we'll be by your side? If critics try to attack you, for some reason I cannot fathom, we'll be with you."

Lilah tried not to side-eye Brooke, but an idea blossomed in her brain and spread to her heart and then came out her mouth before she had a chance to formulate the whole plot. "Emerson, before we fight too much more, do you want to come here for Brooke's birthday party?"

Emerson sounded like he had whiplash from the sudden turn of conversation. "What?"

Brooke said, "She's saying 'birthday party' like we'll wear paper hats and hand out goodie bags. We're actually going to dye yarn and watch a movie."

"Pizza will be involved," Lilah added.

While talking to Emerson, Brooke's eyes had brightened. Her voice was surer. Her confidence had returned.

Brooke didn't have a whole lot of friends. She'd never made them easily, and the friends she'd shared with her ex-boyfriend were gone.

It was time to get her a new boyfriend—and Brooke already liked Emerson. At the two meetings of the Brighthead Crafters Guild, she'd stuck to his side the whole time.

Emerson was perfect: smart, artistic, perceptive... Lilah could go on about him all day. Based on this conversation, he was thoughtful and forward-looking as well, even though she disputed that what he foresaw would come to pass.

Lilah had never set up a couple before, but this looked like an unmatched blend of design and form. Like dyeing yarn, if you just add acid, the dye will strike.

"Say yes, Emerson," Lilah teased. "You know you want to."

"Fine," Emerson said. "Yes."

Brooke beamed. "That's the best birthday gift. You've given us an entire day when we can convince you to keep your art show."

Lilah stirred the yarn in her dye pot, and the water was clear. She turned off the heat to let it cool down before she would pull it out and rinse it. The dye had all gone into the yarn, and now Brooke's heart could go into Emerson's—a worthy man if she'd ever met one.

CHAPTER TWO

Emerson had figured Lilah would hound him for a reason, rather than just accepting his withdrawal. It was who she was.

He flipped on the lights in the bedroom that doubled as his art studio, staring at the paintings dominating every square inch of the walls, floor-to-ceiling, and seeing how every one of them wasn't good enough. The flaws jumped out at him—the way the light didn't sparkle just the way he'd envisioned, the color choices that were too muted, the way an entire landscape should have been reframed to draw the eye in a different way.

How could Lilah understand that? She dyed yarn in a pot, sold it, and left the creation aspect to others. The people who manufactured Emerson's paints and canvases didn't fret about what he did with the paint after it left the metal tube. They just hung around waiting to sell him more.

That wasn't entirely fair, though. Emerson clenched his fists and walked back into his kitchen. Lilah understood the art world, and anything she didn't understand already was something she immediately set about trying to learn.

On the BCG forums, she participated in multiple conversations where you could see at first she didn't comprehend the parameters of the art, and then abruptly during the conversation, her vocabulary would change. Suddenly, she'd adopted the lingo and had walked back her previous misconceptions. She'd recognized the gap between her experience and the artist's, and she'd done some research to expand her vision.

Emerson glanced at a painting on the kitchen wall. Speaking of expanding one's vision, he should have framed this image from further back, creating a better sweep for the eyes and a more amazing scope for the tree he'd wanted to highlight at the center.

His art wasn't on a par with the expectations of the rich tourists who'd bombard Brighthead in July. Well, the specific tourists who felt sufficiently overburdened with money to visit Fruits de Mer. Tourists who'd escaped their urban existence and their busy schedules were not interested in Emerson Charles, city transplant who'd found a government job that enabled him to paint trees in his spare time.

"You could get a government job here in Boston," Grandma had snapped when he'd announced he was moving to Acadia to be a park ranger. "Less bugs."

Not as many bugs, true, and no bears or coyotes. But after a childhood in Jamaica Plain, Emerson wanted out. He'd wanted to look around and see vistas, not buildings. He was tired of the sounds of cars, the scent of exhaust, the jostling, the advertisements. You couldn't rest your senses in JP. Always motion, always vigilance, always so many people to navigate around.

The National Parks Service offered a way out, and now here he was, with the grand title of "Assistant Program Manager," along with benefits and a salary that paid the rent on a one-bedroom apartment—which then got taken over by his easel, paints, chair, art books, sketchpads, computer, and a mile of plastic sheeting.

He slept on a futon in the living room...just in case

anyone wondered about his priorities.

Emerson returned to his easel, but his in-progress painting sat like a failed soufflé, flat and uninteresting. It was ugly. Everything was ugly. Patrons of the restaurant would look at these and think, "How ugly," and everyone would know.

He opened a bag of chips, then texted Lilah. "What should I bring for Brooke's birthday?"

Lilah didn't reply right away, but she'd said she was dyeing yarn, and surely at certain points, the process involved both her hands. Also, he'd need to ask about solar dyeing yarn, what that meant for how he should dress or what he should expect.

When no answer came after another few minutes, the silence grew too oppressive. Mom had called yesterday, so Emerson hit the button to call her back. She answered as if distracted. "Just returning your call," he said.

"Yes, now what was I calling you about...?" Mom laughed at herself. "I didn't maybe leave a hint on your voicemail, did I?"

Emerson laughed. "Tell me what's been going on, and maybe you'll remember."

"Oh, honey, it's been a mess." She was laughing, though, so it couldn't be that bad. She started the recap. His grandma had gone to another appointment with the cardiologist, and now her medication was adjusted down because she was doing so well. "Your grandma walks three miles a day, every day," Mom commented. "She only did two-and-a-half miles yesterday because it was raining, and then in the afternoon, she went back out again to do another half-mile because she said not doing it was making her grumpy."

Emerson laughed out loud. "She's going to outlive us all."

"Don't I believe it? Your dad's on the warpath with an insurance company that stopped covering the tablet form of some medication, only a lot of his customers cut that tablet in half to get the right dose, so he's calling the insurance company every day and asking for exact instructions on how you cut a capsule in half." Dad had been a pharmacy tech for years, and Emerson had heard so many variations on this theme that he could write the rest of the story himself. Dad wouldn't be able to get them to override their decision. People would either have to be undermedicated or overmedicated, or else they'd have to pay out of pocket and be under-cashed.

A text came in from Lilah, but Emerson let that sit. "What about you?"

Mom sighed. "Same old nonsense. One of the team leads is getting in everyone's hair and micromanaging, which is demoralizing the entire staff. Getting further behind means she gets more anxious and tries to micromanage them even more."

Emerson said, "Vicious cycle."

"I know, and I can't get her to believe me to just back off and trust the people she hired to get the work done."

Emerson shook his head. "That's how you get good employees to leave."

"You know it. How's your job? You still working things out with your manager?"

Emerson's mouth twitched. After two entire months in his new position, he hadn't gotten a sense of how his manager wanted him to do things. Every working day reminded him of a childhood trick he used to do on the playgrounds, where he'd walk up the see-saw until he was at the center, and then lean on his forward foot just enough to start the beam tilting over onto its other side. But then he'd lean back enough that the beam wouldn't go all the way down. If he balanced right in the center, not moving at all, he could keep the see-saw parallel to the ground, neither side touching, nothing swaying. But that meant he couldn't move, either.

Mom said, "Ellen's still on your case?"

She wasn't exactly on his case. She just wasn't...well... connecting. "I'll figure it out." He sighed, then noticed Lilah had texted him again. "How's Sonia?"

Maddie Evans

Mom said, "Oh! That's what I was calling about. Sonia's fine, but I'm worried."

Emerson sat on the futon. "What's going on?"

"She had another job interview, and they treated her terribly. They lined her up in a room with a dozen other candidates and left all of them sitting. After two hours, with no one knowing what was going on, she walked. Thirty minutes later, she got a text telling her to go inside, but by then she was halfway home."

Emerson's nose wrinkled. "She dodged a bullet."

"Her friend did stick around to see what would happen, and after they did the first interview, they told her that was a screen, and to go across town to where she might be able to talk to the real interviewer. I think they were testing applicants to see how bad they could treat them. That's when her friend bailed."

Emerson sighed. "You know, you laughed when I applied for federal jobs, but at least they didn't pull this nonsense."

"No, you just get to deal with people that can't be fired." Mom huffed. "Sonia's getting discouraged, though, like big-time discouraged, and I wanted you to maybe help her out."

"Yeah, I'll call the White House and pull strings. *Hello, Mr. President? I'm a GS-5 program director over at Acadia National Park, and my sister needs a job.*"

Mom made a *pssht* sound. "Your sister needs a pick-me-up. Could you talk to her?"

The only talking to her that would pick her up after months of fruitless job hunting would be, *"I'd like to offer you the position."* Emerson said, "Sure, I'll try to think of something."

"Thanks. I've done mock interviews with her. It's not a good time to be looking, but she sees so many others she graduated with already got jobs, and it's frustrating."

Emerson didn't mention the Fruits de Mer exhibit to Mom. Mom would tell him to hang his paintings up on that wall and not think about it twice, but Mom wasn't him. For

18

all that Mom always asked for a detailed list of painting supplies to buy for birthdays and Christmases, she never understood. When he'd still lived at home, he'd sit at his easel with the painting in front of him and Mom standing behind, him telling her exactly how he wanted the viewer to look at the picture or why he was layering the colors a certain way, and Mom would agree. *Oh, I like the sky. That's a pretty lake.* But she never connected with the images.

By the end of the call, he wanted to close his eyes and zone out, but then he remembered Lilah's messages.

"Don't bring anything. We'll take care of the food. It's super casual."

Her second message was, "Oh, wait, you meant like a gift? Don't bring one of those, either. See above about super casual."

He shook his head as he replied. "A birthday party with no party hats, no balloons, and no presents? I feel bad for Brooke."

Lilah replied immediately. "Then you definitely need to come and cheer her up after the worst party in the history of the world."

Emerson replied, "Or you could throw her a nicer party?"

Lilah sent him an eyerolling emoji, followed by, "I've known Brooke since fifth grade. She's wicked low-key."

Fair enough. "I'll trust you that this will make her happy."

"You'll be there," Lilah texted. "That will be enough happiness for us all."

CHAPTER THREE

The best part of dyeing yarn was the moment the dye cleared.

Before the day a sixteen-year-old Lilah had bounced on her toes in the grocery store, collecting packets of Kool Aid to attempt her first dyeing project, she'd never even known what that meant. Dye clearing? What? But she went home and emptied the packet into the water, brought it to a simmer, and dropped in her sheep-colored skein.

It was on impulse, nothing more. A video about how to dye yarn with Kool Aid had popped up in her social media feed. It looked like fun, so she zipped out to the drink mix aisle, found white yarn in her stash, and dumped it all together.

Years later, she could laugh at her naïveté back then, but the fact was, it had worked. Kind of. She hadn't known that acid dyes work best on protein-based fibers, or that you could measure the dye you put in the skein. None of that. Her first project was a natural skein of big box store fingering weight yarn dunked into orange Kool Aid. It emerged brilliant, but the miracle happened when the water went clear.

Clear water. No dye.

When you found the right balance of dye and acid to yarn, that was perfection. All the color bonded to the skein, with nothing left behind.

That night, she'd dived through her stash hunting for anything else she could dye or overdye. She created a skein that was red on one side and blue on the other. She mixed red and blue to make purple, something that previously stopped being interesting in kindergarten and now became the most thrilling transformation in the world.

She'd stood in her bathroom where the skeins were drip-drying (which likewise had stopped being fascinating in kindergarten) and wondered how brilliantly she could paint the universe.

This morning, Lilah arrived at Bright Stitches with a duffel bag full of freshly dyed, tightly twisted yarns that represented four hours' work last night while *The Last Unicorn* had played on the tiny TV. In addition to the sweater quantity of green tonal yarns, Lilah had ten skeins of hand-painted DK in yellow, bronze, and blue. She had four skeins of half gunmetal grey, half goldenrod. She had one gradient that meandered from pink to deep purple—only one of that because gradients took a lot more work. And finally, four skeins of what she called galaxy colors—triple-dyed worsted, in black, purple, and blue.

That was for play. When Lilah meant business—and she'd have to get down to that soon—she dyed what she called the Brighthead Colorways, to be sold as souvenir yarn.

Natalie watched in delight as skein after skein emerged from the bag. "Don't touch those," Lilah chided about the greens. "Already purchased."

"I can admire without touching." Natalie beamed. "You added blue to it, didn't you?"

"Just an eighth of a teaspoon. And lots of vinegar so it struck quickly. It made awesome tones." Lilah set those aside. "I need to package that up to mail this morning."

Natalie said, "Looks like somebody's making a sweater."

The only customer in the shop was a local named Lavender Paul. She picked up one of the fingering weight skeins. "It's May. Not sweater weather."

Lilah said, "I have it on good authority that winter will return."

Natalie added, "It takes long enough to make a sweater that by the time sweater weather returns, your customer will be glad she ordered it now."

Mrs. Paul untwisted the skein to look at the hand-painted yarn. "This one's nice. It needs to come home with me."

Lilah picked up one of the others. "Its twin will be lonely."

Mrs. Paul snorted. Lilah added, "Fiber insurance?"

She shook her head. "One should do. I'm making socks."

To which Natalie replied, "It's also not wool sock weather," and Mrs. Paul snorted again.

After Lavender Paul left with her lonely skein, Lilah started hanging up the rest on her display shelf. "Have you ever talked to Emerson Charles?"

Natalie said, "The painter dude Brooke likes?"

Lilah said, "Exactly. Let's set her up with him."

Natalie turned to her. "Why? I mean, why now?"

"Brooke lights up when she talks to him." Lilah stepped closer and lowered her voice. "Also, I'm worried about him. Emerson was going to have the second exhibit at Fruits de Mer, but now he's saying he doesn't want to."

Natalie's brow furrowed. "Yeah, Colin mentioned that. Did he say why?"

"No, but here's what I'm thinking." Lilah half-sat on the Sit and Stitch table. "What if it's a confidence thing? Well, nothing is better for confidence and artistry than falling in love. He's perfect for Brooke, anyhow. We need to encourage that."

Natalie started unpacking a box of Cascade yarn. "How exactly do you intend to do that?"

"I don't have a plan, but I invited him to her birthday

party."

Natalie said, "Should I bring balloons and play 'pin the tail on the donkey'? Oh, wait, no, spin the bottle. I'll rig it so they're the ones who kiss."

Lilah drummed her manicured fingernails against her opposite arm. Last night while cogitating over this, she'd redone her nails to shades of blue. "You and Brooke are such a pain. She said the same thing, except not about setting her up. She didn't want to call it a birthday party. We're going to have pizza and watch a movie, and she wants to dye something."

"That's exactly the romantic mood that will entice Emerson to fall madly in love. Behold the magic of dye powders so toxic you have to wear a respirator to handle them." Natalie shook her head. "Maybe you need to come up with a better plan."

Lilah's nose wrinkled. "You and Colin didn't need a plan."

"Colin and I needed someone to sit us on a couch so we could communicate, which you may have noticed we weren't all that good at doing." Natalie rolled her eyes. "I'm not sure Brooke is over Hal enough that she's going to play along. Plus, if you recall, Brooke told me I'm not supposed to be a charity for unambitious men. I'm pretty sure she's not going to volunteer as a self-confidence charity for unnerved artists."

Lilah returned to hanging the rest of her skeins. "Emerson doesn't need her charity, and she's over Hal. She never even mentions him."

Natalie said, "That's why I think she's not over him. She doesn't show it when she's sad. She crawls into a cave like a wounded animal, and then when she comes out, she seems fine."

Lilah didn't answer.

"Look, if you want to set them up, try. But don't do it as a magnanimous act of service to the artistic world. Do it because it'll be good for both Brooke and Emerson."

Of course it would be good for them. Emerson needed a

fan who would propel him into the spotlight. Brooke needed someone who'd draw her out of her shell so she could approach the world with zest. Like two puzzle pieces, they'd complete a picture.

Natalie said, "On the other hand, with all three of us surrounding him all day, Emerson will have no choice but to divulge what's keeping him from doing the exhibit."

"Yeah, that's so odd. I was hoping maybe it was something awesome, like all of his paintings got purchased by a museum."

"If it was something terrible, he'd have told you that, too. You know, if his house burned to the ground."

"He said he's not a good fit for the clientele."

Natalie huffed. "Some of the clients I've heard of, they're a good fit for nobody. '*I want the chicken cordon bleu, but substitute prosciutto for the ham, veal for the chicken, no seasonings, no butter, provolone for the Swiss, and make it gluten-free.*' Can you imagine? '*I want to buy this landscape, but change the sunset to high noon, take all the boats off the lake, and change the season to springtime.*'"

Lilah choked on a laugh.

"After four substitutions, Austin will explain that this is an entirely new dish that will be billed as an experiment, and there are no guarantees as to taste." She shook her head. "If those are the customers Emerson wants to avoid, I can't argue."

Lilah opened the laptop and logged into the Crafters Guild discussion boards. She found Emerson's profile, and from his signature line she clicked on his website.

On the landing page was an abandoned house on a lakeside, the front yard overgrown, the paint peeling, but all around, nature bursting with joy. The house was muted, with a deep sense of despondency as it returned to nature. Everything else burgeoned with life: the overgrown driveway, the sweet pea vines curling up the downspouts, weeds poking through the listing stairs. Through it all thrummed the yearning of thwarted potential, but the promise of new growth.

How could this not be perfect for the tourists?

Lilah clicked on "Gallery," and up popped the familiar grid of images. "Slideshow." A new painting filled her screen, a derelict castle on an island in a river. The next one was a typical New England dirt road, autumnal trees lining the way with their crowns interlocked.

She shivered as she clicked through to the next one. This was her favorite, a rose on a trellis, one flower already erupted but the rest of its buds coiled up tight, poised on the verge of beauty.

One at a time, she admired all the paintings and barely registered that Natalie had come up behind her to look as well.

Lilah breathed, "Isn't he amazing? The reason we formed the BCG was to get artists like him into the public eye. Why would he reach the verge of success and backtrack?"

Natalie said, "You're the marketer. You tell me."

Lilah's nose wrinkled.

Natalie added, "You're generally right about marketing tricks. I trusted you about the colors for the overnight shawl back in February."

Lilah kept clicking through. They were all good, so what was she missing? What was Emerson seeing that she didn't see?

Or rather, what was Emerson looking at his paintings and failing to see?

Lilah breathed to steady herself. "Okay, so you're on vacation. You're a flatlander who came to Maine because it's cool in the summer, and we have pretty beaches and plenty of places to walk. There's Acadia, an hour from here. You've spent your day at the beach, and now you're hungry and tired."

Natalie said, "Moreover, you've chosen Fruits de Mer because you don't mind spending money for something that's high-end and well-presented."

Before dating Colin, Natalie would never have thought about 'presentation' or 'plating.' Just a little nudge from

Colin had opened a new world for her, and Brooke could do the same for Emerson.

Natalie said, "Now you're waiting an hour for your table. You've got your drink in your hand, and you're hanging out in the lobby. These are the paintings. What do you think?"

Lilah thought of Emerson's hand on the brush, painting every one of these strokes with boldness, evoking emotion with colors and lines, coaxing three dimensions out of two. His smile and his laugh, his intelligence and his quips.

Except... That wasn't how a tourist would think of it. They'd see, "Local artwork courtesy of Emerson Charles" on a sign by the door, except the name wouldn't conjure a tall man with short locs and a confident stance. It would be a name—a name that sounded reversed, come to think of it: Emerson, Charles. And then they'd see a sad building or a lonely castle. They'd see a beautiful flower, solitary on the canvas.

Was Emerson right? Were these paintings wrong for the exhibit?

Not that they'd hate him. Diners wouldn't post pictures to social media, captioned, "What on earth is this?" No one would storm out of the restaurant, enraged at having to see a fox hidden in the tall grass.

Lilah shut the lid and pressed her fingertips over her eyes. The door jangled, and Natalie walked away to greet the customer.

Last night's yarn had been playtime with color. Lilah's Brighthead Colorways were business, and those she linked to the town. "Lighthouse" featured blues, white, and a little tan, to evoke the colors of the lighthouse on Brighthead Harbor. The "Brighthead Statue" colorway was a greyish sandstone speckled with verdigris and copper. She'd named the yarns specifically to encourage tourists to lay down cash for "souvenir yarn," displaying only one or two of each at a time (and replacing them the minute they got purchased) because tourists wanted to hang onto the peace of their vacation.

Did these paintings evoke peace? Were they going to remind travelers of their Brighthead bungalow long after they returned to their second-floor bedrooms with wall-to-wall carpeting?

Oh, Emerson. He had a point, after all. The paintings were amazing, but they weren't right for the audience.

Chapter Four

"Arrived at destination."

Although Lilah had warned Emerson that she lived in a barn, he hadn't believed her. His mother used to yell exactly that when he left the apartment door open. Lilah sounded like the kind of person to have an "open door policy" for the entire world, so he'd figured he'd arrive at a bungalow to find the front door wide, all the windows open, and three women like the Fates working with yarn on the porch.

Instead he took the driveway past 88 Spring Road to 88 1/2 Spring Road, an actual barn.

With, yes, the door rolled open.

He parked alongside two other cars, then carried his bag through an entrance wide enough to drive in a horse and buggy. Inside were Lilah, Natalie, and Brooke.

Lilah brightened up. "Emerson! We're setting up solar dyeing projects now, and you have to make one."

The barn loomed over him, so woodsy-smelling. When had the last horse set hoof in here? Stalls would have lined the sides, but at least two dividers had been removed beneath the loft to create a wide-open space for Lilah's work tables. On either side toward the back were actual stalls, cordoned off, and behind that was a wall with a regular door, beyond which he could see what appeared to be a kitchen.

At a work table lined with plastic, Lilah gestured to a pile of twisted skeins, all of them a beige-white. "Choose one, and I'll talk you through it."

"Don't worry," Natalie added. "She took pity on us and chose the non-toxic dyes this time."

Emerson set his bag on a futon and approached the trio. "Happy birthday, Brooke."

She smiled and averted her eyes. "Thank you for coming."

The shyness was cute because she didn't have to be. Lilah moved around the table to be next to Natalie, so Emerson took a spot next to Brooke. "I'm ready. What would you have me do?"

Lilah said, "Brooke, you're the birthday girl. You tell him."

Brooke looked up, brow furrowed. "I'm not the professional dyer."

Natalie said, "But this isn't a professional dye job. It's birthday yarn, and it's your birthday."

Emerson said, "If none of you want to tell me, I can just stand here, devastated and un-dyeing."

"We can't have that," Lilah exclaimed. "Brooke, help a guy out."

More than a little baffled, Brooke said, "Take a skein of yarn and a mason jar, and then you'll want a pair of gloves so you're not wearing birthday sprinkles for the next week."

The bare yarns were different thicknesses, but the skeins all seemed to be about the same size. He took one from the middle, then a mason jar. "You'll need to untwist the hank," Brooke said. "I'm sorry, but my hands are colored up."

"No problem." He studied the coiled yarn, then found the tip where two ends seemed to be pulled through one another like an ouroboros. He separated them, and the skein twisted loose into a loop about a foot-and-a-half long, tied at four different points. "I just unleashed a hairy monster."

Lilah said, "Oh, you did, trust me."

He met her eyes, and she grinned. She added, "Knitting's like a vampire: it bites you, and then you turn into a knitter and look for other people to turn into knitters."

Brooke said, "This is an important step because the more people buy yarn, the more the yarn manufacturers will produce pretty yarn for us to turn into projects."

Natalie said, "This is less true of crocheters. We don't care what you knitters do over there." She gave a desultory wave. "Carry on. I'll just be over here, consuming thirty percent more yarn per project and being overlooked."

The three women looked so comfortable with one another. How different would it be to go to work knowing everyone in his office not only cared about one another, but were actively seeking each other's happiness? Five o'clock came, and Emerson couldn't wait to hit the parking lot. He didn't even eat lunch with his co-workers. This trio, on the other hand, worked together six days a week and still chose to spend Sunday together.

Brooke talked him through the dyeing part, which didn't sound much like dyeing at all. He tucked a little of the hairy-hairy loop of yarn into the jar, then took a pinch of one of the colors. He sprinkled that in, and then tucked another bit of yarn into the jar. Now take another pinch of color.

Which, it turned out, was Kool Aid.

Brooke stopped telling him what to do once he got the hang of it. He said, "Should I be taking the colors in rainbow order? Or layering them in a specific way?"

Brooke said, "Whatever you like."

Lilah said, "There are fun things you could do if you wanted, but this is very laid-back. You could do things like shades of blue, or start with pink and then work up to red and then work up to purple."

Emerson nodded.

Lilah added, "Keep in mind though that the skein is a three-foot loop of yarn, so when it gets knit up, the actual yarn wouldn't make a steady progression of color. It's going to loop through the colors every three feet, so you can sprinkle in colors whenever you like."

Emerson tilted his head. "Are you saying you don't have any idea how your project will turn out?"

Lilah looked dreamy. "It's like a lot of life. You can have very specific intentions, but the yarn will do whatever it wants."

Once they had all their yarn sprinkled with colors, Lilah poured water into each jar. They sealed the jars, labeled them, and then with the gentlest movement Emerson had ever seen, Lilah transferred them to the driveway to sit in the sunlight. "The heat is going to set the colors wherever you put them," Lilah said. "If we mix the water around, the colors will turn sludgy, and that would be a shame."

Back inside, Lilah revealed a metal catering tray in which she was soaking a clump of white fabric. As she wrung out a knitted square, Natalie exclaimed, "Sock blanks!"

Lilah turned to Emerson. "This is special for you. We're going to hand-paint some yarn."

Lilah set out a number of dye solutions in squirt bottles, and she unrolled plastic wrap on the table before each of them. They each took one of the rectangular fabrics that smelled faintly of vinegar, and Lilah demonstrated how they could use the fabric as a canvas to paint a picture.

Brooke said to him, "O Great Artist, this is your wheelhouse."

Emerson flattened out the sock blank, fairly sure this wheelhouse was anything but his. If he tried to use a brush on the blank, it would buckle up beneath him. Also, for all that they called it hand-painted yarn, he saw no brushes and no paints.

Lilah worked with the squirt bottles to show everyone how to make designs, and this... This was insupportable. The women kept looking at him, expecting him to make artwork.

Brooke arched her eyebrows. "You're going to show up all three of us by recreating the Sistine Chapel ceiling on the sock blank, right?"

Emerson shifted his weight. "I'll try not to humiliate you with my blinding talent."

Lilah winked. "Bet you do it anyhow."

Lilah "painted" by squirting dye, then working it into the yarn with her fingers (she'd done her nails a sparkly purple color) or with a cotton ball. The dye spread through the fiber when she moved it, and that meant whatever he did, there wouldn't be detail. Impressionist, then. She had ten dye stocks on the table, and although she had all three primaries, he likely couldn't do much mixing. The yarn was white, but given the way the dye spread through the fibers, he wouldn't count on the undyed areas remaining white.

Lilah looked him in the eyes. "Are you up for the challenge?"

Emerson hummed. "Let's see."

Lilah had set a piece of paper towel in front of each squirt bottle with a bit of the color soaked onto it. Assuming he couldn't blend, those were his palette. The blue and yellow were striking. Together, they reminded him of Van Gogh's "Irises."

A long time ago, someone had told Emerson, "Bad painters borrow. Good painters steal." He suspected that line itself was stolen, but it hardly mattered. Today, Emerson would be a good painter. He took the blue and the yellow, then also the green and a lighter brown. His palette chosen, Emerson set to work.

He recreated the painting in his mind's eye and then started in the lower left corner, adding brown. He wanted to create the sensation of "Irises," not an exact copy. Browning up that area gave him a sense of how the dye behaved on impact with the fabric.

Lilah said, "Wait," and ran to one of the cabinets on the wall. She returned with eye droppers and plastic syringes.

"This will give you better control over the dye."

Emerson began adding the blue-purple flowers, each unfurling itself toward the sun, reaching and longing. Each dot landed on the yarn and then spread with fibery fingers until it could reach no further. He used the squirt bottle to create the flair of the S-shaped leaves heading toward the brown, then outlined the stems. One area he left untouched because he remembered a singular white flower in that spot. Toward the top, he added orange flowers, and then more green.

He realized abruptly, all three women had fallen silent. Brooke was just watching, but Lilah stood with her hands wrapped around one another.

Emerson's heart caught. He wanted her to like it—really like it. "Is that okay?"

"Yes," she breathed, then met his eyes. "That's wonderful."

Emerson stood back while they "set" the dye. Lilah had a long explanation for what you needed in order to set an acid dye, but it came down to heat, moisture, and acid. She showed him how to wrap his sock blank in plastic wrap as though it were a burrito, and then she tucked all four yarn burritos into a steamer basket over a simmering stock pot.

Cooking yarn. Not something Emerson had thought he'd be doing this weekend. Nor, ever.

Lilah kept saying to Brooke, "Wasn't his work amazing?" and "Aren't you glad he came for your birthday?" to which Brooke kept agreeing. Brooke was polite and restrained, as she'd always been. It was hard getting Brooke to talk about herself with any enthusiasm, but the times they'd met, Emerson had found her a good listener, and she sometimes broke the silence with a completely random piece of information he'd never realized he needed to know, like, "Do you know human molars have rings just like trees?"

At the BCG meetings, though, Brooke had seemed unnerved. Well, not even seemed—she'd stated that she felt unnerved the first time the BCG met at Fruits de Mer. Today, she seemed comfortable and maybe a bit detached.

"Are you doing okay?" he asked.

Brooke nodded. "Wondering what I might make with this yarn."

Emerson said, "Sock blanks. I figured you'd make socks."

"Sock yarn doesn't always want to become socks." She shrugged. "We'll see. Maybe it will."

He followed Brooke to the barn door. "Yarn wants to become things?"

Brooke chuckled. "It's something you learn after a while. Lilah says the yarn talks to you about what it should become."

He turned to Lilah, who was watching them with a broad smile. "Care to explain?"

"Explain what?"

"Talking yarn."

"Oh!" Her sock blank had become a series of concentric circles, working from red at the center to gold to green to purple to blue, and then more red at the corners to finish it off. "Yeah, sometimes you want to knit the yarn into something, like a scarf, and the yarn refuses to become that thing."

Brooke murmured, "I guess she can't explain it either," and Emerson laughed.

Lilah came closer. "How do you decide what a canvas wants to become?"

"A canvas doesn't want anything." Emerson shrugged. "I decide what I want to paint, and then I sketch out a composition on the canvas, set out my colors, and start painting."

"But doesn't it ever happen that you want to paint

something, only it just doesn't come together?"

Emerson nodded. "But that's not because the canvas is resisting, and if only I took out a different canvas it would be fine."

"Well, yarn resists when it doesn't want to be a thing." Lilah said that the same way his cousin might say, *"My son would only eat mac and cheese for three months last year."* "And then sometimes the yarn explicitly tells you what it wants. I'll see a pattern and realize it's exactly what those two skeins of superwash merino have been waiting for."

"Before you ask," Brooke said, "allow me to introduce you to the concept of the yarn stash—wherein an over-eager knitter or crocheter purchases yarn because it's beautiful and not because there's an immediate use for it, let alone a project in mind."

Emerson used to buy random colored pencils in the art store, not because he needed them but because he loved that dusky shade of blue or the metallic gleam of the copper. "I get that."

"Yarn stashes are ever-expanding creatures, devouring container space and dwelling deep within your mind so you always remember exactly what's in it and vaguely where to find it." Lilah clasped her hands at her chest. "Then one day, you encounter a pattern so perfect that it tells you, then and there, that it must be matched with a specific yarn in order to be happy. So you do it, and it works, and both the yarn and the pattern feel complete."

When Emerson laughed, Lilah said, "I think people are that way too."

Emerson sighed as he leaned against the barn door. "That would be nice to think."

Brooke said, "Granted, sometimes the fight is with the needles that refuse to give the correct gauge."

"You're making it harder than it has to be." Lilah wrapped her arm around Emerson and tugged him away from the door edge. "Sometimes you just need to look at one half of the perfect pair to recognize the other half of it."

Warmth shot all the way through Emerson. Was that a very direct come-on? Had she invited him here today to try hooking up with him?

Instead of looking at him, though, Lilah was reaching for Brooke's arm, and she tugged her closer as well. Then she backed away, leaving Emerson wondering what had just happened.

Brooke turned to Emerson. "I've discovered most yarn is more forgiving. Check out a pattern page online, and you'll see any number of yarns can work for it."

Lilah walked back to the table with the hot plate and the steamer bath. "When I wake up in the middle of the night, and I can see a project in my head—both the yarn and the pattern—I've learned I have to knit it. There will be dire consequences if I don't."

Emerson looked at Brooke. "What's the most dire consequence of not knitting something?"

Brooke said, "You may lose the chance to do something awesome for someone who needs it."

Lilah looked up from the steaming yarn. "There's not enough beauty in the world. When the universe says we need more of it, it's on us to answer."

CHAPTER FIVE

When the light strings turned on throughout Lilah's barn, she relished their pinpoint glow and then snuck a look at Brooke and Emerson.

Natalie was staying out of their way. Not that she was avoiding them, but she had spent most of the day either getting things together or cleaning up afterward. Whenever Brooke tried to help, Natalie had pushed her back toward Emerson. "You're the birthday girl."

Natalie might not have embraced the matchmaking scheme, but she was still a thoughtful partner in crime.

Before sundown, they retrieved their solar-dyed yarn and opened the jars to reveal gorgeous swirls of color. The skeins each got a bath in clear dish soap, and then a turn through the spin dryer.

"Did you see the best part of all?" Lilah asked Emerson. "Look at the water in the jars."

He swirled it around. "What about it?"

"It's clear." She beamed. "All the dye went into the yarn."

"Oh, that's odd." He held a jar to the light. "The water had turned blue and yellow and red. I figured there'd still be color in there."

"Dyeing is such magic." She headed back to the tables again, but instead of leaving Lilah so he could talk to Brooke, Emerson followed. Lilah shooed him away. "Your sock blank is perfection itself. Go show it to Brooke."

"I hardly think it's perfection." He frowned. "What does this want to become?"

"I have no idea." She laughed. "So, the thing with a sock blank is that once you start pulling the yarn apart and reknitting it, you can't tell what kind of design it's going to resolve into. Like my tie-dye effect, I can sort of guess it will have bits of stripes and long blocks of color. But yours —it's artistic just the way it is."

Emerson held it away from himself. "You're saying, once all these stitches come out and then get stitched into something else, it's like you're taking it down to the component atoms. You won't be able to see the original picture in the final project you knit up."

"Exactly. It's going to be a surprise. But the best things in life come as a surprise."

Emerson said, "What's the best thing in your life?"

He should be asking Brooke these questions, not her. Lilah headed back across the barn to sit with Brooke and Natalie. That way, Brooke would be a part of the conversation. "I have so many good things in my life that it's hard to choose. Friends. The yarn shop. The BCG. My dye shop. Health. Family. Maine." She pointedly left open the seat beside Brooke so Emerson would have to sit there. "What's the best thing in your life?"

Emerson frowned.

Brooke said, "Lay off him, Lilah. He doesn't have to rank everything he loves."

Emerson said, "I love my family. I love art."

Brooke turned to him. "Then why are you backing out of the art exhibit?"

Emerson's eyes flashed with anger, and Lilah flinched because while ostensibly they'd brought Emerson here to discuss exactly that, he shouldn't get angry at Brooke. Lilah should have been the one drawing his ire while

Brooke remained his safe place.

Natalie said, "I'm curious, too. Colin thinks your artwork is perfect."

Emerson sighed. "You won't let this rest?"

Brooke said, "Not if you're making a mistake."

Emerson stood up. "It's not the right art for the right place. The pieces I planned to use there—they're all wrong. I could do better, and if I launch these out in the world now, they aren't my best."

Brooke said, "So make new paintings."

Emerson turned to her.

Lilah urged, "Listen to her. Why not paint some of Brighthead's local attractions? The lighthouse and the Myth Brightman statue would be two things that would get a lot of attention."

"For that matter, paint Fruits de Mer," Natalie said with a smile.

Emerson shook his head. "It's not just the paintings."

Brooke said, "You're not thinking objectively. They won't see anything that's not on the wall."

He sat back on the couch, hands between his knees, and looked down.

Lilah's brain tickled. "Have you ever done an exhibit before?"

He shook his head. "Not me alone. A single individual piece in a large exhibit, yes."

Lilah said, "I guess we could muddle it up and have a bunch of artists participate."

Brooke said, "One artist, one waiting area, one limited time. We discussed this." She faced Emerson. "Your work is objectively good. Even if you can do better now than you did two years ago, no one can see your anticipated growth decorating the wall. They're going to see what you actually did, and it's fine work."

Brooke needed to be more encouraging than that. She needed to bolster Emerson, not diminish him.

Lilah blurted out, "Wait, is this about *you*? You think they'll reject you?"

When Emerson looked up, she said, "But they won't reject you."

Brooke said, "You won't even be there. How would they know to reject you?"

No, that was the wrong tack to take. Lilah said, "But they wouldn't reject you anyhow. I want you to be up there in the spotlight so everyone can see the brilliant mind behind the emotions in every one of those pieces."

He looked choked up. Brooke needed to say something to push him into accepting the opportunity. When Brooke stayed quiet, Lilah said, "You have a gift to give the world. We want you to give it to them."

He managed, "I don't think they want it."

Lilah said, "People don't know what they want until they see it! Of course they'll want it. We just have to make sure it's in front of them. But if you want to sell a few pieces, do what Brooke suggested." Had Brooke suggested it? "Make a couple of paintings that are Brighthead-focused. Paint the lighthouse. Paint Brighthead Harbor. Give them some of the things they expect so they'll take a closer look at the others."

Emerson said, "Isn't that selling out?"

Lilah said, "It's selling *up*. You're still creating beauty, but you'll create it in the way they expect."

He still didn't seem convinced. Lilah said, "Come to my barn to work. I've got plenty of studio space. I'll cordon off part of it, and you can wander around Brighthead to find interesting things, then paint them here."

He met her eyes. "You're insistent."

"We really want you to do this." Plus, if he was here, Lilah could get Brooke here with him. Give them enough time together, and everything would happen the way it should.

He sighed. "Okay. You win."

Brooke whispered, "Yes!" and Lilah laughed.

At the end of the evening, Lilah brought out a cake, and Brooke asked them please not to sing to her.

Natalie said, "You never want us to sing to you."

Brooke shrunk a bit. "I don't like the attention."

Lilah said, "What if I like singing?"

Emerson said, loudly, "Let her alone. It's fine if she just cuts the cake," so Lilah let it go. It was good that Emerson stood up for Brooke. He was catching on.

When they were all seated with cake, though, Emerson handed Brooke a little wrapped present. She recoiled. "You weren't supposed to bring anything. Lilah was supposed to tell you that."

Emerson met her eyes. "I also wasn't supposed to do the Fruits de Mer show, so we're even."

Unnerved, Brooke said, "Should I open it?"

Natalie said, "Social custom says you should."

Brooke undid the wrapping paper with care, then lifted the lid to reveal a light catcher in the shape of a butterfly. Lilah exclaimed, "Oh, how pretty," and leaned in to see the blues and greens as they caught the light.

Brooke held it up. "Thank you. I like it."

Lilah beamed. "The colors are gorgeous! Where did you find it?"

Emerson looked pleased. "One of the park gift shops that specializes in sustainable eco-friendly gifts."

"Let me see." She took it from Brooke and held it to the light. "You have great taste, Emerson."

Brooke retrieved the butterfly and nestled it back into its box. "Thanks. I can hang it in my kitchen."

Brooke's studio apartment had only two windows. Brooke then sliced the cake, and they concluded the evening.

"Oh, and you get a goodie bag anyhow," Lilah said, leading Emerson back to the work table where the yarn was now dry. She retwisted his hank of solar-dyed yarn, then took a picture of his Irises sock blank before tucking that into a bag with the hank. She handed him the bag, but when he took it, she didn't let go.

Lilah lowered her voice. "Ask her out."

Emerson's eyes shifted back toward Brooke. "Are you sure?"

"She's into you, but she's also very reserved. You'll make her day." Lilah squeezed his hand, excitement blossoming inside. "She's super thoughtful once she warms up, and you can see how much she appreciates your art. The two times the BCG met, you were inseparable. Ask her."

Emerson looked over his shoulder.

Lilah said, "You could keep the stalemate for months, or you could just cut to the chase."

He looked at her, eyes amused. "I guess it does save time."

"Plus, you'll be in Brighthead looking for good painting spots, so it's convenient." She gave him a nudge in Brooke's direction. "Don't miss out."

"Convenient and cute," he said in a low, almost purring voice. "What more could a man want?"

Lilah snorted a laugh.

He went to say goodbye to Brooke, and Lilah called Natalie over to her at the work table. Scene set. All the players in place.

Natalie sounded uneasy. "You know, this may not have been the best idea."

"It's a perfect idea, and he's onboard." Lilah took Brooke's birthday skein and twisted it eight times, then popped one end through the other. "Now, we watch and wait."

Brooke walked with Emerson to his car, and Lilah shifted to the other side of the table so she could get a better look. Brooke leaned against his car, and Emerson rested a hand on the roof while they kept talking. Brooke looked down and to the side, and Lilah beamed—that had to have been the ask. Then Brooke was nodding, and Lilah bounced on her toes.

Natalie said, "I guess that seems good."

"She's way too reserved." Lilah huffed. "I wish she'd show it when she's interested in a guy. He'd have asked her out weeks ago."

"You know that's not what she does. It's all in the way she watches them and listens to them."

"Good thing I was here to grease the gears." Lilah sighed. "And that butterfly is gorgeous. I'm glad he got her a gift."

Natalie snickered. "It's not Brooke's speed, but it was thoughtful of him."

Lilah frowned. "She liked it."

Natalie shrugged. "She's not going to be rude, but she's not a butterfly person."

Irritated, Lilah didn't reply. She'd known Brooke nearly as long as Natalie, and knowing her better for some of that time probably made up for the shorter length. Natalie was Brooke's cousin, but Brooke hadn't even lived in Brighthead until fifth grade. Maybe Brooke didn't plaster her life with butterflies, but that didn't make them not her speed.

Brooke and Emerson were still talking, and then they both pulled out their phones. Very good: they'd hatched a plan. Maybe their first actual date?

Finally Brooke took a step back from the car, her body language uncertain. Emerson let her go, and then after another moment, he got into the car and Brooke returned to the barn.

Brooke was smiling as she entered. "He asked me to go to the Renaissance Faire with him on the weekend."

Lilah clasped her hands. "That's awesome!"

Natalie said, "Good for you!"

Brooke nodded. "That's nice of him. I'll drive over to his place on Sunday morning, and then we'll go together in his car."

Lilah teased, "Make him win you a large stuffed animal and carry it all around the fairgrounds."

"A stuffed animal?" Brooke gave a half eyeroll. "No thanks. But if they have a blacksmith forging swords, I wouldn't mind one of those."

CHAPTER SIX

Brooke arrived at Emerson's apartment exactly on time, with shorts and sneakers and her hair in a ponytail. She immediately headed into the paint room. "Amazing!" She took a tentative step onto the plastic-covered floor. "This room looks a lot like how I imagine the inside of my brain." With a smile she leaned over his paint chair to study the project on the easel. "I'm so glad you agreed to do Fruits de Mer. You've got so much skill."

She kept looking at the paintings up close while Emerson collected his wallet, keys, and phone. "Could I take a panoramic shot of your studio for Lilah? She's going to be eaten alive with jealousy that I got to see all your work."

Emerson looked back from the kitchen. "Do you hate her?"

"I love her. And Lilah loves everybody, but she especially loves your artwork, based on the way she goes on about it." Brooke hesitated. "On second thought, if I send her a picture of your room, that might constitute an act of reckless endangerment."

Emerson laughed. "I hardly think she'd die of envy."

"I'm not sure why she didn't beat you to the punch and ask you out herself." Brooke stepped toward him. "But I'm glad it didn't happen that way, and the Renn Faire sounds like fun."

Trying to figure out how all that parsed, Emerson backed up a step. Lilah had encouraged him to ask Brooke out, but Brooke seemed like she'd have been perfectly happy if he'd asked Lilah. So either they were the two least-competitive women in Maine, or else he would never understand how women thought.

Brooke hesitated. "Where do you sleep?"

"Futon," he said. "The paintings needed more room, so I got rid of my mattress."

Brooke nodded. "I feel like someday Natalie may need to make that same decision about her yarn stash. It would be bad form to buy a futon cover and stuff that with yarn."

Emerson picked up his backpack with sunblock, bug spray, and bottled water. "Shall we?"

It took forty-five minutes to reach the fairgrounds, and Brooke tended to fall silent between conversational stretches. Not as if she seemed bored, but rather, she watched the world. She'd observe the terrain or the towns they passed, remark on interesting license plates (did everyone in New Hampshire have a vanity plate?) and other state plates in general. "Montana!" she called.

Emerson said, "That's a long drive."

"When I was a kid, my grandmother kept a wooden map in the car, each state with a switch you could flip. We'd start the month with all fifty states down, and whenever we found an out-of-state plate on the road, we'd flip that state. The goal was to hit all fifty before the month ended."

Emerson frowned. "Even Hawaii?"

Brooke nodded. "I have no idea how, but yes. Alaska was rare, but more frequent."

And then, as though the conversation were over, she just stopped talking. Subject matter, exhausted.

Emerson said, "How'd you meet Lilah and Natalie?"

"Natalie's my cousin. Her mother is my father's sister,

and our grandmother lived here in Brighthead. Natalie was in a different school year, though, so when I moved back to live with my grandmother, Lilah made sure I had friends. As payback, I taught her to knit."

Emerson said, "While that's a fair trade, what made you move in with your grandmother?"

"My brother was sick." Brooke's tone flattened, which struck Emerson as odd because her tone didn't vary all that much to begin with. "My parents initially moved us to Boston because he was always having doctor appointments and therapies. That kept them busy all the time. After a while, it was decided I should live with my grandmother. I knew nobody in our class, and I think Lilah felt sorry for me. She got me in tight with her friend group."

Emerson said, "That sounds difficult. What did your brother have?"

"Brain tumor. They needed a pediatric cancer center so he could have surgery and start getting treated. They can do all these things now," Brooke added, sounding awed. "But of course, you can't mess with the brain and not have other things happen, too. It was all about him, and they needed to make sure they spent good time with him and enjoyed having him for as long as they could."

Emerson said, "And...? Did he survive?"

Brooke nodded. "Fortunately, yes. He still needs assistance with things, but he's alive, and that's what's important."

If Sonia had nearly died, would Emerson report it that way? Or would he gush with relief that his sister could have been in a box, only they'd all gotten a second chance?

"He was four when it started," Brooke said. "I was seven. They moved me up here when I was ten."

"I grew up in Boston. Maybe we met."

She laughed. "Only if you were near the hospital. Maybe we were getting fast food at the same time, me knitting while my mother got my brother a frappe, you sketching the french fries, and neither of us knowing we'd both end up in Maine." She paused. "How'd you come up here?"

"My goal was always to get out of Boston. You don't have to get too far out of Boston to see lots of trees, but I just wanted the open spaces. And a job."

Brooke gestured at the windows. "You found it all."

"I spent a few years as a park ranger, then moved into the program development section. I'm not outside anymore, but it's a good promotion, and I like planning events."

Brooke said, "What kind of events?"

"Outreach." He shrugged. "Things like arranging day trips for local camps, busing in kids from Boston, sending park rangers to local schools to talk to the students—oh, and outreach to Scout troops. We also do adult education programs about recycling, sustainability, and fair trade."

Brooke brightened right up. "How does that work?"

He carried the conversation the rest of the way to the fair. She had a dozen questions for him, some direct follow-up but others a little out of left field ("Why is there fair trade coffee but not fair trade tea?") and then she'd come up with a story from an article she'd read ten years ago about how reintroducing wolves to an ecosystem helped change the course of a river.

The fair was crowded, and Brooke stuck close to him. They found a place off to the side to look through the brochure and pick out things they wanted to see, and after she finished marking up the brochure (numbering the areas in order of importance) Emerson suggested they start by watching the jousting show.

Brooke relaxed only a little while watching the royal court process into their boxes. Was she always this tense? More unnerving, Emerson realized she kept checking him as if watching for cues before responding. She did enjoy the show, though, and between jousts, he got a chance to put his arm around her. She relaxed into him.

Overall, it was a great time. Lots of food, plenty of people-watching (although again, Brooke seemed uneasy) and a lot of noise. At the shops and craft displays, she prowled over all the jewelry and then stalled out in front of a yarn spinning exhibit.

"Can you spin?" Emerson asked her.

"I wish. I'd love to have my own wheel, but there's no room." She wrapped her arms around his arm and leaned into him. "Think of how amazing that would be, to make yarn."

"Do you sell fleeces in the shop?"

"We sell fiber twists," she said. "They're gorgeous, but I don't have the first idea what to do with them."

They rode an elephant, and that was a lot of laughter and lurching. When he held onto her tightly, Brooke fit right against him, and he wished he could enjoy having her near him rather than struggling to keep their balance. They waited in line a long time for the axe-throwing—which was a lot of fun—but afterward, Brooke looked pale.

He led her to a picnic table in the shade of some trees, then got her a slushy that was quite assuredly not authentic to the Renaissance. He sat with his arm around her, and she leaned against him.

"You're getting overheated." He rubbed her shoulder. "Whatever we do next, it should be in the shade and sitting."

"I'll be okay." She sipped at the drink. "There's a lot of people, that's all."

Emerson straightened. "Oh! You don't like crowds. That's why—"

He stopped. Brooke said, "That's why what?"

That's why she attached to him the moment they got into the fairground. That was why at the first meeting of the BCG, she'd latched onto him and stayed the whole time. He'd become her landmark. Lilah must have served as something similar when Brooke landed in an unfamiliar class halfway through fifth grade. And that was why Brooke kept checking Emerson before doing anything.

Emerson said, "That's why you're a little unnerved."

Her nose wrinkled. "I've never been to one of these before, and I'm not sure what the rules are. It's fun, though, and I'm glad you invited me."

The rules?

She returned to nursing her drink. Emerson said, "How did you and Natalie and Lilah end up starting a yarn shop together?"

She shook her head. "The shop already existed. Natalie's mom owned it. Both Nat and I used to hang out there, and then when we got older, we'd work for Aunt Ellie during the summers. When Aunt Ellie wanted to sell the shop and move, Natalie asked if I'd go in on it with her, and I thought, sure. Natalie's got drive, but no business sense. I've got business sense, but like you said, I'm not a people person."

Emerson interjected, "I didn't say that."

Brooke waved him off. "Regardless, we asked if Lilah wanted to work for the shop full-time, and here we are." Brooke sipped more of the drink. "Lilah gets premium floor space selling her indie-dyed yarns, and I have a side gig designing patterns. During the summers, we hire one seasonal part-time employee, but otherwise, it's just us. We could get in each other's hair, but it works well. Especially now with the BCG starting up, there's been so much to focus on. Lilah's a whirlwind."

Emerson laughed. "I get that impression."

Brooke smiled. "She's so alive all the time, and when she gets an idea, either get onboard, or get out of the way. That's both good and bad, because sometimes she's convinced something should happen, only it shouldn't actually."

Emerson said, "Should I be worried that she's so emphatic about the Fruits de Mer exhibit?"

"She's not usually wrong. It's just that even if she were wrong, she'd dedicate herself to that cause until it broke her heart." Brooke's eyes were lively. "On the plus side, she'll never give up on you, either."

Emerson tightened his arm around Brooke. "I can see why you've been her friend for so long."

"She's tough as nails. You want someone like Lilah in your corner." She shifted away from him. "But speaking of tough as nails, let's go to the blacksmith exhibit. I want to see them forge a sword."

Emerson's manager stalked past his desk wearing a face etched with irritation.

So—him? What had he done lately?

A minute later, Ellen was heading back to her office with one of his co-workers and the admin, then said, "You might as well join us, Emerson."

Emerson saved his work and followed them as the Afterthought Employee. At least whatever this was, it wasn't his fault.

Ellen sat behind her desk and said, "I just got an email from the falconers who were supposed to be here on the 23rd."

The other program director gasped. "*Supposed to*? They're pulling out?"

The admin said, "Was that what they were calling about?"

Emerson's mind whirled. The falconers had been working with their office for months to put together an exhibit along with an educational program. Not with Emerson, since he'd only worked here a few weeks, but Ellen and the other two had gone above and beyond to create a program that would meet all the falconers' needs as well as help educate the public about the birds and their environment.

And all that to just throw it away? For what?

Ellen glanced at Emerson, but he kept his face impassive. This wasn't his fight. Having him look angry when he wasn't the one harmed by the cancellation was only going to create problems in the office.

Ellen turned her attention to the other two. "One of the

falconers scheduled a knee replacement surgery for the day before the event." She raised her hands as the other two protested. "I'm not heartless. I know people need knee replacements. Why she scheduled it for then is also not my concern. They have time to find another falconer, and they won't do it. They also won't come with one fewer bird. It's all of them or nothing."

Emerson struggled to keep from matching Ellen's scowl.

The admin said, "Given how much we've put into this already, we can work around them being one man down."

"Loretta's surgery was scheduled for the week after the presentation," said the other program director. "We worked out all the transportation arrangements so she wouldn't have to walk, remember?"

Ellen spread her hands. "They worked her in a few days earlier, and apparently this is going to make a huge impact on her health. I'm not arguing with you," she added.

Three more days waiting for a surgery that had been on the books for months was not life-changing. Not in Emerson's opinion, although he wasn't a doctor. And not being a doctor, again, he kept his face blank.

Once more, Ellen looked at him. What did she want? This wasn't his fight, and adding his outrage was only going to call attention to the fact that he hadn't been one of the ones whose work was wasted. If he got angry, they'd wonder what he intended to do about it, or maybe even why he cared since it hadn't been his project in the first place.

This felt so much like dealing with Lilah and Brooke, both of whom kept looking to him to express specific feeings because what he did express wasn't good enough for them. Here, be angry about the falconry exhibit. Here, be excited about this art show.

Instead, he imitated Brooke, with her carefully blank expression and her understated responses, as the others vented. They discussed damage control, and finally they discussed rescheduling.

The other program director said, "I can't discuss this

with them now. I need time to cool off."

Ellen glanced at Emerson. "Any suggestions?"

Emerson kept his voice low. "None. I'm sorry. I wasn't involved enough in the planning to be able to plan a way back out of the mess they created."

"Fair enough," Ellen said, which probably translated as a comment on Emerson's overall usefulness to the team. "I'm giving us until one o'clock to come up with an alternative. At one-oh-one, in the absence of a workable solution, we'll start dismantling the entire thing. That means you'll need to contact the papers and update the website—"

The admin raised her hands. "I'll get on it. But first, I'll figure out if there are any additional accommodations that can get them here with one fewer falconer."

The second project manager said, "I'll look into whether another group can take over the slot, since all the preparations are in place. It's possible we can bring in the wildlife rehabbers again or even an educational ambassador team."

Ellen looked at Emerson, who keenly felt the spotlight. As though he were going to put on a leather glove and reach into the nearest raptor cage to educate the world.

He could paint a falcon. Ellen didn't know that, of course. Why would she?

Instead, Emerson said, "If you give me a list of newspapers we've already contacted, I can send a batch of updated press releases."

Ellen said, "Try not to disparage our fine feathered friends."

Emerson bristled. "As if I would?"

Ellen started, then shook herself. "I'm sorry, Emerson. Of course you wouldn't. I'm frustrated because we've only got a small part of the full picture, and I so much wanted this to work out."

CHAPTER SEVEN

Next Saturday afternoon. Lilah bounded over to Emerson at the Bright Stitches entrance, grinning ear-to-ear. "I heard you guys had a great time at the Renn Faire! See?"

Emerson had a life in his eyes that left Lilah's heart pounding. Oh, he and Brooke were going to be so perfect together. She said, "I've got ten minutes before I'm out of here, but you can talk to Brooke, and then we can go set you up in the barn."

He looked around. "This place is colorful."

Brooke came from the back, and she smiled. "Hi." But she didn't rush up to him, and Lilah wanted to shove her at him. "Are you ready to paint the town?"

"In ten minutes, he'll be painting the town." Lilah hesitated. "Maybe you should take him, after all."

"It's your barn, and it's my shift. I'll drive your car back to you after we close up, like we planned." She shooed them. "You don't need to wait ten minutes. Go on."

They got into Emerson's car, Lilah irritated that Brooke hadn't tried to hug him or even look him in the eye. Maybe Brooke thought it was unprofessional to do that at work, but come on. A gorgeous man walks into your shop not even a week after your first date, and you don't make him feel like a million bucks?

Lilah said, "Brooke's been a bit overworked lately."

Emerson muttered, "Aren't we all?"

Lilah directed Emerson to the pier near Brighthead Bay to look at the waterfront. The tide was out, leaving the causeway visible where you could walk all the way to the lighthouse. Well, if there was enough time. When the tide came back, the causeway vanished beneath the waves, and you'd need someone who owned a boat.

Emerson talked as he gazed, and Lilah strapped in for a front row seat to how an artist thinks. He snapped pictures from multiple angles, but the whole time, he was observing the clouds, the birds, the rocks, the interplay of light and water. "I'll need to come back when the tide's in," he said, and Lilah checked the lighthouse website for the tide conditions. Meanwhile, Emerson clambered down the rocks rather than using the path, heading straight for the causeway.

"We shouldn't walk all the way out," Lilah said. "The tide's inbound."

Emerson stepped onto the gravel and rock path toward the island. Lilah followed, eyes on the water. At some point, the waves would start lapping over the edges, and then he and she would have to be back on shore or else get their shoes wet. They wouldn't have to swim. It didn't get that deep out here... Except, hang on: Emerson kept heading to the lighthouse.

Maybe a fully clothed swim was in the works after all. "I hope your camera's waterproof."

Emerson said, "We'll be back. Doesn't matter if you cut it close, as long as you make it."

Lilah chuckled. "Lead on."

Halfway to the lighthouse, Emerson took more photos. "I need to get all the way out there," he murmured. "There's a painting in that."

Lilah noted the time. "There's also only thirty minutes." In response, Emerson speed-walked the causeway, so Lilah added, "We're going to be getting so wet on the walk home."

Emerson replied, "Skin is waterproof."

Once at the island, Lilah stopped checking the time. They were committed now. They climbed the path spiraling the island up to the lighthouse, and then Emerson took photos right up the side of the lighthouse, far back, every side. He photographed the memorial plaque and then backed up and got it again. That done, he said, "Now—power walk."

They stepped out onto the causeway, which was already getting engulfed. "You know, they do a race out to the lighthouse once a year." Lilah breathed hard as she struggled to keep up with Emerson's longer stride. "I never saw the appeal."

A few families milled about on the beachhead and the pier, probably watching the two poor planners who hadn't figured out that tides come back in the same way they go out: in silence. At least they were getting their afternoon's entertainment while Lilah and Emerson got some cardio.

"I don't want to run, though," she said. "The rocks look slippery."

"We'll be fine," Emerson said. "It's water."

"It's salt water," Lilah corrected. "Much deadlier."

He turned to her and winked. "See you in Heaven."

"Less laughing," she exclaimed. "More walking!"

The walkway wasn't higher in the middle, so it all got engulfed at the same time rather than coming in from the edges. They were very close to the shore at that point, and Lilah laughed as they splashed toward the rocks through a hundred-yard puddle.

"Brilliant." She clambered up a boulder in squishy sneakers. "You got your photos, and we aren't dead."

"Unless you're a slug, death wasn't in the cards." Emerson pulled off his own shoes and socks. "It's entirely your fault. If you hadn't conned me into doing the Fruits de Mer—"

"Conned you?"

"—then I wouldn't have been out in the water in the first place to get a picture of the lighthouse."

"Brazen," Lilah said. "Here I am, risking my life for your art, and you're blaming me for a little sand between your toes?"

He turned to her. "You're an audacious little thing, aren't you?"

"And that," Lilah shot back, "was an expert blame shift."

He frowned. "I would have called it an ad hominem attack."

She glared into his eyes for one long moment, and then they both started laughing.

"Fine." Lilah flexed her toes, glad she'd given herself a pedicure the night before. The bronzy color glimmered in the sunlight as she stuffed her wet socks into her wet shoes and slid down onto the pebbled beach. "I'm an audacious little thing, and I conned you into advancing your artistic career. I admit it."

Emerson followed her up the beach. "What's your nefarious goal, then?"

"Taking over the world, of course. You know how a democracy is rule by the people, and an autocracy is rule by one all-powerful individual?"

Emerson said, "So you'll establish an *audacity*, with yourself at the pinnacle?"

She stuck out her tongue. "I want an *artocracy*, where artists rule the world. Your work is a key component of my diabolical master plan."

Emerson's eyebrows shot up. "Whoa. I do need to make these paintings good."

"No pressure." Lilah shrugged. "It's just that, if you fail, the world ends."

Back on the pier, they left a trail of wet footprints toward the statue, where once again Emerson took a dozen shots, then a dozen more. He wanted every angle, every iteration. Then he started pointing out to Lilah all the lines on the statue, the way it drew the eye and the way it evoked feeling.

Lilah said, "Make sure to capture the plaque, too, because everything about it is wrong."

The plaque was standard enough: Alice Brightman, followed by birth and death dates, founded the Brighthead Point lighthouse when her fisherman husband died during a storm, after which Brighthead was named for her.

Lilah said, "Her name was Alicia Brightman, and that's not when she was born. Brighthead isn't named for her. Her husband wasn't a fisherman, and the statue is based on a photo of her sister. I'm not sure she even raised the money. There's more, but all of that is why we call her Myth Brightman." Lilah giggled. "We live in trepidation of the day the Brighthead Historical Society gets full of itself and pulls off the plaque to correct it."

Emerson said, "And you know why they haven't done that very simple thing?"

Lilah raised her eyebrows. "No, why?"

"Because everything about Myth Brightman feels like truth. Her posture, her longing, her determination. It's the way she rallied herself as an individual to do something good in the face of tragedy."

Lilah cocked her head. "The statue of truth... accompanied by the plaque of myth?"

"Exactly. If it was just the mistakes and the lies, no one would care. A plaque is maybe fifty words and costs two hundred bucks to replace, but the statue is worth well more than a thousand words, and the mythology is priceless." He took another picture, focusing on the statue's face. "Art at its best spins a higher truth than the facts can tell. What people take away from great art is the humanity and the heart."

"Speaking of heart," Lilah said, "there's another place I want you to see."

They drove (barefoot) back to Brighthead center, where Lilah directed Emerson to park in front of an old church with boarded-up windows and peeling white paint.

"This property's been abandoned for a decade," Lilah said, pulling her wet sneakers back on. "I've talked to the town, and the BCG has a chance to buy it. They want it off their hands, and we want to turn it into our headquarters."

She punched in the code for the lock on the back door, then unsealed it so they could squish their way into a narthex that smelled of old wood and mildew.

Light streamed through the uppermost windows, but none through the boarded ones on the first floor.

"What would you do with it?"

Emerson's voice echoed.

Lilah spoke softer, and hers didn't. "Everything. Pull out the pews, and we'd have prime studio space. There are rooms in the back, plus downstairs there's a kitchen and a bathroom. We could host meetings, and we could teach classes, and we could even have an artist-in-residency program." She clasped her hands. "That's been my goal for a while—being able to offer artists a place to stay and work in peace. Lift the regular cares of the world off them for a while, and they can produce their best work in a spot free of stress."

Emerson's mouth opened. "That's what the apartment is for, then?"

He got it! "It's the same as offering you part of my barn to paint. We can offer artists from all over the world a chance to work in a studio surrounded by other artwork and visited by brilliant crafters and artisans, and they can work on their own pieces." She opened her arms. "This could be ours!"

Emerson said, "Other than the hundreds of thousands of dollars it would take to buy and restore such a place."

"It doesn't need a lot of restoration, and the town doesn't want much money. The BCG has been applying for grants. We can do this. It's my dream, and it's right here." She clenched her fists. "I needed you to see it because we're not telling everybody about it yet. But I had to talk to someone."

Emerson walked into the center of the church, then turned in a slow circle, looking up at the rafters, the stained glass, the wide spaces. "You can feel the history.

These buildings were designed to elevate the spirit, so repurposing this one for artwork is the next best thing."

Warmth spread through Lilah as he saw everything that Lilah saw. His mind was attuned to all the beauty of the world. He'd picked up the same hints of potential that she had, and as with dating Brooke, just a nudge was enough to commit him to it.

He turned back to her, eyes alight. "I want to photograph this place, too. I want to capture it on canvas, and then I want to show the world what we've found."

CHAPTER EIGHT

Back at Lilah's, Emerson hauled his painting gear out of his car. True to her word, Lilah had cleared out an area and arranged lights to create the perfect workspace.

Looking at the barn, it was easy to see why Lilah had attached so hard to that abandoned church. Both had high ceilings. The barn had a hay loft, and the church had a choir loft. Age permeated both buildings, but both had been encroached on by modern upgrades.

Lilah gave him the Wi-Fi password, and Emerson was good to go.

Sitting at the easel, he swiped through his photos, debating which landmark to paint first. He'd have to do the lighthouse, no question. Brighthead Harbor was another that seemed obvious, although he wasn't sure what angle was best. Lilah had taken him to all the best spots, including Sky Ridge Drive where the richest houses looked over the water. He'd photographed a couple running with their border collie. A landscape could be breathtaking, sure, but Emerson loved giving each scene a human touch. Even a bicycle leaning against a tree humanized a photo just enough to tell a story and draw the viewer closer.

He'd snapped a photo of two boys sitting on one of the boulders, heads bent over the same phone screen. That was nice.

He swiped again, and there was Lilah.

He hadn't meant to get that picture. She'd stepped into the frame unexpectedly while he was photographing the town green, and then she'd apologized as though she couldn't just step backward and let him take the picture again. She was a little blurred, her mouth open in a half-gasp as she realized her mistake, so he moved his finger to delete it—and then stopped.

Lilah's hair had been in motion just as she was. Her hand was extended as she tried to draw his attention to something else he might want to capture, only in that moment, he'd captured her: the spirit of Lilah was digitized for eternity, dedicated to an afternoon of picture-taking in a town she'd lived her whole life, finding newness among familiar landmarks.

He glanced at Lilah across the barn, on the futon, working on her laptop. Where did she find the energy to do all this? The zest?

She and Brooke were so different that it was hard to see why they'd clicked, but maybe Brooke needed Lilah for her passion, while Lilah leaned on Brooke to keep her on the rails.

Emerson kept swiping through his photos, but he kept thinking of Lilah's photographic intrusion. Thinking of how he'd photographed so much beauty today, and how well she fit with the rest of it.

Then Emerson forced himself to turn away from her because of Brooke. Lilah wanted him to date Brooke. Lilah, who had an instinct for how things should fit together, thought he and Brooke were a good fit. Lilah wasn't interested in him.

Lilah looked up. "Which landmark do you want to paint first?"

Emerson paid close attention to his tablet. "The harbor.

That feels like a slam dunk."

Working on a sketch pad, Emerson roughed out how the piece would look. *This isn't selling out. It's still beauty. It's a means of smuggling my other art into people's lives.* He combined the harbor with the outline of two people sitting on a rock, heads together, looking at the same thing. A heron. Would a boat add too much visual clutter? What time of day should it be? Should the causeway be visible?

And hadn't that been fun, losing a race against the water? Lilah had his sneakers on her boot dryer right now, and his socks were stretched out on the hood of his car.

He wouldn't draw the children. That felt wrong, no matter how anonymous they were. Two adults, then. Two adults looking at something, maybe a phone, maybe a pamphlet the way he and Brooke had looked over her marked-up pamphlet at the Renn Faire.

Emerson stopped then because the figure he'd sketched had hair in frizzy waves like Lilah's.

It had been automatic. She'd just shown up there in his mind, her in that accidental photo, her now accidentally on his sketch.

He fleshed out the second figure quickly: long dark hair, with a little lean toward the other figure. That could be Brooke. They were friends. At some point, they must have conspired over a phone screen.

He decided against the boat. A heron, though, felt right. Peaceful. He'd have the causeway fully visible, a pathway to the light.

After a couple of sketches, he decided on the layout and sketched again, this time onto the primed canvas.

Lilah's car pulled into the driveway, visible through the open barn door. Brooke hopped out, removed her bike from the back, then retrieved a pizza from the front. Lilah bounded out to her, all enthusiasm. "I'll tuck this into the oven until Emerson's at a good stopping point."

Brooke went to his side, then picked up his discarded sketches. "This is amazing. Exactly what Lilah wanted." She gestured to the pair on the rock. "That's me and Lilah."

She smiled shyly. Emerson said, "I didn't intend it that way. I guess you were on my mind."

"That's sweet." Brooke rested a hand on his shoulder. "You were thinking of beauty, and you unconsciously immortalized the two of us."

Emerson drove home at ten o'clock with a painting in Lilah's barn, and a sketchpad full of thoughts on the passenger seat. *Don't drive and draw,* he kept telling himself as the blacktop approached beneath his headlights and then vanished away beneath the tires. He didn't ever text and drive, but now his head was full of sketches and his chest ached with the need to draw them all.

And iterations of them all.

And then he'd have to decide which ones to paint.

Lilah had said he could return on Sunday morning, as early as he liked. "I have an open-barn policy," she'd quipped.

Emerson suspected that if he'd said he would stay up painting the whole night, that she'd have shown him the coffee maker before retreating into her apartment to sleep. That led to burnout, though. Best to close the tap on the inspiration right now and awaken with the well replenished. Ideas developed in the dark. His unconscious mind could play with the images in a way his conscious mind couldn't. A drive, a solid sleep, and another drive would work wonders that coffee and an all-nighter could never.

Besides, there was magic in that barn. Lilah had filled it with creative energy and decorated it with her heart. If she could do that, alone, in a barn, what would she accomplish with an abandoned church and a community of crafters?

Right before he'd left, Emerson had taken one more

picture: Lilah's kitchen sink. It was just a regular sink, but on the window ledge she was growing things. She'd taken the bottoms of a few lettuces and set them in bowls of water where they could extend long leaves toward the light. An onion top was stretching toward the sun. Carrot greens, too.

She'd noticed him looking at the plants. "They have life in them. I wanted to give them a chance."

She said not all of them made it, but for the ones who responded to water and light and love, she gave them a second chance in the soil.

Of all the Brighthead photos Emerson wanted to paint, that one burned hottest in his mind: a kitchen window full of vegetable cuttings. Outside the window could be anything, but what mattered was the tiny plant nursery with second life being coaxed from scraps.

He got home with his brain alight and still not ready for sleep. He checked his phone to see who had texted during the drive, and it was his sister. He replied, "Are you still awake?"

She sent, "It's only ten o'clock, old man."

He hit the button to dial her, and when she answered, he said, "If I'm such an old man, then you'll talk to me on the phone rather than having me figure out this new-fangled texting contraption."

"Do you have your cane and your prune juice?" She laughed, but she sounded tense. "I thought you tucked into bed at eight-thirty every night, so where were you?"

Emerson pulled the sketch book from his bag and paged through everything he'd done today. "You know the crafters guild I've been talking about? They gave me an exhibit in July, and they convinced me I needed to do a few commercially viable ones."

"Money," Sonia said. "Money is good."

Emerson reached the first blank page, and he set Sonia on speaker phone. "I hate the idea of selling out, but they said it's not selling out if it's opening the door to new patrons. So—"

"So do it. You can paint amazing stuff, but you can also paint amazing sellable stuff, and that's totally fine." She laughed. "What's on the board right now?"

He opened the pencil case. "I'm doing Brighthead harbor, since the showcase is going to be in Brighthead."

"You said it's a French restaurant?"

"I didn't think they'd want me there, but Lilah insisted."

Sonia said, "Yeah, well, don't put your photo next to the paintings. Let them think Emerson Charles is a stodgy white dude with a well-combed beard and a law degree he's no longer using."

Emerson sighed. "Lilah didn't get it at all. She's like, *If you put up your work, they'll see the real you,* and I'm thinking, that's not what we want. I'm not about grandstanding. She had a point about giving tourists pieces they'd want to take home to remember their vacation, though, so that's the current project."

Sonia said, "Will you die of boredom painting the harbor over and over?"

"Lilah drove me all over Brighthead today to show me the sweet spots. I'll be painting those and giving everyone a slice of their peaceful vacation to carry back to their stressful lives."

Sonia laughed. "Whoa. Those words didn't come out of your mouth. She's way in your head."

Emerson finished framing up Lilah's window on the page. "She had a point. If you're going to pin a price tag to something, make it something they want to buy as well as something you want to sell."

"No joke, but you always shut down Dad when he said the same thing. I've got to meet this woman someday, hopefully before the wedding."

Emerson stopped. "What?"

"I'm liking your new girlfriend. Visits Renn Faires and makes you this excited about painting? She's a keeper."

Emerson said, "No, Lilah isn't my girlfriend. She's the one who set me up with Brooke."

Sonia fell silent. Then, "Oops."

"Brooke's more laid-back." Emerson swiped through his photos past the harbor, past the church, past Brooke's bicycle leaning against Lilah's barn door. There, the kitchen sink. "She's thoughtful and observant, and she agrees I should be doing the commercial stuff, too."

Sonia said, "But she's not supportive?"

"She is. She sat with me tonight while I was painting, and we talked."

"Okay." Sonia sounded off-balance. "Well, I'd like to meet her, too."

Then, after a pause, Sonia said, "I need to get out of the city. Any chance I could crash on your couch for a few days? Just get my head together and stop hunting like crazy for a job?"

"Absolutely." Sonia had long since claimed she could never live out in the middle of nowhere like Emerson. The fact that she was even asking left Emerson unsteady. "I don't have a lot of room, but I'll get an air mattress, and we'll make it work."

"Thanks. It's so frustrating. I put in all these applications, but I never hear back. Dad asks every day if I've gotten any good leads or if I'm networking, and it's just pressure all the time."

He started drawing a bowl with Romaine stems growing from it. "I get it."

"You don't get it. You were in the process for a government job before you even graduated, and then you wandered around with your friends camping for three months while you waited for the G-men to call your number."

That wasn't a fair characterization. Emerson had spent those months painting, too, while his friends had slowly grown disenchanted with the, "We'll live out of a van" lifestyle. Not him. Every so often, he'd stop off at a postal center and ship home any of the paintings he wanted to keep, and then he'd prime over the ones he didn't and make new ones.

Sonia went on, "I can barely even land an interview, and

when I do, they don't call back. I'm losing it."

Thinking of Lilah's barn and how it filled him with artistic energy, Emerson said, "Come up here, and find it again."

"I didn't go to college to wait tables." She huffed. "I'm pulling down decent money, but that's not what I want. I'm living in one of the easiest places to get a job, and I'm even applying as far out as Worcester, and there's nothing."

Shaking his head, Emerson set down his pencil. "I don't even have any advice because—"

"That's the thing. I don't want advice. The career center is giving me advice. Dad is giving me advice. Mom is giving me advice. Even Grandma is giving me advice. What I want is a floor to sleep on."

Emerson took up the pencil again and started drawing carrot greens. "Then let's get you up here. Give me some dates, and I'll put in for days off. We'll get you some floor space and some quiet, and maybe you'll sleep better surrounded by art."

CHAPTER NINE

Lilah awoke the next Saturday morning with a tremor of excitement. Her barn was filling with art, and Emerson was coming today to make more.

She had the morning shift at Bright Stitches, so she'd leave everything set up. He seemed comfortable in the barn, but even so, she didn't want to risk he'd feel like he couldn't get milk for his coffee, or like he couldn't have coffee at all. Instead, she turned on the string lights, wrote out a list of things he could find in her kitchen, and made suggestions of places he could drive if he needed a mid-day creativity break.

Just before heading out, she texted him. "I'm leaving the barn unlocked. Just go in."

He didn't reply. Maybe he was driving.

At Bright Stitches, Lilah checked her yarn display and made note of which colors were low. Natalie or Brooke would be keeping track in the computer so they could pay her out at the end of the month, but it made sense to replenish as the pieces sold. Tourists were already trickling into Brighthead now that Memorial Day had passed, although not the gush they'd expect in late June,

July, and August.

Natalie was already at work. "I hear things are going pretty good with Emerson."

Lilah nodded. "He's going to be painting in the barn today, and Brooke will visit after work. I can't wait to see what else he's done. He was working on a painting at home all week, too."

Natalie said, "Sounds like you found his magic formula."

"All that talent deserves to thrive." She sighed. "You should come for dinner. I assume Colin's tied up at the restaurant."

"He kissed me goodbye on Monday and said he'll see me after Labor Day, and I'm still not sure how serious he was." When Lilah flinched, Natalie added, "I'll find a way. If nothing else, I could pop into the restaurant after work and roll silverware for an hour."

Before lunch, a customer entered and marched up to Lilah. She looked familiar—vaguely—in the way people did when you lived in the same town all your life. Not a tourist. She was steely and small, grey-eyed and grey-haired. The woman looked her up and down as if finding every fault with her, from her open-toed sandals to her fingernails done in five different colors. "Lilah Marcille?"

Was she looking for hand-dyed yarn? "That's me. Can I help you?"

"No. I'm Michelle Hargrove, the president of the Brighthead Historical Society, and it's come to our attention that you're trying to buy the Old First Church on Main Street."

Lilah nodded. "Not me, specifically, but the Brighthead Crafters Guild."

Michelle frowned. "You can't do that."

Taking a step backward, Lilah said, "Why not?"

Michelle folded her arms. "It's an historic building—a landmark."

"That's why the town wants to sell it to us," Lilah said. "We'll repair the building, keep it in good shape, and restore it to life at the center of Brighthead."

Michelle drummed the fingers of one hand against the opposite arm. "You're going to be changing the character of the building."

"A church is designed to raise our consciousness to something beyond this world." Good thing Emerson had said this because it worked perfectly right now. "Art does the same. If anything, repurposing an old church for an artists' community will be enhancing the character of the building."

Natalie drew closer as Michelle shook her head. "Repurposing the building will rob it of its original design and usefulness. That building was constructed in 1892, and it's interwoven with Brighthead's history."

Lilah forced a smile she wasn't feeling. "Our guild will ensure it's interwoven with Brighthead's future."

In a smooth voice, Natalie said, "What exactly is the historical society's objection?"

Natalie had a way of calming down a situation. Good thing Brooke wasn't here yet, or she'd have started arguing. Which, to be fair, Lilah was on the brink of doing.

Michelle pulled up a list on her phone. "The stained glass windows would require full restoration."

Lilah said, "Of course. That's not even a question."

Natalie said, "I suspect a lot of the Historical Society's concerns are concerns we have as well. What else?"

Michelle said, "Many items in the church were donated and have memorial plaques attached to them."

Lilah said, "Those can be retained."

Michelle said, "You're keeping the pews?"

Lilah said, "No. The pews would have to be rehomed."

Rehomed sounded better than removed, especially in the face of someone who was so rooted in keeping everything the same.

"Then you can't take over the building because the pews date back to the original church construction and need to stay with it."

Lilah said, "And the altar?"

Michelle huffed. "You know as well as I do that the altar

71

was removed to a church in Ellsworth after the church was decommissioned."

Lilah tilted her head. "You're saying that the seating is more integral to a church than its altar."

"We had nothing to say about what the church leadership decided to do at the time they closed their doors," Michelle said. "But the pews are there, and they need to remain."

Natalie said, "In the past ten years, how many organizations have shown an interest in taking over the building?"

Lilah said, "Does the Historical Society realize that if the building collapses after decades of disuse, the pews will be destroyed anyhow?"

Natalie added, "Also, unless I'm mistaken, one reason the church closed its doors was a leaking bell tower, which the Historical Society filed an injunction against them removing."

Lilah said, "The Economic Planning Board has discussed the abandoned church building at several meetings over the past three years. That's prime downtown space, and the town doesn't benefit from having it stand as a gravestone to the past. Our guild will ensure there are lights in the windows and open doors for anyone visiting Brighthead. What's wrong with that?"

Michelle sighed. "What's wrong is the removal of historically significant features from the church. I've spoken to people who were baptized in that church, married in that church, and whose parents were buried from that church. To turn it into a drug den for artists would break their hearts."

A drug den for artists?

Fortunately, Natalie spoke before Lilah. "Removing the benches is a far cry from cooking meth in the basement."

Lilah said, "Also, have you ever met our local artists? Our typical meetings take place in Fruits de Mer." Well, both of them so far. "You can contact the owner to find out how we behave. Our members are knitters and crocheters, jewelry designers, a woman who makes bead mosaics, painters who work in oil and acrylic, photographers, sculptors—and yes, some of us are a bit odd, but any church worth the name also welcomes members that are a bit odd."

Natalie said, "I have the Fruits de Mer owner's personal cell phone number if you'd like his endorsement."

Michelle shook her head. "The last thing we need are a bunch of counter-cultural iconoclasts smearing the interior of the church with whatever subversive imagery is currently getting the most clicks and views on social media."

Lilah's hands shook as she opened her phone to show Michelle one of Emerson's pieces. The one she landed on was the abandoned white house, vines climbing the sides. "Subversive?"

She said, "No matter your membership now, you can't guarantee who will join in the future. Since you can't promise the church will remain the same, we can't permit the sale to go forward."

Lilah said, "How do you intend to prevent it?"

Michelle said, "Two of the Historical Society members are lawyers. We're filing an injunction Monday morning to stop you from proceeding."

Natalie said, "Then thank you for the warning, and please, feel free not to remain in our shop any longer. It's our personal policy not to speak to individuals who are suing us."

Lilah's ears rang. You shouldn't be able to feel your own blood pressure, should you? This woman with her petty concerns and her bored attorneys that needed something to do—willing to save a bunch of benches at the expense of the building standing around them—willing to let a building die and a dream die just because someone might paint the walls—

Natalie walked to the front door. "Thank you for your time." The door jingled as she pulled it open. "Please, don't let us detain you further."

This was unreasonable and ridiculous, and why? For what? Because someone might look at her grandmother's wedding pictures and think, "Where that bench is in the picture, there's now a sculpture of a willow"?

Michelle Hargrove said, "I'll be in touch."

Natalie said, "To repeat myself, since you're taking legal action, I'd prefer to hear only from your legal counsel," and then waited with the door open until Michelle finally walked out the door.

Lilah struggled to unclench her fists. "Can they do that?"

"I have no honest clue if they can do that, but she thinks they can." Natalie started typing into her phone. "I'm asking Colin if he's ever heard of anything like this. He may also know something about historical structures."

"It's not declared a historic site. We checked that." Lilah closed her eyes. Breathe. One deep breath, two, three, okay. The first thing she needed to do was email the BCG leadership team.

The church was perfect. The Historical Society was a nonprofit group, like the BCG. It didn't matter if the Historical Society was against them. They just needed to get the town onboard. The town would see it was for the best. If it went to a judge, the judge would agree with her.

CHAPTER TEN

Lilah walked through her barn door looking so devastated that Emerson nearly dropped his brush. "What's wrong?"

"Keep working." She hurled her backpack onto the futon. "I'm too angry to tell you now."

She stalked into her apartment. Should he go after her?

Better to wait her out. By now he knew Lilah well enough to guess that in a minute, she'd be back and start doing something to burn off her own energy, either throwing herself onto the futon to knit or else heading over to her dye table to colorize something.

Sure enough, two minutes later, she was back in the barn, flipping on the hot plate and then hauling the large pot to the utility sink.

Emerson listened to her working behind him. Another basin got filled. Yarn got plopped into the water. Cabinets opened and then banged shut. Her tongs clicked as she retrieved them, then other metal clanked as she set up all her tools.

He said, "What colors go well with outrage?"

"I intend to find out." She came up behind his shoulder to look at his painting of the statue. "Yeah, not those colors. Sorry," and she headed back to her table.

"She didn't mean anything by that," Emerson reassured the canvas.

"Your paintings are never angry," Lilah replied as if he'd been talking to her. "I've recognized peace and yearning and despair and relief, but never anger."

She'd seen all that?

Most people looked at his paintings the way Brooke did. "Oh, pretty!" Maybe he'd get more from the ones who wanted to fill up the silence: "I'd love to see scenery like that!" or "Where is this supposed to be?" Sometimes someone broke apart the symbolism of a specific color or a design choice.

Lilah, meanwhile, went right for the heart: peace and yearning and despair and relief.

He looked at her as she retwisted her yarn hanks. "Your yarn has different emotions attached to the colors. Joy, curiosity, wonder."

"Well, buckle in, because tonight, we dye with fury."

He said, "Will the wool hold up to that?"

Her mouth twitched. "Maybe."

It turned out what she was doing this afternoon wasn't the same kind of dye job she'd done at Brooke's birthday party. That had been playful, but it had also been very hands-on. For this one, she strangled the yarn hanks until the strands were so tight they screamed, and then plunked the tight hanks into the boiling dye-water with everything on a timer.

Afterward, she came up to him. "Is this what you were working on at home?"

The painting on his home easel was her kitchen window. "It's making good progress," he said, hoping that deflected her.

She'd left the apartment unlocked for him today, along with a note that he could go in there for anything he needed. Good, becauase he'd needed to see her window again.

He hadn't stayed long—long enough to put his lunch in

the fridge and refill his water bottle. He'd gone into the apartment to use the bathroom, aware all the time that he shouldn't snoop but at the same time aware of how much he wanted to. He wanted to crawl through all the books on her shelf. He wanted to learn what art she'd hung on the walls of her other rooms. Had she strung her bedroom with lights the way she had the barn?

He hadn't indulged the curiosity beyond taking more pictures of her kitchen window. Lilah had done a lot for him already. Repaying it by violating her privacy was wrong, no matter how unworried she seemed about leaving a man alone in her home all day.

When her timer rang, she turned off the heat under the pot. Eventually the yarn came out, and he crossed the room to look at the result. Once again, the water inside the pot looked clean enough to boil spaghetti (he knew you don't do that—all this equipment was no longer food-safe) and the yarn wore varying shades of a vivid blue, with some parts bare because they hadn't absorbed any dye at all.

He said, "It didn't all get dyed."

"Those are called resist points. If the yarn is tight in places, those parts don't absorb anything. That's why I'm retwisting before I re-dye it."

Lilah spread out the hanks to cool in the catering tray, then measured more dye into the pot. "We're going purple this time."

"Same skeins?"

"Yep." She re-twisted the slightly cooler hanks of yarn, and once the water boiled, plunked all four back in the pot.

Again she set the timer. Again Emerson returned to the easel. She drifted over to the harbor painting he'd hung the wall to dry. "I love this. Someone's going to snap it up."

The figures on the rocks were no longer Lilah and Brooke. He'd obscured their features enough that they could be any two people sharing a confidence. He'd reached for the feeling you'd have if you'd met a friend on vacation. He'd wanted them to seem comfortable together. The viewer should notice the pair and remember being on those rocks, remember double-checking a schedule or showing off a photo on the phone screen.

She took a picture of his finished painting. "Your eyes only," Emerson said.

"Of course. Being painted in my barn doesn't make it my intellectual property." She shrugged as if that were obvious and went back to her yarn pot.

Emerson thought of all the photos of her kitchen window and decided fair was fair.

When the timer went off, the yarn came out of the pot and got spread out to dry. Again, there were resist points, but they were smaller. Again, new dye got measured into the pot. Again, Lilah retwisted the yarn. She looked happier now, so Emerson kept working. He had the statue painting roughed out and was wondering which way he wanted to go with the plaque of lies, whether he should make some of the letters readable or just leave it blurred.

He could correct the plaque, but that felt vile. Brighthead had—intentionally or unintentionally—created the legend of a woman who, in the face of unfathomable loss, had rallied herself to prevent others from experiencing the same. People bonded to their stories, and tourists were already a highly emotional, highly bondable class of people. If their resolve strengthened when reading about Myth Brightman's one-woman fight to secure the harbor, why should facts rob them of their inspiration?

"Knock knock!" Brooke stepped inside the barn. "Everyone's so busy."

She paused to admire Emerson's paintings, first the work in progress and second the finished painting of the harbor. "These are amazing. You're so talented." Then she stepped over to Lilah's dye station. "Gosh. What are you making?"

"Kettle-dyed three times," Lilah said. "I'm so over people."

Brooke said, "Yeah, I heard from Natalie."

Emerson set down his brush. "Do you want to tell me about it, too?"

Lilah spooned up some water, and it was, once again, clear. So weird, that the yarn drew up all the pigment and left the water pure. Emerson never ended his paintings with clean brushes or a clean palette. If anything, he spread plastic all over the place because the colors went everywhere.

Lilah shut off the heat. "Yeah, I'm calmer." She faced Emerson. "The same historical society that couldn't be bothered to make sure the Brighthead sign was correct is going to court to prevent the BCG from acquiring the old church building, on the grounds that it's a historical landmark of great significance." She spoke over his startled exclamation. "We'd do terrible things to the building like showcase experimental art or remove the seating from the nave, so yeah, they can't tolerate that."

Brooke said, "Natalie talked to Colin, and he said sometimes things like this happen, and if we have a lawyer involved with the BCG, this very seriously is a matter for them to handle."

"*Obviously* sometimes things like this happen," Lilah muttered. "It happened to us, so it stands to reason things happen."

"I mean, people getting prickly about historical buildings. One of his mentors had continuous fights because his restaurant was set up in old railway cars, and every time he wanted to expand, it was yet another fight to move a train car onto the lot. Because apparently it was going to destroy the area."

Emerson said, "We had a situation back home where an office complex wanted to put up a parking garage near Route 9, and the neighbors complained it would block their view. Their view was, weirdly, a strip mall across the street, but I guess they couldn't stand to lose their vista of the auto dealership and the fast-food place."

Lilah said, "I already put out a call within the group asking if anyone's a lawyer or related to a lawyer. But that woman said to my face she'd rather the building collapse into a heap of stone and shattered glass than shelter a bunch of bohemian artisans sipping tea and knitting."

Emerson said, "You mean Black artists."

Brooke and Lilah both froze, then turned to him.

Emerson opened his hands. "Come on. How hard is it to read between the lines? She doesn't want deviants and strangers to sully the purity of their abandoned church. Which one of us has a quality that stands out in Brighthead?"

With eyebrows in an inverted V, Lilah shook her head. "I showed her your art! She said your art wasn't the problem. She's afraid of future art that may never even come to pass."

Brooke lowered her voice. "Do you think she would say, 'Actually, dear, I'm a racist'?"

Lilah's fists clenched. "Well, now I have another reason to pound her into the ground. Legally."

Emerson said, "And again, for legal reasons, she'll never mention her real concern."

Brooke sighed. "I could almost understand if she was actually concerned for the historical building."

Emerson couldn't resist adding, "If you'd removed me from the initial lineup, you'd have had the building by the time the historical society rallied its defenses."

Lilah said, "Stop it. For now, she's just saying she objects to subversive art created by artists who don't exist. Let's keep it at that level. As you said, she won't mention race in a legal case, so we'll have to fight on the grounds they're introducing. If they're racist on top of being hidebound, then they're the ones who can't lay their heads down at night."

When Lilah removed the dyed yarn from the pot, Brooke let out a gasp that was more enthusiastic than anything she'd shown during the Renn Faire. "That's amazing! What colors?"

Lilah said, "Cerulean blue, midnight blue, and amethyst. I soaked the yarn in vinegar so the dye would strike quickly and unevenly."

"Tell me you have plans for these." Brooke's hands clenched as she watched Lilah spreading out the skeins on the tray. "Otherwise I might end up buying them."

Lilah snickered. "All four? I'm not sure they classify as the same colorway. This one's more blue than the others."

"I'd treat them like a gradient." Brooke bounced on her toes. "You could totally sell them as one colorway. It'd be a shame to split them off from one another."

Where had that excitement been when they'd watched the jousting, or just having a meal together? Brooke said, "Add a little pink next time, and these would be galaxy colors."

Lilah said, "Oh, I like that. This is more like midnight in the forest."

Brooke nodded. "Is that the colorway name?"

"This took a lot of time. I don't think I'll make it an official colorway." Lilah shrugged, then looked at Emerson. "What do you think?"

Emerson quelled the urge to reach for the yarn because it was still too hot to touch. He studied it, then changed position and looked at the interplay of colors from a different angle.

"I like it more than I thought I would," he said. "At first it looks like regular yarn, but the longer I study the way the parts work together, the more interesting it becomes."

CHAPTER ELEVEN

Emerson and Brooke went for a walk while Lilah got on the phone with the only attorney the BCG had to offer. "Our attorney specializes in tree law," Brooke added, "but at the very least she probably knows someone who knows someone who can help."

Emerson said, "Networking at its finest."

"That's the whole point of the BCG. If we can't somehow scare up a lawyer, maybe we don't deserve to exist." She stretched as they passed Lilah's landlord's house. "Isn't that a gorgeous farmhouse? When Lilah first told me she wanted to live in a barn, I said, 'What, like a horse?' and offered to start her a straw registry so she could outfit her first stall and buy a feed bag of oats. It's worked out well for her, though."

"It does seem to fit her perfectly." Emerson chuckled. "Where do you live? In an airplane hangar?"

"Nothing so exotic. I have a studio apartment in a complex up Route 188. If you've ever been in a hotel room with a kitchen, you've got the idea." She brushed the hair back from her forehead. "I don't need a lot of space. I'm one of those rare creatures, the low-stashing knitter.

Because we've got the shop, I figured out pretty quickly that I don't need to keep one of every pretty yarn on hand just in case it vanished, never to be seen again. There's more out there than I can ever knit. A bed, a couch, a desk, a kitchen table that folds up, a dresser, a closet—and with that, I'm all set."

Emerson said, "You could buy an RV and drive around Maine, knitting wherever your heart desires."

Brooke's eyes widened. "Why would I want that?"

Emerson prompted, "Wake up in a different part of the state every day...?"

She shuddered. "That's a nightmare, not a dream. Every day, having to figure out again where you are and what you're doing...? I like my routine. Everything is right where I put it. Start the coffee maker, toast the bagel. Bagel comes out of the toaster at the same time the coffee finishes brewing." She laughed as they turned onto the road. "Not to say I don't get any variety. Sometimes I get a sesame seed bagel instead of plain. Also, I check the weather to see if I should drive to work instead of biking."

He raised his hands. "Whoa, take it easy there. You don't want to go crazy, party girl."

Brooke grinned. "I know my limits. Everything's comfortable."

"Comfort breeds stagnation."

"I haven't stagnated." Brooke shrugged. "I get that you're up for adventure every day. As a park ranger, you'd have had all that and more, not to mention the huge change you made moving from Boston to Bar Harbor. That may be where you get your creative energy, but my creativity is structured."

Emerson frowned. "There's a lot of structure in painting."

"Absolutely, but your inspiration is emotional. Lilah sat with your website on her tablet after the first BCG meeting, showing me all your paintings and telling me about the emotions behind every one of them. I'll promise you now, no one talks about the emotions inspired by my shawl patterns."

Emerson nearly stopped in his tracks. "She did that?"

Brooke nodded. "You and I talked a lot at that first meeting, and Lilah wanted to make sure I understood you weren't just a painter, but a great painter. I said I wouldn't have the first idea how to talk art criticism, so she went through and explained every image on your website."

Emerson didn't respond.

"Here." Brooke took his hand and turned off the side of the road to a place that looked barely like a road at all. "Have you ever seen one of these? It's an antique road."

After ten feet, they emerged onto a much wider path that cut through the woods. Brooke said, "This used to be a road, or a path, or something. It never got made into an official road, but everyone uses these to move between the actual roads."

Emerson craned his neck to look around. "We're basically off-trail here."

"We're on-trail, just not an official trail. There isn't a full map of these anywhere, but the locals know the ones near them, and some of them have official names. There's a Facebook group called Bright Hearts in Brighthead where you'll see some of the old-timers posting things like, 'Anyone go up to the Island lately?' and it turns out it's just a place deep in the woods that happens to be a bit higher than the rest, where the high school students 'used to' go to drink." Brooke snickered. "As if they don't still. You'll find campfire remains sometimes, along with a thousand cans. And the occasional sink someone's discarded because it's cheaper than paying a disposal service."

Emerson shook his head. "Yeah, there's nothing like this in Jamaica Plain."

"It's neat, seeing the underside of Brighthead's history." She took his hand as they climbed down a steep part of the path, then let go as they kept walking. "You'll want to check for ticks later, by the way."

"Yeah, I'm up on that part of nature."

She said, "Sorry. Park ranger. Forgot."

"I'm a desk jockey now, so it's a good reminder." He hadn't brought bug spray, and the black flies were annoying. He should be ashamed of himself for not having thought of that. "Hang on."

He photographed the trail, then turned around and got the area behind with the rocks they'd just climbed down. Then they kept going further until they ended up on a much wider path—still not a road, but with a well-maintained gravel surface.

"Behold, the rail trail!" Brooke stepped out into it. "It starts at the mill buildings and the high school, and it heads on toward the interior for about ten miles. Good for biking or running or walking."

Brooke led him out even further. They emerged by a pond, and here Emerson photographed everything he could, taking a panorama of the entire body of water. He took pictures of the ducks, and Brooke laughed when a frog plunked into the water nearby. "We've even got otters," Brooke said, "but I've never seen one myself. I usually go through on my bike."

Emerson said, "You bike everywhere."

"My grandmother didn't want to drive me all over. A bike was an expensive birthday gift, but she realized it was worth it not to have to cart me to lessons or to my friends' houses."

Emerson added, "And it's fun."

She said, "That, too."

After another mile, Brook turned them off the main trail onto another "antique road," and shortly they were back on a paved road, walking single file along the side whenever a car came. They didn't speak much while Emerson's head filled with images from the pond and the rail trail. Did tourists come to the rail trail? If he painted one of these, would it be a "for love" painting, or a "for money" painting?

Lilah's landlord's farmhouse came into view, and Emerson realized they'd circled back to the same road he'd driven in on. Brooke dropped back alongside him as they turned up the driveway. "I had a good time at the Renn Faire," she said. "I was wondering if you'd like to go somewhere tomorrow, too."

"Sure. What were you thinking of?"

"There's a hiking trail about half an hour away with a decent view from the summit. We could meet at the trailhead. I'll pack lunches. You can bring your painting gear if you're the kind of painter who likes to paint with the subject in front of him."

Emerson said, "And then when you die of boredom, I'll carry you back down?"

Brooke shrugged. "Knitting and a book. I'll never die of boredom."

That sounded like an enthusiastic endorsement if Emerson had ever heard one. "Sure, then. Tell me when and where."

"Awesome." She squeezed his hand just before they re-entered the barn.

Lilah looked up from her futon as Brooke and Emerson returned from their walk. They seemed happy. "Thanks for giving me some space. I needed to be less prickly."

Emerson raised a hand. "Not prickly at all. Although, entirely understandable if you had been."

Brooke said, "That sounds like a toddler's excuses: *I didn't do it, and if I did, it wasn't that bad, and if it was that bad, they deserved it.*"

Lilah laughed, and Emerson did too. Lilah said, "Hey, while I'm waiting for advice from legal counsel, why don't we plan something for dinner? Maybe get Natalie over here, too."

Emerson said, "And Natalie's boyfriend?"

Lilah shook her head. "We aren't going to see Colin until the end of tourist season, at which point he takes a three-week nap. If it's a fun time to get together, or a holiday, he's working."

Brooke said, "But that means Natalie will be free, so I'll text her."

While Brooke did that, Emerson sat on the opposite side of Lilah's couch. "Are you getting any good advice from the guild?"

Back to the frustrating stuff. "Yes and no. Legal advice from a pottery-maker isn't what we need, but we have a lot of that. On the other hand, I have a few recommendations on decent lawyers, plus someone's brother is going to call when he gets a chance." She shook her head, and with a glance at Brooke, she said, "But at least you two got a nice walk out of it."

"Brooke showed me the rail trail." Emerson didn't have dreamy eyes, and he didn't look as if he'd snuck a kiss with her beneath the pines. "We walked out past a pond and then made a big circle of it to get back here."

"Burnett Pond. It's pretty, isn't it? Although not later in the summer, when it's covered in green and looks disgusting." Lilah snickered. "Don't paint it that way."

Emerson shot back, "If I don't paint it that way, the July tourists won't recognize it."

Lilah slapped a hand over her heart and crumpled into the couch. "Touché! Then you'll need to re-paint it in the fall when it's brown with rotting leaf debris."

Brooke sat criss-cross on the floor in front of the couch. "You should thank me, Emerson. I brought you to the pond for the fifteen minutes of the year when it's not a sodden mess."

Lilah said, "He has to paint it that way because paintings aren't supposed to be photographs. They're supposed to capture the best of a place. Leave reality behind, and give everyone the emotions of clear water surrounded by tall trees."

Brooke said, "Isn't it better to paint things as they

actually are, rather than the way you convinced yourself they ought to be?"

Lilah grinned at Emerson. "I'd rather he does what he does best, and paints the right emotions into existence."

Chapter Twelve

Emerson awoke to a patter of rain.

He checked his phone to find a text from Brooke, sent ten minutes ago. It was an emoji face, looking irritated. Must be raining in Brighthead, too.

It was hard to haul himself upright, but eventually Emerson started the coffee maker. He'd text Brooke when he was thinking clearer. First he went to his studio door and looked at the painting on the easel—the painting he'd finished last night, then sealed with a coat of glossy varnish.

Lilah's kitchen window looked out on a sunny field, while alongside it was his bedroom window with a view of the drizzly parking lot. He knew which one he'd rather see, but reality hadn't given him a choice.

The coffee maker beeped, so he poured the cup and started drinking it straight, checking the weather app on his phone. The rain should stop shortly—it shouldn't have been raining at all—but the sky would remain overcast.

He texted Brooke. "I'm up for a muddy hike if you have waterproof gear."

After a minute, she replied, "We were doing this for the

view and so you could paint it."

Was that why they were doing it? Not to spend time, but to facilitate Emerson's career?

Brooke's second text read, "I'm going to guess you have any number of canvases in your house that already look like what the view from the top is going to look like."

He replied, "I don't use grey primer."

She shot back, "Maybe you can do that and call it modern impressionism. View From the Top of Mount Mistyfog."

He drank more coffee, then texted, "Let's go anyhow. Not for the paintings, but for the adventure."

Brooke replied, "I don't want to waste your time."

He replied, "We can talk and hike together. That's not time wasted."

A hesitation, and then she replied, "I guess so, if you don't mind."

For all that Lilah seemed to think Brooke was into him, Emerson couldn't detect enthusiasm. He said, "We're on. I'll meet you at the trailhead."

Brooke was reserved, sure. Lilah had said as much, but then she'd added, *Trust me, she likes you.*

Except, how could Lilah know? They'd been friends since fifth grade, but did that instill in Lilah a telepathic sense of Brooke's attraction? Or did they gather in that yarn shop like middle school students, heads together over a desk, giggling about which cutie was their crush this week? Then some girl would come over to Emerson to ask him what he thought of her quiet friend. Brooke did seem to think Lilah had made friends with her because of pity.

Which... It worked, but he kind of wished everyone could outgrew that immaturity, that's all. Or that Brooke could have a little of Lilah's expressiveness and expansiveness.

Mist rose off the road as Emerson pulled into the dirt lot near the trailhead. Brooke was already there, wearing khaki shorts, hiking boots, boot socks, and a tech T-shirt. Looking cute in a ponytail and backpack, she handed him the bug spray and then took a picture of the trail map. "There's two routes to the peak," she said. "I assume you're an expert hiker, but if you don't mind, I'd rather take the longer trail that's less advanced."

Theirs were the only cars. The tourists must have seen the early rain and opted for an afternoon hike instead of a muddy morning.

The going was sloppy toward the bottom, but once they got under the trees, the ground grew more solid. The area silenced. Brooke didn't talk much during the hike, keeping her eyes down on the trail and focusing on keeping pace with him.

Emerson, on the other hand, kept observing the trees, the rocks, the underbrush. He pointed out the mushrooms they passed (and which ones were safe to eat). "These are ghost pipes," he said of some eerie pale plants jutting up from the leaf litter. "They're not actually mushrooms. They're a kind of plant that grows in the wet and the dark, and they have no chlorophyl."

She would examine anything he showed her, and then ask questions. Are these safe? How do these grow without sunlight? Emerson would answer while taking pictures, and they'd continue along the posted trail.

He said, "This feels so tame. We're walking the same way thousands of others have walked, on marked trails that have been cleared and shored up for safety."

Brooke said, "Tame isn't bad."

"We say we come out here to get exposed to nature, only it's not really."

Brooke was breathing hard as the climb steepened. "It's real enough for me."

Except it wasn't real. It was structured and carefully composed to give the veneer of the wilderness. In reality, it was safe. Safe and boring.

At a clearing halfway up, they stopped for a snack of water and fruit while sitting on the remains of a rock wall. "Have you heard of the year without a summer?" Emerson asked. When Brooke shook her head, he continued. "1816 was the coldest summer on record. Frosts in May killed off a lot of the crops, and there was snow in June. There was ice in the rivers. The corn crop was devastated, and people were starving."

Brooke's brows contracted. "What caused the cold?"

"A volcano went off in 1815—"

Brooke straightened. "Oh! Mount Tambora! It was the strongest volcanic explosion in recent history. Dutch East Indies, right? You think the ash stayed in the air that long? All the way around the planet?"

She remembered that? "A lot of farm families couldn't make a go of it with their crops wiped out, so they moved. They didn't know it was like this everywhere, so they headed for the Midwest hoping to start over or at least not starve."

Brooke glanced along the length of the rock wall. "And that's why these exist. Because once upon a time, these rock walls were marking off the edges of people's property. Only the people left." Shaking her head, Brooke said, "And you complained that this was too tame? I'm glad it's tame. Untame leads to snowfall in June and frost killing the corn in July. Wild leads to abandoned rock walls."

Emerson pulled out his phone and texted that to himself. *Wild leads to abandoned rock walls.*

Brooke sipped more from her water bottle, then mustered a smile. "Shall we keep going?"

The climb was muddy again, and both of them slipped at least once. Emerson didn't mind. He'd done his share of mud in his first year at Acadia. He was worried for Brooke, but she laughed it off as much as possible. "As long as you aren't painting *me*," she quipped.

Emerson said, "Skin washes off," but then he remembered dashing to the lighthouse with Lilah and saying nearly the same thing. *Skin is waterproof.*

He shouldn't feel guilty. It wasn't as if he was sneaking around with Lilah. Neither was he exclusive with Brooke. In fact, Brooke had sent him off with Lilah precisely so they could go do that. Why, then, did that guilty feeling keep creeping up on him? Was it just that Lilah racing the tide had looked enrapt, whereas Brooke climbing the mountain looked...okay?

They climbed through a heavy mist, and then at the peak, somehow, they emerged into clear air.

Brooke shone with a delight he hadn't seen before, other than after Lilah's triple dye-job. "We walked through a cloud!"

The peak was an expanse of bare stone with some brush and a little dirt, and cracks running through the granite. They ate their lunch near the edge while Brooke kept watching the floor of mist that lay thirty feet beneath them like a phantom sea.

"You were right to come here." Brooke carefully picked apart her orange, wiping her fingers between slices as though their legs weren't covered in dried mud. "I didn't know this could happen."

He said, "To be honest, I didn't know it would happen, either. We could just as easily have reached the top and had five feet of viewing pleasure."

"Which would make your painting a whole lot simpler." She leaned forward, frowning as she looked down the side. "You can't paint this, though. People would think you're making it up."

Emerson got out his camera. "That sounds like a challenge."

"I was talking to a writer who said the only things people told her sounded unrealistic in her stories were the things that actually came from real life. That's because fiction needs to make sense, and real life doesn't." Brooke hugged her knees to her chest while Emerson got to his feet to get more pictures. "People will tell you clouds don't look like that from the top side because it doesn't look like what they think it should look like."

Emerson said, "They do that already. 'Wisteria doesn't grow that way.' All right, then—go look at someone else's painting."

The whole time he walked around the peak, looking for photographable moments, Brooke watched. She rubbed some of the mud off her shin, but mostly she watched.

They were alone on top of a mountain. It should be romantic and sweet. He should be sitting at her side, an arm around her shoulder, both of them in companionable silence as they rested for the trip back down. His heart should be thrumming as he wondered if now was the best time, and then he should have turned toward her, and when she angled her face toward his, he should have leaned in for a kiss.

Except none of that was there. Brooke was nice. She was pleasant and smart. She was cute, and in all ways, she seemed willing to make this work. But in terms of sparks, nothing was flying. At least, not from him.

What did Brooke feel, anyhow? Her face showed so little emotion when they were talking or walking. Not that she seemed bored. More like, studious. And Emerson disliked being studied.

He said, "Did you have a good time on the climb?"

She nodded. "I did! Thank you for sparing me by taking the longer way around."

He chuckled. "Well, it made sense not to have to carry you back down."

She shrugged. "You could have dragged me, but I do prefer it this way."

Even joking with him, Brooke wasn't igniting a spark. Nothing. Emerson put away his camera.

Brooke tightened her boot laces and hefted her bag, then checked to make sure they hadn't left anything behind. She'd even tucked her orange peels back in her bag to carry out again, of which Emerson approved. Too many people had the idea that "biodegradable" meant you could just leave it there.

Was that where he'd find the attraction? In her attention to detail and her caring for the environment? Except, no. Whatever spark Lilah had foreseen between them, it wasn't catching.

Brooke tightened the straps on her backpack. "Ready?"

"Ready." They headed down the same trail, back to earth.

CHAPTER THIRTEEN

Lilah laughed when Emerson came in through the barn door. "Did you roll down the side of the mountain?" She pulled him inside while he tried stomping the mud off at the threshold. "Dude, it's a *barn*. It's seen a lot worse than dirt."

Emerson backed off as though protecting her. "You were warned. I wanted to head back to my place."

"And I, in my wisdom, told you not to worry about it." Lilah folded her arms while he unlaced his boots. "I've got everything ready to go."

"Everything?" Looking confused, Emerson let her tug him into a walk.

It wasn't until they were halfway across the barn that Lilah realized she still had her hand on his arm, but she didn't let go. He was tall and warm and limber, and he'd just ascended a mountain. "Yes, everything. Brooke went back to her place to shower, and behold." Inside her apartment, she gestured to the bathroom. "I have a shower, too. I asked my landlord if he had a pair of shorts and a shirt you could wear, and he let me borrow them for you."

Emerson took a step back. "Wait a minute."

"I have my washing machine at the ready." Lilah thrust him a towel and a washcloth.

Emerson looked at the shorts and the shirt, concerned. "They're not stylish," Lilah admitted. "But it was the best I could do, and I don't think you'd fit any of mine."

He looked her up and down, which made Lilah's skin prickle. "Yeah, I'd probably stretch out the shirts." He gave a nervous laugh. "But still—"

"Go!" She nudged him toward the shower, then followed. They were close in here because it wasn't a large room. "You pull this lever to the side to increase the water pressure, and this is the temperature. I've got three different body washes, so if you've always wanted to smell like hydrangea, today's your chance."

He faced her with a smile, and Lilah's breath caught.

Emerson tilted his head. "How did you know my most secret desire?"

His eyes. His relaxed expression. The scent of dirt and pine and energy that faintly filled the tiled room.

She swallowed hard. "I'm telepathic. I know everyone's secret desire."

Emerson's eyes narrowed. "What's yours?"

Lilah forced a laugh. "If I tell you, that defeats the purpose of it being a secret."

Emerson said, "But then you have a chance of it being fulfilled."

Lilah took a step backward out of the bathroom. "I guess I'm doomed to a life of miserable frustration," and from there she fled.

What was that all about? Yes, Emerson was an amazing specimen of a man, plus he had a whip-sharp wit and a way of seeing right through her—but come on. He was Brooke's, and if anyone was going to nurture a secret desire for Emerson, it should be Brooke.

If Lilah had one too, then Lilah needed to take it to her grave because cheating was not in the cards. Not now, not ever, not with Emerson, not with anyone. No man was worth jettisoning her self-esteem and torpedoing the longest friendship of her life.

The pipes hummed as Emerson's shower turned on, and Lilah returned to her work table where she had three separate dye lots going.

It was okay. She'd had a momentary flash of attraction, but that was to be expected in the presence of an attractive man who was—entirely through her own fault—about to take off all his clothes. Without her. Behind a locked door, a door she had no intention of unlocking. Temptation wasn't evil. Giving in to temptation was evil, and she'd walked out on temptation. If this were a video game, some NPC wizard would hand her a jewel and inform her she'd opened the next level, and maybe give her better armor.

Like maybe armor around her emotions.

Brooke texted her. "I'm out and cleaned up. Should I bring anything?"

Unable to come up with what they'd even be doing next, Lilah replied, "Just yourself."

Please take your car. Please get here soon.

Lilah's dyes saved her. The timer went off before Emerson emerged, and although she shut off the heat on two of the pots, one hadn't cleared the dye yet. She added a quarter cup of white vinegar, and she didn't turn away from her work when she heard Emerson return to the open space.

"Sorry, the yarn is being fussy."

"Brooke says fussy yarn can be the best yarn."

No, that's my quote.

If Brooke had said that, Brooke had been quoting Lilah. Brooke hated fussy yarn. Lilah was the one who enjoyed fussy yarn because of the challenge inherent in matching the yarn's fussy qualities with a pattern that would show it off to best effect.

Mismatching the pattern and the yarn could result in chaos. Sometimes the different colors in a skein would stack over one another, an effect called pooling. A low-twist yarn used for a high-friction garment would get worn out right away. A fuzzy yarn might bury an intricate stitch pattern so all your work became invisible. An itchy yarn that worked well as a hat would be a disaster as a cowl.

Brooke's response was usually, "But a sturdy workhorse yarn with a high twist works well for all those things too." Which, well, yes. The thing was, with a boutique yarn, fuzzy, or boucle, or twisty—sometimes it made a masterpiece.

Lilah checked the yarn again, and now the dye had cleared, so she shut off the heat so all three could cool. "Hey, the hiking clothes—you left them in the bathroom?"

"I dropped them right into the washing machine," Emerson said.

Lilah fled to the laundry machine where she could throw in her own clothes and get the cycle started. Clothing could tumble around together in sudsy water all it wanted without causing trouble. That would be fine. And in the end, everything would come out clean. Which was how it should be with people, too.

Back in the open barn, Emerson had ventured back to his easel, and Lilah snuck a look at him.

Okay, no more strange urges. It was fine. Just a momentary loss of balance, and everything was back to normal.

It was okay to find him attractive. Part of the reason she'd set him up with Brooke was because he was attractive, and because Brooke seemed to be attracted to him. Plus, he was smart and funny and knew how to tell a good story. Brooke had latched onto his conversations during both BCG meetings, so it made sense that Lilah would find his conversation interesting too.

Lilah had her balance back by the time Brooke arrived, looking fresh and clean and more energetic than Lilah would have figured after climbing a mountain—yes, even a small one. She stopped at Emerson's easel and complimented his progress on the current painting, then paused. "Ah. New clothes."

Emerson gestured to himself. "Horribly unfashionable, too."

"It's a crime," Brooke said.

It was annoying. Brooke should be all-out flirting right now. *"You make anything look good."* Right? How hard was that?

Instead Brooke came over to the dye area. "Hey." Lilah smiled. "When I saw the rain, I figured the mountain was out of the running."

"So did I. Emerson knew better."

While Brooke watched, Lilah pulled the skeins from their respective pots and laid them out in the catering trays.

"Are these orders, or stock?"

"One's an order. The others are stock."

Brooke said, "And did you get any more information about the church?"

"Nothing yet. We won't be able to know more until they actually file on Monday. I've talked to one of the Town Hall folks, though, and—" Lilah sighed. "I bet, legal issues or not, they're going to scuttle the deal. They don't want the bad press of being against the Historical Society."

Brooke said, "People are stupid," which—well, Lilah wasn't going to argue. But people weren't *only* stupid. Sometimes people were driven by urges they didn't understand. People were churning balls of potentiality, energy ready to be discharged once they discovered their purpose.

Emerson said, "I don't know if people are stupid as much as they're afraid."

Brooke gestured to Lilah. "How can they find her scary?"

Emerson approached. "Not Lilah, but they find artists scary, and they find strangers scary, and they find the act of creation scary."

Lilah said, "You get it."

Brooke interjected, "They're joking when they call knitting witchcraft, that we wave sticks and string to create a blanket."

Lilah said, "But we keep the yarn magic confined to the

Bright Stitches shop. The guild will be in its own building, summoning all sorts of weird artistic vibes that they can't even comprehend. Mosaics? Sculpture? The horrors!"

Emerson said, "I bet if you hosted the BCG in any random storefront for three years, or even this barn, and then tried to move it to the old church, the Historical Society would be less willing to go to court."

Lilah sighed. "So it's our fault we're new?"

"You're not a known quantity." Emerson shrugged. "Mainers are awesome, but you guys tend not to like things that aren't familiar."

Lilah lowered her voice. "I get it."

Brooke said, "You guys don't get that as much at Acadia, do you? I mean, it's a government job, so you probably have people transferring in and out, and you're up to your eyeballs with tourists."

Emerson said, "It's not as bad for me, true, but I get looks in the community during the off season. Like, why didn't I go back to Jamaica Plain? And I'm sure that's why my sister's having trouble finding a job."

Brooke raised her head. "You didn't mention that."

Emerson pulled out his phone, and Lilah cradled it in her palms, looking at a young woman with deep brown skin and a gorgeous smile. She had waist-length braids gathered into a ponytail behind her head, dotted with beads, and her hair went from black to bright red at the tips. "She's gorgeous," Lilah breathed.

Brooke said, "What field is she in?"

"She's waiting tables right now, but her degree is in finance."

Brooke said, "And you think racism's at play?"

Emerson said, "That and the way she doesn't look like a financial analyst."

Lilah said, "Which means, racism."

Emerson said, "The hair. The clothes. She doesn't look the part, and she's getting judged. If she were a known quantity—like her professors were the ones hiring her—she'd have five job offers already. She's a hard worker. She got a slate of scholarships and worked two jobs to get through school. But until employers know her, her looks frighten them off."

Lilah sighed. "She shouldn't change who she is just to get a job."

Emerson said, "Cutting your hair or not dyeing your hair isn't changing who you are. Wearing a tailored business suit for a job interview isn't changing who you are. It's providing the front an employer expects to see. Or do you think the kids behind the counter at the fast-food places are changing who they are when they put on a hat and a name tag?"

Lilah said, "Cutting her hair is modifying her body. Yes, I consider that changing who she is."

Brooke said, "And yet you're saying putting the BCG into a storefront for a few years won't change who we are, and that will get the town used to our existence enough that they welcome us taking over the church?"

Emerson shrugged. "It'd be worth a shot."

Lilah said, "By that time, someone else will have taken over the building. I want to do this now."

Emerson shook his head. "Do you understand that by grandstanding, you're risking that we lost everything? We don't have the money for a court battle."

"It's not going to be a court battle. It's a matter of us filing back with the court that we aren't going to do any of the things the Historical Society is afraid we're going to do, as well as pointing out that the government can't refuse to sell us a building because someone may go into that building and paint an objectionable picture. The Historical Society is trying to police artistic expression." Lilah put her hands on her hips. "It's hardly grandstanding to want a place to meet. And it's absolutely not grandstanding to be who we are."

Emerson said, "I'm saying to let them get used to you, first."

Brooke took the phone from Lilah's hands. "Sonia's beautiful the way she is. You can see the intelligence in her eyes. I'm sorry the interviewers won't look past her hair to see that."

Emerson took back the phone. "She wants to come up here in a couple of weeks."

Lilah said, "Oh, I'd love to meet her!"

Brooke said, "Where's she going to stay? You don't have room at your apartment, and it's tourist season."

Emerson's nose wrinkled. "I haven't quite figured that out."

Lilah said, "Couch?"

Brooke said, "His apartment is as small as mine, and he already sleeps on the couch."

Emerson shrugged. "My painting area needed to be the bedroom, so—"

"Ah." Lilah gestured to her barn. "I'm not the Hilton, but if your sister wouldn't mind sleeping in a barn, I'm the one with plenty of room."

Emerson's brow furrowed. "Are you sure? That's a huge imposition."

"Dude, you're here already on the weekends. Let's have her here too."

Brooke said to Emerson, "Will you be working while she's visiting? If so, it's better for her to be with us because Lilah and I can schedule our hours to stay with her most of the time. Lilah can open, Natalie can come in for the afternoons, Lilah can leave earlier, and I'll still work evenings. Between all of us, Sonia will have someone available all the time."

"Don't be so clinical," Lilah muttered. "She doesn't need babysitting."

Brooke said, "But she'll want a car. I'm not the world's best hostess, but I know she'll want to go places, and she'll want to eat."

Emerson gave a semi-embarrassed smile, and it was cute. "I didn't mean for you guys to take over. I live in a tourist hub. I can figure out something."

Lilah giggled. "Except we figured it out for you. What were you planning on doing once she was here?"

"She just wants a break. I thought I'd take her camping, but somewhere a bit more free-form than Acadia. Also, somewhere that hasn't been booked solid since March."

Brooke intoned, "That sounds wild and dangerous," and Emerson laughed. An in-joke. Lilah hated when her friends hit that phase of a relationship.

Lilah said, "I've got camping gear if she needs it."

"Oh, we've got camping gear. We used to camp in the Berkshires and in the White Mountains."

Emerson wore an easy smile again, relaxed and genuine. Lilah's heart shivered. He was at loose ends about his art, and he was worried about his sister, and he was wearing her landlord's clothing—but still, he looked good.

A little too good.

Lilah returned to her yarn, which should have been cool enough by now to handle, except it still was a bit too hot. "It's a good thing she's in finance, because we may even teach her to knit."

CHAPTER FOURTEEN

Lilah had heard her current situation described as a "fence slat problem." Basically, if you needed to repair a few warped slats on a fence, you'd pull off the worst ones and replace them. But then once those were replaced, invariably you'd see another slat that could stand replacing. Removing the worst one only made room for another warped slat to be the worst.

Waiting for Sonia to arrive, Lilah had been cleaning all day, and every time she finished one task, she'd turn around and find another thing that was out of place even though it had been good enough before.

Her anxiety made no sense. Lilah had people over all the time. Emerson had been practically living here on the weekends, and Brooke or Natalie popped in and out without texting. Lilah liked it that way. The first time she'd seen the barn—the very first—she'd looked at that big rolling door and thought, "I could leave that open."

Sure, the apartment in the back was wicked awesome, but the big space all around was much better. It's just—it was a barn.

Sonia knew it was a barn. She wasn't expecting the Four

Seasons. Still, Lilah wanted her to like it.

Lilah's eyes fell on a pile of paperwork on her counter and thought maybe she should put it away, but then she heard a car crunching up the gravel driveway. Prep time was over. With a deep breath, Lilah headed outside.

Emerson was getting Sonia out of the car, and in person? She was even more vibrant than in her picture. "Lilah!" Sonia rushed up and wrapped her in a hug. "Thank you for putting me up this week."

Lilah laughed. "Not a problem!"

"Look at this place!" Sonia opened her arms. "This is amazing! I didn't believe him when he said a barn. Do you have horses?"

Lilah led her inside. "No horses. Just me."

"Bummer. I always wondered if they really nicker and neigh like in the books." She beamed. "This place is the best. I love the lights. Oh, and my brother's paint area. Because of course he's got that. He squeezed us into a corner back home, then he moved out and squeezed himself out of his own bedroom, and now he's taking over here, too."

Emerson shook his head. "You realize I was invited."

"Lilah's a good-hearted soul who didn't realize she'd give you an inch, and you'd just keep on taking." Sonia put an arm over Lilah's shoulders. "Now, you tell me all about your barn, because I love it. What made you live here?"

"Look at all this space." Lilah gestured around. "How else is a girl like me going to afford twenty-five-foot ceilings?"

Sonia never let up, and Lilah matched her energy. Sonia loved the little apartment, didn't notice the pile of paperwork on the countertop, admired the art on the walls, asked about the bookshelves, and then stopped dead in the kitchen, looking out the window.

Lilah said, "It's just fields back there. This used to be a farm, and my landlord doesn't want to develop it. He likes having just the one tenant because my rent pays the property taxes."

Sonia stepped closer to the window, but she didn't seem to be looking through it as much as at it and all Lilah's resurrected plants. "Yeah, it's real nice," she said, almost distractedly. Then she drew herself together. "Well, now where do I set up? That sweet barn stall?"

Lilah said, "I'm giving you my bedroom. It's the best room," she added over Sonia's protests. "I can't invite a guest over and then have her sleep in a stall. You're not an animal."

Sonia said, "And you're saying you are?"

Emerson was leaning against the doorway, a grin plastered over his face. Lilah said, "You're enjoying this."

Emerson said, "Only about ten times more than you think I am."

"Tell your sister she's my guest, and therefore she gets the best."

Sonia said, "Tell your little friend she's doing me a favor, and I'm not putting her out of her bed."

Emerson rolled his eyes. "Since when have either of you ever listened to me?"

Both Lilah and Sonia exclaimed in disgust. Lilah said, "Tell your sister my house, my rules—and my rule is I treat my guests well."

Emerson snorted. "You can tell her yourself. You've got a mouth on you."

Sonia huffed. "Does she ever!"

Emerson added, "You told me that if I wanted to crash here, I could sleep on the couch in the barn or in one of the stalls."

Lilah huffed. "That's different."

Sonia said, "If it's good enough for my brother, it's good enough for me. Or does my brother deserve second-best?" And she strode back into the barn.

Lilah caught up to her at the stall. It wasn't a bad room. In the winter, it would get chilly because the walls weren't well insulated, but for summer, it was airy and cool. "It's not that I thought it was good enough for him, either." Lilah put her hands on her hips. "But he was up late painting, and I was going to bed. I'd rather he crash here rather than crash his car into a ditch."

Sonia smirked at her. "You didn't tell my mooching brother to sleep in his car?"

Lilah rubbed her chin and raised her eyebrows. "Come to think of it, he could have driven his car into the barn and slept in here."

Sonia turned to him. "Why didn't you?"

Emerson was still leaning in the doorframe—he'd just pivoted positions. "I'm not saying anything. You two are entertaining enough without me."

Brooke entered. "Sounds like the party's already started."

Lilah brightened. "Sonia, this is Brooke, who's going to tell you to take the bed I'm offering you."

Brooke dropped her backpack on the couch. "Sonia, I'm Brooke, and I'm going to tell you I don't do triangulation."

Lilah narrowed her eyes, and Brooke added, "Nice try, though."

Sonia folded her arms. "What's triangulation?"

Fighting annoyance, Lilah said, "When one person is telling another to take the better bed, and she asks her best friend to back up her opinion. Apparently."

Brooke approached Sonia and extended a hand. As Sonia shook it, Brooke said, "It's good to meet you." After that, she glanced at Emerson as if she wasn't quite sure what to do with herself.

Emerson approached. "Is Natalie going to join us, too?"

Brooke regained her equilibrium. "She'll come later. We wanted to give Sonia the grand tour of Brighthead, same as Lilah gave you."

Sonia said, "And then I can see all those amazing landmarks for myself, and why you love them."

Emerson tensed unexpectedly.

Brooke said, "Is it love, or is it recognizability?"

"All the best artwork comes from love, not from familiarity." Sonia patted her brother on the arm. "Even if he doesn't want to talk about it."

Emerson looked even more uncomfortable, but Sonia spun on her toes and headed back to the paintings. "Is this the plain vanilla stuff you're selling at the exhibit? Because no wonder you're nervous. These people are crushing you down."

Emerson stiffened. "What?"

Lilah said, "They're beautiful!"

"They're *domesticated,* honey. You took a wild thing, and you tamed him."

Lilah marched over to the paintings. "I did nothing of the sort."

"Well then maybe it's Brooke who tamed him. No offense."

"None taken," said Brooke, "because I'm confident you're wrong."

Emerson choked on a laugh.

Lilah said, "Brooke and I did not domesticate Emerson. We talked about marketing and merchandising. He nearly backed out of the exhibit *until* we told him to do local scenes."

Sonia turned to him, glowering.

Emerson said, "Entirely true."

"You put a leash on your art." Arms folded, Sonia tilted her head. "Are you afraid of not making your rent? That's why you need to cater to the rich people who are about to have their entire meal smothered in cream sauce?"

Brooke laughed. "Oh, wow, if Colin heard you say that...?"

As if she weren't trying to find the knife Sonia had just embedded in her soul, Lilah grabbed the change of subject and leaped right onboard. "Austin would agree. Not sure about Colin."

Brooke narrowed her eyes and changed her stance, and it was a dead-on impersonation of Colin. *"While that's an overgeneralization, you're neglecting to consider the many varieties of cream sauce."*

Lilah laughed while Emerson shook his head.

"But this!" Sonia gestured with one hand. "This is stuff

you'd find in the mall. Where are you? In all these paintings, where are you?"

Brooke wasn't about to say anything, so Lilah strode forward. "Excuse me, but of course he's in there. He's there in the way he set up the images, the way he selected the elements, and the way he put his heart into them. There's a touch of humanity in each of these paintings, and it all came from his heart. There is nothing wrong with marketing."

She said, "Do you think I don't know about business?"

"Well, he's got to do business first. Lead them in with this, and then once they're looking at him, they'll see the rest of him. The real him."

Sonia glared at Emerson over Lilah's shoulder. "You don't want them to see the real you, huh? That's why your real paintings are at your apartment? The ones that show where your heart is?"

Brooke said, "I've seen those paintings. They're amazing. He's going to include elements of both."

"You saw them?" Sonia pivoted to Emerson. "She saw *all* of them?"

Brooke looked to Emerson. "Well, anything that was up when we went to the Renn Faire."

Sonia wasn't taking her eyes off Emerson, and it made Lilah nervous enough that she looked back at Emerson—who himself looked nervous. What painting was Sonia referring to?

Sonia said, "These paintings, they're good—but you're hiding the deep ones. The true ones."

Emerson shook his head. "It's better this way. Scratch the surface, and no one wants to see what's under there."

Brooke didn't object, so Lilah had to. "That's not at all true." She returned to Emerson and gave him a quick hug. "We see what's there, and that's why we want the show to go on."

CHAPTER FIFTEEN

Sonia and Brooke couldn't have been more different. As much as she loved Brooke, Lilah still had to admit it was fun being with someone who always said what she was feeling, always felt things in a big way, and had no trouble taking center stage. Brooke and Emerson both faded into the background, but Sonia? Everywhere they'd gone in Brighthead, she'd strode onto the scene, owned it, and then when she was done, exited stage left without waiting for applause.

In his sister's wake, Emerson seemed tentative. She was loud, and that made him seem quieter—or else it made him actually quieter. In the shadow of Sonia, Brooke went silent. Lilah had let Emerson handle the narration for the grand tour, but over and over, when Sonia did things that drew attention to herself—and, to be honest, Sonia being amazing drew attention to herself—Emerson would speak lower or try to shut her down with statements that sounded very final.

Sonia loved the Myth Brightman statue. She'd laughed loud and long about the mix-ups that led to the plaque of lies. She'd stood with her phone at the head of the causeway, demanding to return at a time when the water drained away so she could walk to the lighthouse. When she saw people staring at her, she waved big, and Emerson shrank.

He loved *Sonia*. After bringing in Chinese food and sending both Emerson and Brooke to their respective homes, Lilah began to realize it was the attention Emerson didn't love. Public attention. Private attention was fine, but on the street? On the pier?

Being the star of an art exhibit? That meant lots of attention.

While Lilah was redoing her nails in a red to match the one in Sonia's hair, Sonia walked around the barn again, admiring all the lights, the wind chimes, and her brother's paintings. She wanted to know about yarn dyeing. She asked about Lilah's business plan, which wasn't the question Lilah had expected to come out of Sonia's mouth, and they talked about profit and loss, tax write-offs, and what it would take for Lilah to fully support herself as a dyer.

"I don't want to work at the yarn store forever." Lilah capped her nail polish bottle and returned with Sonia to the dyeing station where she had some hand-painteds waiting in the catering tray. "Fortunately, I can do some of my own work while I'm on the clock, and they give me a lot of free advertising by putting my yarn in a prominent place."

Sonia said, "Have you thought of a subscription service?"

Lilah nodded. "You need a theme for it to work well. There's a dyer I admire who creates geeky themes around specific science fiction and fantasy fandoms. There's another who's doing a great job by picking vacation spots and dyeing skeins in colors to match those places."

Sonia huffed. "I imagine Boston as this grey and blue colorway. Or New York as grey and black."

"I do a Brighthead line every summer, and we display it under a banner that says Souvenir Yarn." Lilah laughed.

"Hang on." She very carefully pulled up the photos on her phone, making sure not to smudge the polish that was still drying. "See? Brighthead Harbor. The Lighthouse. The Statue. Those sell well, but they only sell well locally because why would anyone want to buy Brighthead-themed yarn if they're not in Brighthead?"

Sonia said, "Could you do Acadia themed yarn?"

"It wouldn't sell *here,* though, and I don't have any contacts in Bar Harbor."

"You could make some. For goodness sakes, how about I walk into all the gift shops in Bar Harbor and tell them what they need to sell?"

Lilah imagined Sonia doing exactly that—brilliant in her approach, unapologizing in her demeanor. Again, such a contrast to Emerson. Emerson, who fled from the spotlight. Who didn't want to get noticed.

Lilah had noticed him. She'd noticed him every time: noticed him being kind to Brooke, noticed him making suggestions to the BCG, noticed his keen observation of the world around him. For that matter, she'd noticed him too much when he was standing in front of her shower.

Sonia leaned back on one leg and folded her arms. "Are you still dead-set on giving me your bed?" When Lilah nodded, she said, "How about we make a deal? I'll take your bed if you let me play with your hair because whatever you're doing with it, you're doing it all wrong."

Lilah recoiled. "Excuse me?"

Sonia said, "You've got curly hair, and you're treating it like it's not. If you let me use my products on your hair, I'm going to guarantee you love the result."

Lilah trembled, but this was Emerson's sister. Surely she wasn't going to do something horrific. "Your hair is amazing, but I can't expect anything like that. Are you going to cut it?"

"I'm going to wash it, maybe wash it a couple of times with different things." Sonia raised her eyebrows. "If you don't like it, no biggie. You wash out my products with your waxy shampoo and conditioner and let it get frizzy again."

This sounded like it should be an insult, but after an entire afternoon of listening to Sonia telling it like it was, Lilah didn't have it in her to feel offended. Sonia was looking at her hair the same way Lilah looked at a neutral skein of yarn and thought, "Do you know what I could do with that?" Maybe Emerson felt the same way when he looked at a blank canvas.

Ten minutes later, Lilah was bent over her tub while Sonia washed and rinsed her hair for the first go-around. "I'm stripping out all the silicone. You won't have to do this every time, only if you mess up." Sonia's fingers felt strong and firm on her scalp, and Lilah closed her eyes to enjoy the massage. She rinsed out the first shampoo and then used a different one. "Oh, honey, you're going to love this." Again she massaged the shampoo in for well over a minute, and Lilah melted against the tub.

I wish this were Emerson.

Tensing, Lilah squeezed her eyes shut and gasped.

Sonia said, "Sorry, did I get some in your eyes?"

"No." Lilah swallowed hard. "It's fine."

Except she wasn't fine. She fought tears and kept her eyes as tight as possible. Her head was facing away from Sonia so Sonia couldn't see.

Emerson's touch would have relaxed her. Lilah would have let Emerson rinse her hair and then touch her skin, and she'd have let him do whatever he wanted to her head. His sister was brilliant and bold and brave, but Emerson was thoughtful and kind and perceptive. Sonia commanded the room, but Emerson commanded himself. And in doing so, he'd taken command of Lilah's heart.

The tears seeped onto Lilah's arm, and she let them stay because there was enough water coursing over her head that Sonia wouldn't notice.

Lilah had feelings for Emerson—for her best friend's boyfriend.

Were Brooke and Emerson exclusive now? Not that it would matter to Brooke. Brooke was always exclusive when she dated. Would the two of them even have that conversation?

It didn't matter. Lilah would never divide Emerson's loyalty. He was an amazing guy, and Brooke deserved the best. They were together because Lilah had done everything in her power to keep Emerson coming back to Brighthead, not thinking that the more time Emerson spent here, the more time he was spending with Lilah. The more opportunities Lilah gave Brooke to see Emerson's amazing qualities, the more opportunities that gave Lilah to see them as well.

Sonia jetted water over Lilah's head while Lilah tried not to drown. Not from the water, but from the feelings. Did Brooke appreciate Emerson enough? But again, it didn't matter. Lilah would never hurt Brooke. She'd rip out her own heart and dye a thousand skeins of yarn red with her own blood before she'd harm Brooke.

It's not real. Lilah didn't say anything while Sonia explained the next step, a huge glop of gentle conditioner. *It's just infatuation. Emerson doesn't feel anything like that for me because his attention is on Brooke. All I have to do is shut up and leave them to one another. I can distract myself. I can put distance between me and Emerson, and everything will ease off. What I'm feeling isn't love. Love would require Emerson loving me back. His focus is on Brooke, exactly where it should be.*

"Touch this," Sonia said after she finished rinsing the conditioner. "That's how you want it to feel. Don't rinse it all out."

If only Lilah could rinse out the unwanted emotions. She could use whatever stripping shampoo Sonia had just used, rendering her heart clean and bare.

The only one who's going to hurt is me. That's fine. This had happened before, when a guy in high school had started off liking Brooke and had pivoted to liking Lilah. Lilah had turned him down flat, but here it was even easier: Emerson didn't feel attracted to Lilah, so there was no need to turn him down. No one ever had to know.

Better still, he and Sonia were going camping for a few days. That would give Lilah a chance to get her head on straight.

Sonia squirted some styling product onto Lilah's hair. "Not talking much. You're exhausted," Sonia said. "You were driving us everywhere."

Driving with Sonia taking shotgun and Emerson and Brooke in the back. Maybe they'd held hands while Lilah drove, maybe whispering to one another or exchanging glances.

Lilah said, "It's hard to talk when I've got my head down."

"Getting my hair done, wow, no one ever shuts up." Sonia laughed. "Here."

She pulled Lilah's T-shirt up over her head, then used the shirt to capture all her hair on the top of her head before twisting it up. "Leave it there for a bit. We're not going to touch it until it's a bit more dry."

Lilah sat back on her heels. "And this will make my hair less frizzy?"

"Girl, you're going to love this." Sonia dangled a few of her own braids between her fingers. "My hair is 4C hair. You know how curls get graded? You're thinking you have 2A hair, and you've been greasing it up and coating it with waxy conditioners, but I bet you're more like a 3B."

Lilah scooted back against the wall, then sagged against it. "None of what you said makes the slightest sense." Fair enough, though. Nothing in Lilah's heart made sense either.

Sonia stood. "Nah, come on. While it's drying, show me how you knit. Brooke was knitting the whole time today, and I need to know more about this ancestral magic."

Lilah found Sonia a pair of straight needles and a ball of yarn. "I'll cast on for you so you can jump right into the fun part." Then she went ahead and sat alongside Sonia, showing her how to insert the needle into the right-hand stitch from front to back, wrap the yarn, tug it through, and then slip the old stitch off the left-hand needle.

Sonia watched her for a while, and Lilah told her about tensioning the yarn and how to keep the stitches the same size as one another. Lilah had been teaching friends to knit, and sometimes classes to knit, ever since Brooke had taught her how to do it. Back in school, Brooke used to get tongue-tied about explaining knitting, but Lilah could explain it just fine. Once Brooke had led the way, Lilah could take over. Then Brooke watched Lilah teach, and Brooke learned how to do it, too. In fact, many times when Brooke taught, she used Lilah's actual phrases. Kind of like she'd used Lilah's phrase about fussy yarn with Emerson.

Then Sonia took the needles back, and she laughed as she couldn't make it work. "You're doing fine," Lilah assured her. "There's a lot to keep track of at first, but once you get it all in your head, your muscle memory takes over. It becomes natural a little bit at a time."

Natural. Like falling for a handsome, smart, observant man.

Sonia kept at it until the end of the row, then handed it back. "This is first-class witchery."

"Stitchery," Lilah corrected.

Sonia said, "Well, that settles it. You have to come with us when we go camping."

Lilah froze. "What? Why?"

"Because I need someone to keep teaching me how to knit so I can go home and make blankets and scarves."

Lilah recoiled. "I hate to break it to you, but you're making a washcloth."

Sonia waved her off. "You need to come camping. We've got a big tent, and you've got a sleeping bag there in the barn stall. Pull on a pair of hiking boots, and you're all set."

No. Not alone with Emerson and without Brooke. Not her and Emerson out in the woods, climbing and seeing beauty and spending late nights in front of a campfire.

Sonia could read her mind. "Fine, have Brooke come, too. Then all three of us can sit around the fire doing sorcery with needles and yarn to make Emerson feel left out."

Lilah said, "The yarn will get smoky."

It was the only thing that came out of her head right then. So near to the fire, the yarn would absorb the smell of the smoke. So near to Emerson, Lilah would absorb more of those feelings she wanted to send away.

As if that were a joke, Sonia laughed. Then she untied the T-shirt from around Lilah's head and roughed up her hair. "Girl, look in the mirror. You're fabulous."

Lilah found herself looking at herself, and her hair really was fabulous—bouncy and curly and shiny. But her heart felt dull, and inside her spirit, everything was limp.

Emerson. And Brooke. And she loved them both.

Chapter Sixteen

Sonia must have told Lilah something terrible about Emerson. It was the only conclusion he could reach. They'd been camping one entire day now, and Lilah wouldn't look at him. She wouldn't stand near him. She only spoke in terms of logistics. "Where should I put the food?" and "Should I set up the camp chairs?"

The first time Emerson had suggested camping with Sonia, Lilah had been excited. Wouldn't it be marvelous? He and Sonia could explore! Hike! Swim! She'd sat on the floor cross-legged while he'd painted, knitting and telling him about camping trips she'd taken as a girl. Her family had even brought Brooke a few times. "What's the good of living near all these woods if we aren't going to engulf ourselves in them?" she'd asked, and for a moment Emerson had felt just as immersed in the woods as he had back when he'd worked as a park ranger rather than a program director.

Not that he disliked his job. He liked it fine—and he liked the extra money even more. Even so, fluorescent lights and filing cabinets weren't the same as pine trees and granite.

Neither was it the same now, with Lilah only available on the surface of herself. Everything else was locked deep inside, and Emerson wasn't wrong: she was avoiding him.

Not only that, but she'd gotten rid of her manicure. Any polish on her nails right now was clear.

Roundabout questions with Sonia hadn't turned up anything. Sonia was having a blast. For someone who'd come up here with the intent of forgetting her job search, she'd succeeded. Although every so often she'd come up with a marketing suggestion for Lilah's dyes or Bright Stitches, she wasn't checking her email for interview requests. She checked her phone on occasion, but mostly for responses to her social media where she kept posting photos of Lilah's barn or their campsite or the crooked knitting Lilah was teaching her to do.

"You have the best friends," Sonia said as she unrolled the sleeping bags in the four-person tent. "Brooke's a bit fussy, but Lilah's a riot. And together? They're a lot of fun."

Emerson said, "I'm worried about Lilah. Is she feeling okay?"

Sonia hesitated. "She's acting a bit strange. I don't know. Maybe she's tired because I kicked her out of her room."

Lilah put her head into the tent, then recoiled. "Oh, sorry."

Sonia said, "Don't be sorry. We're just setting up the sleeping bags."

Lilah said, "Put me near the edge on that side, okay?" Her voice was a little higher pitched than normal. "Then Brooke, then you, then Emerson."

Sonia laughed. "Not both you and me between Brooke and Emerson, like judgmental old ladies keeping them apart?"

Lilah laughed, but it sounded forced. "You stay between them, but I'll be on the other side to hold Brooke back."

Sonia laughed loudly, and Lilah fled the tent.

Emerson said, "She's acting odd. None of that is her."

Sonia went back to setting out the sleeping bags. "She's fine."

Lilah *was* fine—but not quite the way Emerson wanted to mean it. Sonia had texted him photos of after she'd done Lilah's hair, and then other things she'd done with it the next day, and Lilah looked even better now than before. Any frizziness to her hair was just gone, and instead her hair rippled with curls. Had her hair taken the bounce from her spirit?

That left Emerson with one conclusion: Sonia must have told Lilah something about him that left her scared. It was just that, for the life of him, Emerson couldn't come up with what that could be.

Back outside, Brooke was shifting stones to create a keyhole ring for their campfire. She said, "I strung us a clothesline, and I also found two trees that will support the hammock."

Sonia rubbed her hands together. "Then we're set. Let's go for a walk. We can head down to the pond and check it out, then see what else is around here. Brooke? Lilah?"

They made their way down to the pond, Lilah skittish and still avoiding Emerson.

Lilah shouldn't have come. She should have delivered an Oscar-worthy performance and faked being so sick that Sonia would not only have left her in Brighthead but would have counted herself lucky not to be gasping on death's doorway.

It should have been okay being here. Emerson didn't know. Emerson didn't even suspect Lilah's feelings, so all this trip required was to behave exactly as Lilah had been behaving, and no more.

Every minute, though, was another reminder of just how awful a friend Lilah was. Every attempt at distraction ended back up at the self-conscious realization that she was distracting herself from an amazing man.

While they hiked down to the pond, Lilah could only plan how to keep two people between herself and Emerson at all times. When they arrived at the lake and Sonia wanted to swim, Lilah didn't want to strip down to her swimsuit. Brooke didn't help matters by doing what she always did when she swam in a lake: wearing beach shoes against the slippery rocks *and* an oversized T-shirt over her all-black swimsuit. Lilah should have thought to do the same, but she only had a teal and bronze one-piece suit. Of the two of them, Lilah was more eye-catching, and there was nothing she could do about it.

The trouble was, Emerson did keep looking at her. Whether it was her imagination or her fear or her ardent wish, Lilah couldn't decide. She caught him glancing away from her multiple times, though, as if he didn't want his looks to be spotted. Lilah wasn't even trying to flirt with him, yet somehow she was winning his attention away from Brooke.

Sonia said, "How deep does this go?" and Lilah replied, "Let's find out," because that at least covered her body with water. Brooke would never swim out that far, would she? Emerson would have to stay on shore with Brooke.

Except Brooke pulled on a pair of goggles and said, "Let's go!"

Lilah said, "Swim at your own risk." Brooke hated risk.

Brooke said, "Aren't you the one who says the best things in life happened because you took a risk?"

Sonia waded out to her waist. "Oh, gross! The rocks are slimy. Tell me about risk-taking, Lilah."

Emerson wasn't going to enter until they all went in, so Lilah went out to Sonia and then kept going. "It was a risk moving into a barn. Everyone said it would be too cold in the winter, and it would be a lot of upkeep. Plus the landlord had a reputation for being a jerk."

"She means me," Brooke said. "I told her all that, and I was wrong."

"The barn gets cold. The apartment is fine." Lilah started

swimming gently, more a dog-paddle than a forward crawl. "Starting my dyeing business was a risk."

Emerson said, "But that's working out."

Sonia said, "And I'm telling you new risks to take."

"Yeah." The lake was chilly, but she'd warm up to it soon. "The BCG was a risk. And it's still a risk. Getting the church building is going to be a huge risk because it's a lot of money to get ahold of it."

Brooke said, "That one, I'm still not onboard with."

Sonia said, "How about love? Love is the biggest risk of all."

Lilah couldn't answer. The water was cold and the lake bottom was dropping away beneath her. There was a floating dock toward the middle, and she aimed herself toward it.

Love was a huge risk. Every time Lilah had fallen for someone, she'd given her whole heart without reserve because when she fell in love, her partner deserved that much. Some people could date with the idea of just having a good time for a little while, but why distract yourself with fun dates when you could be bonding with your soulmate? When you could open your heart and receive all of someone else's in return?

That meant the fall was hard and total, and when it came, the rejection gutted her like a fish. But the potential... The potential was worth the risk every time.

Lilah murmured, "Love is inherently risky."

Not with Emerson, though. Emerson was taken.

At the dock, Brooke hauled herself up the ladder and then sat with her goggles on her head in the afternoon sunlight. That T-shirt left a puddle around her, but she'd always gone swimming that way, every body part shielded that could be. Sonia went up next and sprawled alongside Brooke, glorious in her bikini and her hair piled on top of her head. That left Lilah with nowhere to sit other than alongside Emerson. She went right to the corner and looked over the side, giving Emerson as much space as possible to sit near Brooke.

Sonia peered into the water. "So deep. Do you think it's thirty feet here?"

Emerson said, "The website said it gets to forty."

Lilah wanted to just drop down into the water. Let the water flow over and through her until the pain flowed away. Maybe Emerson was her soulmate. It didn't matter.

CHAPTER SEVENTEEN

The sun went down at nine o'clock. Brooke sat on the ground near the campfire, a flashlight wrapped around her neck as she knit a pair of socks. True to her word, Sonia had also brought her knitting project, and Lilah kept setting aside her own in order to approve of Sonia's stitching or technique, or occasionally to show her where she'd gone wrong and how to repair a dropped stitch.

The fire popped. Every so often, Emerson would get up to add wood. He'd been a marvel at cooking over the fire, and they'd all washed up together afterward. If anything, cooking outdoors helped Lilah appreciate the barn even more. In the barn, she didn't need to purify the water. In the barn, her oven kept a steady temperature.

Now, the fire was going low, and Lilah's eyes were getting heavy. Between the hiking, the camp setup, the swimming, more hiking, and the cooking, she was too exhausted even to knit the project on her lap.

Emerson sat near the camp lantern, reading with the aid of a flashlight.

Sonia said to Brooke, "What are you making?"

Brooke lifted her project. "Pair of socks. Lilah, you

recognize the yarn, right?"

Lilah smiled. "It's my birthday yarn!"

Sonia said, "You gave Brooke yarn for your birthday?"

Emerson said, "It was Brooke's birthday, and Lilah threw her a yarn-dyeing party. I told you that."

"Oh, right." Sonia frowned at him. "What are you going to do with that yarn, anyhow?"

"Haven't decided. It's pretty in the skein."

"No, no, no." Sonia stood up. "Get over here and learn to knit so you can use that yarn."

Lilah's heart jumped out of her body. "He doesn't need to learn to knit."

"Why? Because he's a guy?"

Brooke said, "We have plenty of guys who come to Sit and Stitch. Most of them are recovering from heart attacks." When Sonia stared at her, Brooke added, "Knitting lowers your blood pressure. What other treatment for blood pressure has no side-effects and can also provide Christmas gifts?"

Lilah said, "When a guy in his sixties turns up for the first time, any other guy at the table will say, 'When did you have your heart attack?'"

Sonia said, "Emerson, get over here. I'm not having you keel over of a heart attack."

Emerson gestured to himself. "Do I look like I'm going to keel over of a heart attack?"

Sonia said, "Grandpa died of a heart attack, and no one knew it was coming."

"Grandpa was also seventy-eight years old and hadn't told anyone about his chest pains for two weeks."

Sonia stood up. "Emerson Charles, you sit yourself right here and learn to knit!"

Brooke met his eyes, and she offered a smile. "Knitting isn't a requirement for dating me."

Emerson said, "Glad to hear it."

Sonia said, "Then let Lilah teach you."

Lilah said, "Brooke can teach him. She's the one who taught me in the first place."

Brooke said, "You're definitely the better teacher. You can hear the way your students are hearing your instructions. I get too technical."

This was ridiculous. "I'm not teaching your boyfriend to knit." Lilah stood up. "Anyway, I'm exhausted. If Emerson wanted to learn, he'd have asked weeks ago."

She fled into the tent, yanked off her shoes, and crawled into her sleeping bag feeling selfish that she'd just left all the takedown for the other three. Teaching Emerson to knit would put them right next to each other. She'd be touching his hands or reaching around him. She'd take in his dusky scent every time she breathed, and her whole body would tingle with his nearness. It wasn't right or fair, and if anyone enjoyed his presence that closely, it needed to be Brooke.

The other three were moving around outside, and Lilah huddled around herself. They'd be banking the fire and extinguishing the lanterns, making one last visit to the latrine, and maybe Sonia would enter the tent first. Brooke and Emerson could talk alone beneath the stars, holding hands, and they could kiss goodnight. They'd linger, maybe whispering or just holding one another. That was the reality that needed to happen, not the other one.

Lilah awoke in the dark needing to pee, so she worked her way out of her sleeping bag to exit the tent. By flashlight she found the designated spot, and afterward she checked her phone. The sky was beginning to brighten, and a cacophony of birds began calling. It was about five.

She tended the fire, which Emerson had banked well enough that it returned to life without too much effort. She filled the kettle, and when she looked up, Emerson was in front of her.

Startled into a smile, Lilah said, "Morning."

Sleepy-eyed, Emerson sat where Brooke had been sitting last night. "You feeling better today?"

Lilah bit her lip. "I'm sorry I went to bed so quickly last night. I didn't mean to worry everyone."

Everyone. Keep it to everyone.

"Not a problem. You seemed a bit 'off' all day, and I was worried."

Lilah's heart surged, but she tamped it down. Yes, he'd noticed her. No, that didn't mean anything. "Sorry."

"I was afraid maybe you were having cramps and we'd forced you away from your couch and a hot water bottle."

Lilah shook her head. "No. But you're funny. Or are you saying I'm moody?"

"I was afraid you were in pain and hiding it." He picked up his backpack. "Come with me."

"I was going to start breakfast."

"We won't go far."

They climbed a ridge to the edge of the woods, where he sat on a rock. Next, he pulled out a sketch pad and some charcoal pencils. The sun was just peeping over the horizon, but he didn't turn toward the horizon. Instead, while the birds called, he looked back toward the camp and started to sketch.

Lilah edged closer to watch as a world burgeoned beneath his fingertips. With rapid strokes, he roughed out the clearing where they'd camped: the tent, the keyhole firepit, the laundry line, the food storage. The trees at the edge. The brush.

He had a beautiful soul. Here was a beautiful man, and when surrounded by beauty, he amplified it. The sketched campsite snuggled into the forest, and Lilah's hands clenched to keep herself from moving toward him.

Wake up, Brooke. Wake up. You need to see this.

Emerson turned to her. "What do you think?"

"You drew us a home."

He smiled, then flipped to a clean page and handed the notebook to her. Lilah took it, but then he handed her the pencil, too.

Lilah frowned. He said, "Your turn."

She laughed. "I can't draw."

"You can try." He gestured to the rock. "You know how you told me, 'It's just yarn'? Well, it's just pencil and paper. Give it a shot.

"I haven't drawn anything since high school, and I was lousy at it, then." She edged toward the rock, and when he stepped away, she sat gingerly. She gasped. "Wait a minute —this is revenge for us threatening to teach you to knit last night!"

"That was Sonia. I knew you weren't going to teach me." Emerson folded his arms. "But fair's fair. You wanted Sonia to experience the joy of knitting, so now I want you to experience the joy of drawing."

Lilah closed her eyes. *I can't do this. I can't put lines on paper while you're watching because you'll see my soul. You'll figure it out.*

Emerson put a hand on her shoulder, and Lilah went warm. "Give this a try. If you hate it when you're done, you can pull the page out of the notebook and stick it right into the fire."

Heart pounding, Lilah tried to figure out where she'd even start. It was like the first time she tried to knit a sweater: how do you begin? How do you make sleeves or a collar? How do you make buttonholes?

Well, that was actually easy. A sweater was mostly a rectangle for the back and a rectangle for the front, and the sleeves were two tubes. The collar was a circle. Yes, there were fiddly bits like the armscye or the yoke, but you could break down almost everything in knitting into basic shapes. A sock was a tube with a ninety-degree bend and a tapered finish. A scarf was a long rectangle.

Well, a tent was a bunch of triangles and rectangles. Lilah started with that. Okay, and the fire pit was a keyhole, so she could do that too. The metal bin with their food was a rectangle.

This wasn't art. It was more like a map. "When you do this, people recognize what's important," Lilah said. "I'm only drawing what I see."

Emerson said, "You'll train your eyes and your brain to see past the images to what the images really are. That comes with time."

That came with time, the same way knowing what yarns

paired with what patterns came with time.

Time, of course, being the thing she and Emerson would never have.

"I'm sorry." She ripped out the page and handed back the notebook. "I'm going to take you up on that offer." She slipped off the rock and headed back to the fire, then used a stick to shove her nascent drawing into the red coals.

Behind her, Emerson said, "You were doing fine."

Lilah poked the paper down until the edges ignited, and then the whole thing went up. "Some things need to become ash."

CHAPTER EIGHTEEN

Emerson had planned a long hike for the second day. Lilah was still quiet, but not as skittish. Brooke was also quiet, but she seemed to be enjoying herself. Sonia, of course, embraced every second. She had questions, and she had observations, and most of all, she had peace from the job search.

Emerson kept thinking of Lilah, destroying a sketch that wasn't at all bad or embarrassing. She'd ripped it out and burnt it with a finality that told Emerson she'd never draw anything again. Only, really, she should. She'd taken in the setting and reduced it to shapes, and that was a good start. She'd drawn without any self-consciousness once she'd begun, and then all at once she'd retreated as though Emerson's presence were the most vile thing in the world.

On the second night, they returned to the camp exhausted, but Brooke made dinner, and Lilah washed up. Emerson made s'mores for Sonia because she'd always liked him making her s'mores when they were kids. Over the red glow of the embers, he toasted marshmallows for all three women (no, actually, Lilah insisted on toasting her own) and told stories, and they all laughed a lot. Someone should have brought a guitar, but none of them knew how to play.

"Well, I used to play the piano," Brooke noted, looking up from her book. "You didn't happen to bring a campfire piano...? Or maybe a pipe organ?"

How wild, to imagine quiet Brooke sitting before one of those massive instruments and filling a church with chords. If he'd had to choose, he'd have guessed Lilah.

The third and final day was low-key: a shorter hike, followed by swimming, after which they'd pack up the camp.

On the beach, Brooke again wore nearly as much clothing to swim as she did to hike, and Emerson didn't understand why. Maybe afraid of burning? Except if she was worried about sunburn, why not a rash guard? It wasn't that she didn't want him to see her body because the first day, after getting out of the water, she had taken off the shirt so she could sun-dry. Still, there she was again, wearing goggles and a huge T-shirt and beach shoes as if the water shouldn't dare touch her.

At her side, Lilah looked like a model in an orange swimsuit, toes in the pebbled beach, snickering because it pained her to walk on the rocks and yet walking anyhow.

Lilah turned toward Sonia. "Are you coming in? I'm sure it's not exactly as cold as it was yesterday."

Sonia said, "Because it's colder?"

Lilah laughed. "Live a little!"

"I'd rather live a lot longer!" Sonia pushed Emerson. "You go swim. You're the genius who wanted to go camping in Maine."

Emerson said, "Because this is where I live."

Lilah added, "—a little."

Sonia said, "And I could live a lot longer if I didn't freeze to death."

Emerson marched past his sister. "You're not going to freeze to death."

Sonia followed. "You're saying I'll freeze half to death?"

"As you deserve."

Lilah laughed. "Hey, you bully! Treat my roommate nicely or I'll splash you!"

Brooke watched from waist-deep in the water, where the wavelets lapped against the edge of her T-shirt.

Sonia laughed. "You threaten him, girl!"

"I have a lake," Lilah declared, "and I'm not afraid to use it!"

This was the Lilah Emerson had missed for the past few days, so he grinned at her broadly. "Is that so? Because I thought you only knew how to use your mouth."

"Rude!" Lilah exclaimed, then pivoted. "Brooke, defend me! He's being mean!"

Brooke said, "You did threaten to splash him, so I'm on his side."

"Wow. I spent my whole life with you, and then you turned on me for a guy." Lilah made another theatrical pout, then dove into the water and swam away.

Brooke followed her. They were heading toward the dock, so Emerson stepped out into the water to join them.

Beside him, Sonia said, "You're dating the wrong one."

Knee-deep, Emerson stopped.

Their voices could carry all the way to the other side of the lake, so Sonia kept hers low. "You and Brooke have nothing in common. Brooke doesn't make you laugh, doesn't make your eyes light up. You don't talk about her. I thought from your texts that it was Lilah, and then I saw you together and I knew it. You're dating the wrong one."

The urge to dive into the water was strong like a current tugging toward a waterfall. Emerson braced himself. "Lilah put us together."

"Why would she do that?" Sonia looked just as puzzled as Emerson felt, and it was a relief because even with nothing making sense, at last Emerson maybe had someone to be confused with him.

"Brooke's nice." Emerson fought the pain in his own voice. "She's smart. She knows all these odd facts, and she's thoughtful."

Sonia lowered her voice even further. "You can't build a

life together on *nice.*"

I don't want to build a life together, Emerson nearly said, except he caught himself because that wasn't right. Dating Brooke was...well, it was okay. She was okay. She was nice.

He kept defaulting to that. She was nice, and Lilah had said Brooke had been hurt in the past. Emerson didn't want to hurt her, too. He just...

...just wasn't attracted to her.

No, that wasn't it. It wasn't that Brooke was unattractive. It hadn't happened yet, that was all. He—

He said to Sonia, "Not now."

Not now, as in, don't break up with Brooke now? Or was it, not now, don't talk about it now? Not on a trip where they still had to be together for a while?

Emerson walked into the water and dove forward the second he could, subsuming his body in the shock, trying to strip off the guilt that clung to him like trail dust after a hard climb.

Lilah must have seen it. Lilah, who saw everything. Lilah had seen even before Sonia that Emerson was gravitating toward the wrong woman. Lilah loved Brooke and would go to the end of the earth to protect her, and here was Emerson not valuing her. That's why Lilah was so distant. She was angry.

If Lilah hated him for this, he understood. He hated himself for it, too.

He swam like an Olympian, breathing every second stroke and propelling himself as though he could outdistance his thoughts. Sonia was right: Lilah was the one he thought about. Lilah was the one he wanted to draw, the one he wanted to show his paintings to. Lilah's opinion was the one he craved, and when she gave her approval, hers was the one that boosted his ego.

Lilah. He'd waited for the feelings to come for Brooke, and instead they'd come for Lilah.

This wasn't right or fair. This was betrayal, when he'd never intended to betray anyone. It just snuck up on him with all the things he'd noticed. Lilah's jokes, her insights, her zest for the world. Her care for little things. Her empathy. Her care for him.

She'd cared more about his art career than he had. She'd looked at his paintings and seen all the things he'd wanted the world to see. It wasn't Brooke's fault that she hadn't seen it. But when Lilah saw his paintings, she'd understood to a depth that made his heart swell.

Meanwhile, on the other hand, Brooke was nice.

Breathing hard, Emerson put a hand on the dock ladder. He looked up to see Brooke on the dock, and Lilah coming around the corner.

"Oh!" Eyes wide, Lilah swept her arms and legs forward so she shot backward—backward further and faster than she had to. "Sorry."

Emerson's heart rebelled. Lilah hated him, and soon Brooke would as well.

"I didn't mean to startle you." Emerson kicked off the ladder. "I'm going to swim back."

Brooke called, "You can come up and dive," but Emerson was off, stroking as hard as he could for the shoreline. He passed Sonia on her way to the dock. He reached the rocky beach, and there he stood, lungs burning and glutes aching.

Was this fixable? Emerson had training in how to deal with emergencies as a park ranger, and some of that had to be useful. First, assess the danger. Next, get the bystanders to safety. Prevent the danger from spreading. Make a plan. Call for help as required.

He was the danger. Brooke and Lilah were the bystanders, and the way to prevent further damage was to limit contact with them. That would be difficult to do because even after they went home from this trip, he was technically still dating Brooke, and he was still painting out of Lilah's barn, and they all worked together for the guild.

Difficult, but not impossible.

He could come up with a plan. He'd never be able to make it up to Brooke. He'd lost all chance with Lilah, but that was his own fault. Lilah deserved someone who respected the things she loved. With her iron idealism and confidence, Lilah knew that. She'd never go with someone who seemingly expected her to be the hypotenuse in a cheating triangle, let alone a triangle where her best friend was one of the other sides.

He wished he'd never met her. Never met them both. Wished he'd never started painting in the first place. Maybe someday he'd have wandered into a knitting shop and met a curly haired girl with lively eyes and said, "I was looking for a gift for my mother," and that would have been a better chance than where they stood now.

Lilah took another dive off the dock while Brooke and Sonia stood on the edge. Then she swam back around to the ladder while Brooke dove.

Sonia looked across the water at Emerson. From this far away, it was impossible to read her expression, but then Lilah turned to look at him too. In Emerson's heart, he knew what Lilah's face would say.

CHAPTER NINETEEN

At the door of her barn, Lilah saw off Sonia and Emerson with a mixture of relief and grief.

Brooke waved as they left, then turned to Lilah. "That was a great trip, wasn't it?" When Lilah nodded, she added, "And your hair is amazing. Whatever Sonia did to it, we need to send her flowers once she's back at home."

"It's too bad we can't find her a job up here." Not that Sonia would take it. She'd made it clear that she was a city girl, and Brighthead held nothing for her. To hear her talk, it was a surprise Emerson himself had come up here.

Except he had, and Lilah had let him move right into her heart.

The silence of the barn felt numinous. Yes, there had been silence at the campground, but there had also been Sonia and Brooke and Emerson. Emerson alone would have dwarfed the trees, smothered the mountains, and extinguished the stars.

Emerson plus the weight of her feelings was more than the weight of the earth. Lilah had carried it for too long.

Brooke should want to go home. Brooke craved silence and time to herself. Even during the camp-out, she'd managed to find alone time every so often. "Oh, I'll go get more water," and Brooke would be down at the lake, pumping and filtering. Or, "I think we need more rocks to border the campfire," and that was another fifteen minutes stolen for herself.

Lilah got some space right now by checking her phone for the first time in three days. Her email and voicemail and text apps filled with messages. From just a glance, she could tell the Historical Society was being a pain, and no one had resolved a thing.

Instead of leaving, Brooke followed Lilah deeper into the barn. "Can I ask you a question?"

Lilah went cold.

"Was Emerson angry at us on the drive home?"

Lilah tried to loosen up so her voice wouldn't be an octave above where it should be. "Why do you think that?"

"He was quiet when we took down the camp. That, and he wouldn't swim with us." Brooke sounded tentative. "I'm not good at telling what's going on inside his head, but you're telepathic, so I figured you might know."

Lilah forced a laugh. "Telepathic?"

"You know what people are feeling. It's always a mystery to me, so I lean on you for that." Brooke shrugged. "Like the way you like Emerson."

Lilah jerked up. "What?"

She hadn't kept that jolt out of her voice. How could Brooke to say she couldn't tell what people were feeling, and then come right out and say the thing Lilah had been hiding?

Brooke smiled. "You disliked Hal, but you and Natalie both like Emerson, so that's reassuring."

Mouth dry, Lilah nodded.

Brooke said, "Although I'm a bit concerned because, well, he's considerate, but he's never tried to kiss me. I tried to hold his hand when we were walking back to the car, and he tolerated it for about fifteen seconds before pulling away."

Lilah cocked her head. "You've never kissed?"

Brooke shrugged. "I get that he's taking it slow, and maybe he was self-conscious because Sonia was here. But we've had opportunities."

Lilah stepped closer. "Did you want him to kiss you? Have you tried to kiss him?"

Brooke shook her head. "You know me." Yes, Lilah did. This had come up between them so many times, where Brooke wondered what was wrong with her because everyone else in the high school would look at a hot guy and want to do things with him, whereas Brooke wanted to hear more about how he'd changed the rims on his tires. "I don't want to kiss or make out until I feel safe with someone, and maybe he was the same way, so I shouldn't push him. But I would have let him if he wanted to."

Lilah dropped onto the couch and slackened her head into the cushions. Staring at the rafters, her mind spun. "Okay, then." Brooke wanted to feel safe, but the barn was Lilah's safe space, too. The little lights. The wind chimes. The LED candles. This was where Lilah could make her heart free. "We both saw he was upset, so what happened right before we went swimming?"

"The hike, but nothing weird happened there, either. You and Sonia had dropped back, and Emerson and I were up front. I didn't talk much because we were going at a pretty good clip." Brooke took up a tiny space at the end of the couch. "You and I swam to the dock, and then he swam out after us. He turned at the dock and just...never came back."

Having counted it as her good fortune when Emerson had returned to shore, Lilah hadn't considered it again. He'd met her eyes as she got back to the dock from her dive, and he'd darted away. They'd been joking on the shore just before swimming out. Joking about what? About Lilah splashing him? And about the water being cold, and Sonia not wanting to swim. Then Sonia had joined them on the dock, and Emerson hadn't.

Sonia and Emerson must have fought. That made more sense, and Emerson was staying quiet because you keep family fights in the family. Lilah had seen Brooke's family do that on occasion, and Brooke had only broken down and told her afterward. Long afterward. Meanwhile, Emerson had let Lilah and Sonia hug and exchange enthusiastic goodbyes and promises to keep in touch, all without divulging whatever had put him and his sister at odds.

He was an upstanding guy who wasn't going to put Lilah in the middle where she didn't belong. He'd hate knowing Lilah had inadvertently put herself in the middle.

Brooke seemed unnerved, though, so Lilah rallied herself. "It'll be okay. You'll talk to him tomorrow, and it'll turn out he was just tired of campfire food and wanted to stop for a takeout coffee."

Brooke's eyebrows raised. "You think so?"

Lilah struggled to settle the uneasiness in her gut. "Trust him. He's a good guy."

This whole boondoggle had started because Lilah wanted to boost Emerson's career. That's all she'd wanted: to give him the confidence to step into the spotlight. Not that Fruits de Mer was a major gallery, but it was an opportunity he'd been ready to ball up and toss into the trash.

Tonight, the barn echoed without Sonia, without Emerson, without Brooke. Lilah reheated some leftovers for a lackluster meal and then wandered with her bowl and fork over to Emerson's paint area.

On the trip, he'd taken so many pictures. He'd have more ideas for paintings. Even that sketch he'd done on the rock, gazing at the campground, had been amazing. He looked at reality and saw beyond it, then framed it in his mind and gave expression to it with his hands.

She blew off a breath, then went back to eating reheated frozen casserole. This disaster had started out for business, so the way to get out of it was to focus on business. The BCG. The church building. The networking. How she could boost Emerson's career.

Art had a business side. That's what made art so strange: you had to on the one hand have a vibrant zest for life, and on the other hand you had to think like an accountant.

Colin had this going on, as well. Natalie said Colin was constantly looking at ingredients and getting excited about what he could do with them (fifty pounds of chanterelles) and then dialing back to what he could do that would sell. Sonia had been doing the same, talking to Lilah about how to turn her regular customers into "super customers" who'd spend their first fiber dollars on her.

Lilah took that most-recently finished painting from where it stood against the wall, the Myth Brightman statue, and at her work table, she studied it for a long time before settling on what to do.

First, she turned on the *Pride and Prejudice* mini-series for background noise.

Next, she filled a basin with vinegar water and set two skeins to soak, one fingering weight and one DK weight. If worse came to worst, she'd have a couple of experimental skeins to put up on her storefront. Some of her customers snapped up the one-of-a-kind colorway failures the moment they appeared.

Wearing her goggles and her mask, Lilah mixed colors and tested them on paper towels. A few grains of this color or that, and then she finally had every tone she wanted.

With that done, she spread out the fingering weight yarn on a sheet of plastic wrap. With Myth Brightman propped on a folding chair, Lilah spread the dyes on the yarn to mimic the colors in the painting.

A tonal metallic for the statue. Blue for the sky with bare patches for the clouds. Deeper blue for the water. Brown along the bottom for the dock.

She stepped back. Not bad. Then she flipped the skein over and made sure all the dye had penetrated to the back. Careful—don't smudge. Make sure everything is where it needs to be.

Now she'd just have to hope for the best. Lilah wrapped plastic wrap around the wet yarn, and with it secure, she tucked it into the dyeing microwave on high for five minutes.

She could have steamed it, but given the precision she needed, wrapping the unset dye in a plastic burrito seemed the better option.

It emerged hot, but wearing rubber gloves, Lilah squeezed the plastic. The water inside the plastic wrap was clear, so she unwrapped the scalding yarn and raised it as if it were hanging from a peg.

There in her hands was a ghost image of Emerson's painting. Side by side, they were twin arts: hers dangling and filled with movement; his fixed in place but deep with emotion.

She'd need some process improvement. For one thing, she should secure it with more ties. She'd need a zip tie for the top so it would hang better and make the image look more natural. But absolutely, she could do this.

Lilah tackled the second skein, and the second time around, it came even better. After half an hour, the ghost of the myth hung in her hands, a smudge of the pier beneath, the hint of clouds and the lighthouse behind.

Was it useful? No, but it was memorable. It was heart-tugging. It was another way to draw attention to Emerson's artwork, and in her purest moments, that's all Lilah had wanted.

She couldn't pretend to be pure like that any longer, but she could revert to it and hope it would be enough. Emerson and Brooke would be happy, and Lilah could attend to business.

CHAPTER TWENTY

In the three empty, lonely days since Sonia had gone back to Mom and Dad, Emerson hadn't visited the barn to paint.

He hadn't texted Lilah to chat, either. They'd communicated in the chilliest exchanges possible. "Are you coming to paint today?" "Not today." "Okay, I'll lock up." The warmth he'd come to expect was nowhere, and he had only himself to blame.

Sonia, however, was texting up a storm, ample follow-up to the barrage of words she'd unleashed after they'd gotten back from camping and before he'd sent her back to Boston on her own. "You're going to ruin everything," she said.

She was wrong.

He already had.

Emerson couldn't bring himself to think about the exhibition date looming on the calendar. When he'd had Lilah and Brooke at his back, putting himself and his work "out there" had seemed doable. Now? With Lilah furious, Brooke wouldn't be too far behind. They were in tight with the restaurant owner. Would he claw back the offer?

Lilah's eyes kept haunting him. Face-to-face with him at

the edge of the dock, she'd shown first fear, and then revulsion as she'd swept her arms and legs to shoot herself backward in the water.

He'd never harm Lilah. She'd acted as though he would.

At his office in Acadia, he planned programs and dealt with his irritated supervisor, and he thought about the loathing in Lilah's eyes. He called the local Girl Scout councils to verify the details of an upcoming program, and he remembered Lilah jerking away from him. Even worse, on the drive home from work, he'd think about Lilah during those first two days at the camp as she'd kept skittering aside. She'd burned her own drawing.

She wanted nothing to do with him. It was obvious in a way that was both breathtaking and horrific, and Emerson had no idea what to do.

The first step, however, was obvious. He asked Brooke if she'd be around on Saturday evening.

She sounded reserved, but not more than usual. "Where do you want to meet?"

Here Emerson had to tread carefully. "Would you mind something low-key?"

Brooke said, "You could come here for dinner. I'm not the best cook, but I'm unlikely to kill you."

"That's an endorsement," Emerson said, although maybe she should.

"Lilah says I ought to be more confident, on the grounds that my cooking hasn't yet killed me." Brooke laughed. "But erring on the side of safety, I'll treat you. How about Sparrows?"

Emerson volunteered to bring dessert, and now they were sorted.

Saturday evening came. Five minutes before Brooke said she'd be back, Emerson was pacing her parking lot, a box of cupcakes in his hands, and his heart in his throat.

Brooke had biked home. "Hey! You beat me here. I need to lock up my bike."

He held the door while she carried her bike up the stairs, and as she hung it on the wall, he looked over the studio. Spare and well-apportioned, every part of the unit was divided from one another, military in its precision. She said, "I'd give you the tour, but you've basically had it."

He shook his head. "It's a much better use of space than my place."

She laughed. "If you were painting here, you'd spread the paints out over the whole thing and sleep in the tub." That's when she looked him dead in the eye. "What's wrong?"

He tried to hand off the cupcake box, but she shook her head. "Don't sandbag me. What's wrong?"

What had Lilah told her? "Why are you asking that?"

"Because you look determined. Actually, you look grim. Did I mess up?" Her eyes widened. "I hope I didn't offend your sister. Sonia was a lot of fun to listen to, but I didn't have anything to contribute."

Emerson said, automatically, "You have plenty to contribute."

Brooke didn't have much furniture, but she did have a large desk covered in graphing paper, a laptop, a calculator, and a basket of yarn.

"Did Sonia have a good time?" she pressed. "I didn't want to bring up the job thing, but she and Lilah kept talking about Lilah's dyeing business. If I jumped into the conversation, I knew I'd say the wrong thing."

"She's fine. It's not about Sonia."

There was no moment when Brooke's expression changed. "Then it's about me?"

He would have waited until after dinner. He would have eaten with her and shared a cupcake, and then afterward, he'd have delivered the lines he'd rehearsed in his head.

Her voice ticked up. "What did I do wrong? I thought everything was fine."

"It was." Emerson wanted to sit on the couch with her to talk slowly and clearly. "You didn't do anything wrong. It's just, I'm not feeling it. You're a great person, but we're not clicking."

Brooke averted her eyes. "Doesn't that take time?"

Emerson said, "It should have happened by now."

"Not always." Brooke's brow furrowed. "I mean, I get it. Was tonight supposed to be my last chance, or were you going to break up with me by asking for separate checks?"

Emerson's chest felt tight. Brooke still hadn't changed expression. She was a self-contained universe, hooking her thoughts into details that made no sense to him but apparently made sense to her.

Emerson said, "I don't see us going anywhere. That's all."

"Well, yeah." Brooke shrugged. "I feel bad that you had to drive all the way over here with a box of cupcakes just to say you'd made a decision." She gestured to the plastic box. "You might as well take these home with you. I'm not a cupcake fan."

He said, "We can still—"

"No, we can't *still*. I've got chicken in the freezer. I'll be fine." She stepped toward the door. "Thanks for helping me get my bike up the stairs, and thanks for bringing me to a Renaissance Faire. That was fun, at least."

Emerson said, "I'm sorry."

Brooke folded her arms. "I'm sure you are, but I'm also not in the mood to hear it right now. Thank you for the respect of not stringing me along."

She stepped back, a clear signal that he was allowed to proceed back out the doorway. As he went, she said, "Just for my own edification, what did I do right before that last swim to turn you against me?"

Hand on the doorknob, he said, "Nothing."

"Humor me. This is the only question on my exit interview, but that's the moment everything changed, and I can't even parse how I blew it."

He faced her. "You didn't do anything wrong. At some point, I realized we were better off as friends."

Her mouth tightened. "I wish you'd do me the credit of not lying. But since that's how you want it, head off. I'll give you space. I won't show up unannounced at Lilah's when you might be painting."

"You don't have to—"

"Of course I have to." Her eyes narrowed to match the tightness of her mouth. She wasn't exactly angry, but she wasn't exactly sad, either. This was more emotion than she'd shown the entire time they'd been dating. "You need to finish your paintings, and there's no reason to be in one another's hair. By the time the exhibit's ready, everything will be okay again."

In other words, she'd be over him in a couple of weeks. Maybe she hadn't felt any more spark for him than he had for her.

He exited into the hallway. "I'm sorry. I did want it to work out."

Brooke shrugged. "I guess it's like you said about paintings. Sometimes, you just have to primer over the whole thing and try again with a different subject. It's not the canvas's fault or the painter's fault. Sometimes, it wasn't going to work."

Shaken, Emerson stopped at a burger place to grab food.

Breakups were never easy. She hadn't screamed or thrown things or sobbed—but then again, he hadn't expected her to. He'd expected to have the whole evening to work up to it, and instead she'd gone for his heart with a straight knitting needle. He'd assumed she would blame him, but then she'd defaulted to blaming herself.

That wasn't fair. Once Brooke calmed down, she'd see she'd done nothing wrong. She was logical, and she'd work her way through it. Although actually, she had been calm. It had been Emerson getting emotional. If anything, she'd seemed more irritated that he'd made plans for the evening instead of dropping her a text.

How would that have worked? "Hey, Brooke, I've been

thinking. Let's break up. It's not you, it's me."

His phone buzzed on the table, and he shut it down without checking the screen. Whoever it was—Brooke, Sonia, Lilah—he couldn't deal with them right now. Eventually he'd drive home and paint for a while. First he'd level out his blood sugar, and then he'd level out his head and heart.

The food wasn't great, but it was warm. Then it was gone, and Emerson had to leave. He shoved his phone into his back pocket, feeling uneasy-queasy whenever he thought about what messages might have come in.

He buckled in and started the car, but then he hesitated.

What would a brave person do? A brave person would look at the phone. It might not even be Brooke. It might be Sonia. It might be some random scammer texting him about an extended auto warranty. It might be his mother texting him about his grandmother's most recent doctor's appointment. He didn't need to be stressed the whole drive. He should look at the messages still on the lockscreen. In the worst case, that still wouldn't change the message to "read."

His hands shook as he turned the phone back on, and the messages were all from Lilah.

"Emerson, talk to me!"

That was the last of the messages. The two beneath it were in reverse chronological order.

"I don't understand. Call me."

"What did you do? Why?"

Lilah was escalating, and once again Emerson recreated in his mind the moment she'd rounded the dock and found herself face-to-face with him, the currents from her swim mixed with the currents of his, their bodies facing one another, and her repulsion prominent as a lighthouse.

His paintings were in her barn. Every time she looked, she was going to see more evidence of him and get angrier —and not without justification. Emerson should have realized that in the aftermath of the breakup, he'd need to rescue his equipment, or at the very least his art.

Brooke hadn't gotten angry. Instead, like the teammate she was, she'd deflected her emotions to Lilah.

Emerson plugged the phone into the jack, and at a red light, he hit the button to call Lilah.

"Emerson? What's going on?"

"I broke up with Brooke." As though Lilah didn't know.

"But why? What went wrong?"

Lilah had been outraged that Emerson was double-timing Brooke in his heart. Why would she be angry that he'd broken it off? Why pretend she didn't know?

Emerson said, "Can I come over? I'm still in Brighthead, and it'll be easier to explain in person." He should grab his paintings. The breakup would have torched his exhibit at Fruits de Mer. One text from Brooke to the third member of their triad, and then one from Natalie to her boyfriend, would be all it took to get the invitation yanked.

Would Emerson have to leave the BCG?

Lilah was saying, "I don't need you to come over. I need you to talk."

Brighthead wasn't big. He was close to the barn by now. "What is there to talk about? I told Brooke everything. We're not sparking. It wasn't there."

"It could have been! You took her to the Renn Faire, and you both had a great time!"

He was close now. Get in. Grab the paintings while Lilah pelted him with hypothetical questions and memories, and then get out again. "We did have a great time. I don't regret going out with her. Look, can I just come talk to you?"

"We're talking now!" Lilah's voice ticked up. "I don't understand, and neither does she. What happened on the camping trip that turned you off?"

"Nothing! I said the same to Brooke." He hesitated, having an awful thought. "Is she with you now?"

"She wanted to work through this alone. She's probably graphing a shawl pattern." Yes, that did track, Brooke positioned at her huge desk with its calculators and three floor lamps aimed toward it. "She wouldn't let me go over to her."

That meant the coast was clear. Emerson pulled onto the side road. "Do you think she'll be okay?"

"Fine time to think about that now." Lilah's voice was low. "She was excited to take you to dinner, and then you dumped her."

"She wasn't excited to go to dinner. She never gets excited about anything." Emerson huffed as he pulled onto the driveway. "And I did intend to go with her. She jumped the gun." Past the landlord's house. "She demanded to know what was going on."

He pulled up in front of the barn, and while he was unbuckling, Lilah stalked out of the barn.

He hung up while she shoved her phone in her back pocket. "Was I only thinking loudly when I told you not to come here?"

"You're angry, and I wanted a chance to explain." She was blocking the door, leaving no way to get past to his paintings. "I intended to go to dinner, yes. I had a whole conversation mapped out, and I was going to lead her up to the obvious conclusion that—"

"That you're a jerk."

"—that we just weren't clicking. She's nice, and she's thoughtful, but that's where it ends. She's nice. She thinks I'm okay. Is that how you'd want to build your future? With someone who's okay? Someone who's nice?"

Lilah kept scowling, arms folded. "That's the best you can say about her?"

"She's a lot of things, but she didn't deserve to have someone string her along hoping that one day he'd fall in love." Emerson tilted his head. "She wasted what, a month of her time? She got some exercise? She had a few days of vacation?"

"She got attached to you."

Emerson said, "And if I burned more of her time, she'd have become less attached?"

Lilah looked away. Her eyes were glistening.

Emerson's heart bottomed out. "Lilah, I'm sorry."

"You're not sorry. You planned it. I kept having you

come over here because I thought you'd be good for her."

She pivoted and headed into the barn. Emerson followed, saying, "So you were lying when you said you wanted to help me with my art? It was all an act of philanthropy?"

He got one step into the barn and laid eyes on his paintings. They were all safe. All right where he'd left them. All—

All accompanied by a skein of yarn.

"I did want to help you. I wanted to help both of you." Lilah swiped her hand over her eyes. "You two could have been so good together. You're both smart and insightful and full of integrity."

Integrity? "Integrity" wasn't what Lilah had been thinking when she glared at him out by the dock. More like, "Duplicity."

"What did you do?" This time it was Emerson saying it, but with awe rather than accusation. He approached his paintings. The statue. The harbor. The town green. Each had beside it a skein of yarn in the same colors and similar proportions, a free-flowing after-image as if his paintings had been rendered in a dream onto the tail of a unicorn.

He touched the statue skein, letting the strands roll over his fingertips.

His voice emerged in a hush. "I thought you were angry at me."

"I wasn't angry at you *then*." Lilah huffed. "I didn't do these two minutes ago. I wanted to figure out a way to promote your exhibit."

"But—" He turned to her. "You were angry at me on the camping trip."

She approached. "Why would I be angry at you then?"

"At the dock. You were furious. I thought—" Emerson moved to the harbor painting, with the silhouettes on the rock. "You couldn't stand to be near me."

Lilah's voice broke. "Because you were hers."

Emerson turned, and Lilah was close enough to touch. Her eyes, tearful. Her mouth, just a little downturned. Her

151

hands clenched by her chest. "You were hers," Lilah repeated, and Emerson realized what she was saying. "I needed to give you distance." Or rather, what she wasn't saying. "I couldn't get in between."

He reached for her and kissed her.

Lilah tensed in his arms, but then before he had a chance to draw back, she had her arms around his shoulders, pulling him closer, pulling his mouth against hers. She had one hand behind his neck with her fingers in his hair, the other around the small of his back. He inhaled the scent of her, cherished the feel, crushed her body against his until he could feel all her curves. *Lilah. Lilah.*

She hadn't wanted to get in between. She'd been fighting her feelings the whole trip. That was why she'd stayed away. Right here, in his arms, was the one and only reason for her uneasiness, her skittishness, her unwillingness to talk.

He ran his mouth over her neck. "Oh, Lilah."

She clenched him closer, and he nuzzled her ear, then returned his lips to hers. This wasn't the blossom of his imagination. Lilah was warm and solid in his arms. The scent of her. The sound of her little gasps and the hum in the back of her throat when he kissed her hard and tightened her waist against his.

They paused, breathing in bursts. Lilah whispered, "Wait."

He ran a hand over her curls. "Shh. We're here now."

She tucked down her chin and pressed her face into his neck. Leaning against the wall, he struggled to tread water with the feelings rising all around him.

He'd dated Brooke for nearly a month, and not once had emotion carried him away like this. All the zest from the woman in his arms, the gush of her feelings returning to him—he couldn't breathe. He couldn't fathom it. Couldn't plan.

Would she kiss him again? Weave her fingers into his belt loops and tug him toward her? Whisper his name in the way that sent warmth shooting from the base of his spine up into his throat?

So quiet. So, so quiet, and then she shook her head against him. "Why?"

Why? Because the universe was amazing, and because Lilah was brilliant, and because that unmoored part of Emerson's heart had just found an anchor in her belief in him.

She breathed, "I can't. This—" Before the words reached Emerson's ears, she pushed away. "We can't do this."

One look at her face, and Emerson's heart crashed back into his chest.

"Brooke's my best friend." She swallowed hard. "You just broke up with her." Tears spilled over her cheeks, but Lilah clenched her fists. "I need you to leave."

CHAPTER TWENTY-ONE

For the next twenty-four hours, Lilah battled shame and grief and doubt. Her eyes burned, and even Natalie asked if she'd managed to sleep at all. "*Brooke* broke up with him, not you."

When Brooke turned up in the afternoon, she was quiet and efficient. She set up the laptop at the Sit and Stitch table to update their website, then arranged a promotion for one of her patterns. Other than reassuring Natalie she was okay, Brooke didn't mention Emerson at all.

Well, not for the first hour. Then, with Natalie about to leave, she winked at her. "Don't go to war for me or anything."

Natalie paused while packing her backpack. "Don't go to war?"

Brooke returned focus to her computer. "Don't have Colin rescind the exhibit. Emerson was as nice about it as he could have been, other than wasting my time last night. It would have been worse if he'd strung me along until after the exhibit."

Natalie's eyes glinted. "Fine. We won't go to war."

Lavender Paul approached the Sit and Stitch table, and

she was probably just as glad that Lilah had pushed her out of the number one position for Brighthead's Most Hated Citizen. Mrs. Paul said, "But you would."

"Of course she would." Brooke shrugged. "But since we're all playing in the same BCG sandbox, we need to share the pails and shovels."

Lavender Paul plunked a bag on the table. "Something's wrong with my yarn. Go to war with this."

Indeed, the yarn that came out of her bag had endured some kind of tragedy. Instead of being a cylinder-shaped cake, with criss-crosses stacked up the edges, it was a misshapen ovoid, slumped sideways.

"Oh, dear." Brooke shut her laptop. "I hope you brought your ball winder."

Lavender removed that from the bag as well. "Nat," Brooke added, "stay a minute so you can learn how to do this."

Lilah pushed closer, too. "What went wrong?"

"The teeth popped out of each other." Brooke removed her key ring from her back pocket, and among the keys was a tiny Philips head screwdriver.

Lavender said, "And I'm paying you."

Shaking her head, Brooke said, "You brought an education opportunity for Natalie and Lilah, so that's payment."

Lavender said, "Then I'll pay you with advice. Whoever you're getting revenge on, nominate them for the BCG Executive Committee."

Lilah flinched. "Mrs. Paul!"

Brooke, however, was laughing so hard that the light had returned to her eyes. "You're brilliant! I'll put Emerson in charge of taking minutes for the newsletter. He'll be working off his debt to my broken heart for generations."

Lavender grinned. "That's my girl."

Brooke nodded. "The poor man will show up for every single meeting for the rest of time, just to make sure we don't volun-tell him for other jobs. We'll wait years for the one time he misses a meeting due to a hundred and five fever, and then we'll elect him guild president for life. Okay, so here." She removed the swivel from the winder base and pried apart the top and bottom. "You see the teeth attached to the winder handle? They popped out of the teeth on the swivel base, so the base was turning but not swiveling. The swivel keeps the yarn from stacking up on top of itself, which as you can see, eventually makes it a sad, slumpy egg shape."

Natalie watched over Brook's shoulder as she went to work with the screwdriver inside the winder. "Lilah, you won't mind getting demoted to vice president, right? You'll just have to sit around waiting for Emerson to run for the hills, and you'll be back on the throne of power."

Lilah clutched the pen in her hands. "Some throne of power. I won't be surprised if the entire membership votes me out after this."

Brooke pushed the top of the winder into the teeth with a hard crack. "After *what*? No one in the BCG cared that I was dating Emerson except for you, me, Nat, and possibly Emerson himself, though that's not a given." She flashed a V sign with her fingers. "You're taking this harder than I am."

Lilah folded her arms. "I mean about losing the church on Main Street."

Well, Lilah did also mean about breaking them up. If she hadn't drawn Emerson's attention, he'd have kept going out with Brooke until he developed feelings for her. Without incentive to switch to another woman, Emerson would have stayed with Brooke at least until the exhibit started. Except then Lilah had come along, temptress extraordinaire.

She didn't even know how she'd done it. Apparently, keeping her distance from a man was a potent aphrodisiac. *Driving Men Wild: How one woman won her man by only talking to him in groups and never flirting at all.*

Lavender huffed. "The only reason you 'lost' the church on Main Street—and you haven't lost it yet—is you were the only human being with the vision to see that building's potential. No one else would have lost the building because no one would have tried to have it."

Brooke's head shot up. "Now that you mention it, Mrs. Paul, that makes sense. We could also cancel everyone's exhibits to assure that no member ever gets a bad review."

Natalie said, "We'll shutter the yarn shop, that way we can't go bankrupt."

Lilah sighed. "You're not helping."

Lavender said, "She wasn't trying to help. She was trying to make you sound ridiculous."

"Stop." It was better to have them talking about the BCG than about Emerson, but everything was falling apart at once. There was an emergency injunction keeping them from getting the building, and an emotional injunction keeping Emerson away from Lilah—well, hopefully. Hopefully.

Lavender pointed to the winder. "You see how those teeth came apart, and without the click, they didn't turn right? That's how it is with people. You've got teeth. They've got teeth. And if you've got weird teeth, it's hard to get them all to fit together, especially people with regular teeth."

Natalie shuddered. "Well, that got awkward."

Lavender said, "You and them, you don't click, because you're artistic, and they're rule-followers hog-tied by tradition. You need someone artsy like yourselves to see what you see."

Brooke finished screwing the winder shut. "Mrs. Paul is right. I don't think you realize how high the degree of difficulty is for everything you're attempting. In the space of what, five months?, you've started a regional artists' guild, tried to expand your own business, attempted to set me up with a soulmate, and joined the Economic Planning Board. What more do you expect?"

Lilah's eyes burned. "I didn't expect to be terrible at all of those things."

Brooke said, "You're hardly terrible at all those things."

Natalie said, "You did get elected to the planning board,

and you did start the guild."

Brooke clamped the repaired winder to the table. "It's not your fault Emerson wasn't my soulmate, either. I'm not that interesting."

Natalie sighed. "There's nothing wrong with you. And there's nothing wrong with you, either," she added to Lilah. "You're a dreamer, and you've got ambition, and you want to save the world. No one's going to fault you for that."

Brooke huffed. "Except the Historical Society."

Lavender Paul said, "Any time you annoy the Brighthead Historical Society, you're doing something right."

Brooke took a tiny ball of yarn and threaded it through the yarn holder, then started winding. It immediately formed a cake, the lines crisscrossing perfectly. "We've got this," she told Lavender Paul. "It's going to be tricky to re-wind the first cake, though, so take it slow."

The door jangled while Lavender packed up her stuff, and another customer entered. Shelly Novick, who had gotten semi-famous around Brighthead for knitting the dress for her wedding next December. Natalie chatted with her a minute before leaving, and then Brooke looked over her dress pattern while they discussed how to modify it.

Lilah sat at the Sit and Stitch table, staring at her tablet. Gutted.

Brooke was right there discussing a wedding dress as though nothing had gone wrong. She and Natalie had been slinging jokes. Fine, but they didn't know the whole story.

Lilah went through her planning notes, but everything felt insurmountable. She'd head home in an hour and hand-paint Brighthead-themed yarns while eating dinner standing at the table (only pre-mixed dyes—she had to be careful with food around) and then tonight she'd attend the Economic Planning Board and force herself to care about the economy of a town that didn't care about her.

"Excuse me?"

Lilah looked up to find Shelly hovering at her elbow. "I wanted to give you a heads-up about the board meeting."

When Lilah frowned, Shelly said, "My fiancé knows a few members of the Historical Society. They're planning to bring up the old church during the meeting."

Lilah frowned. "That's not even on the agenda."

"They've got people lined up to give speeches." Shelly huffed. "Lucas thinks they're nuts, but they're not exactly reasonable."

Lilah rested her forehead in her palms. Of course. Of course they'd be hungry after getting the court injunction. Of course they'd go for every other thing of hers they could break. She was lucky they hadn't started review-bombing her yarn dyeing business. *"Horrible yarn, plus Lilah Marcille defiles churches!"*

Time to brave up. There was nothing else to do.

Lilah hadn't needed to warn her other committee members about the Historical Society crashing the board meeting. There were already seven people gathered in the room when she arrived, including Natalie and Brooke, plus one other member of the BCG. The rest were Historical Society members. By the time they started, there were twenty in the audience.

Normally, they had two onlookers, and one was the husband of the committee chair who didn't like to drive at night.

For all that the chair didn't like to drive at night, she did drive a tight schedule. She began the meeting right at eight, starting with, "Thank you all for coming. Keep in mind that open questions are at the discretion of the committee, and we will take care of all other committee business first. The secretary will now review the minutes of last month's meeting."

Where else would Lilah have rather been right then,

other than this meeting? How about anywhere? She'd rather be in her barn with all the lights off except the strings of twinkle lights, the barn door wide open while she listened to the motion of her chimes as the air currents lazed through the room. In that sweet twi-dark she'd lie on her couch, the barn heavy with the presence of Emerson's paintings. She'd remember the fervor of him kissing her, the urgency of his mouth on hers and his arms around her waist, the simultaneous relief and terror as she felt an overwhelming longing.

Then the grief, followed by the shame.

She'd felt it repeatedly all day, but maybe in the dark, in the silence, in the presence of his creations, she could reconcile it all. His creative energy would mix with her yearning, and she'd decipher where she went wrong so she could figure out how to make it right.

Natalie and Brooke were tucked into their chairs, but not next to one another. They'd spread out a bit. Lilah thought she recognized another BCG member, but what were they going to do? Start a brawl?

Then the door opened again, and in stepped Emerson.

Lilah went cold to her core.

The chair said, "Now, on to the discussions about signage at the town green."

Early in her knitting journey, Lilah had bought an expensive ball of laceweight yarn from Bright Stitches, back when Natalie's mother still ran the store and Brooke hung out after school doing her homework at the Sit and Stitch table. "I can wind the yarn myself," Lilah had bragged, the vision of a lacy pink scarf hovering before her as she squished the hank in her hands. She'd wound the entire cake into a center-pull ball, and then she'd cast on.

By the end of the night, she'd been in tears: the yarn wouldn't pull right. It kept getting stuck to itself. It would come out of the center in big chunks, and then she couldn't stuff the chunks back into the middle. None of it was working right even though she could still see that fuzzy, lacy scarf in her mind. Soft and light and delicate, it was perfect to wear on a brisk day, paired with a light jacket. Except nothing paired with it. Not the needles, not the pattern, not the yarn.

Just like Brooke and Emerson. Just like herself and Emerson.

The chair said, "With that settled, next up, the industrial park at 245 Washington Street."

The next day, Lilah had slunk into Bright Stitches with her ruined project, trembling with frustration, and she'd even started angry-crying when she explained to Mrs. Prescott. Natalie's mom had gotten one look at the yarn and said, "Oh," then sat down to figure out a solution.

Nowadays, of course, Lilah could have diagnosed the problem just as quickly as Mrs. Prescott had. The yarn was the issue, although not so much the yarn as the way it was wound. Yes, it would make a light, airy garment that would also be warm—but that same fuzziness meant it would catch on itself wherever it touched. If Lilah had pulled the yarn from the outside of the ball, she'd have been fine. Instead, she'd wound the cake very tight, and then she'd pulled from the center.

Mrs. Prescott said, "You should cut the yarn and rejoin from the outside of the ball."

Lilah, instead, decided to re-wind six hundred yards of fuzzy laceweight yarn in the hopes of not having to rejoin yarn in the loose, lacy pattern. She'd used the ball winder at first to pull as much off the ball as she could, but then she reached the clumps in the middle where everything began to stick to itself. Yard by yard, she hand-wound the yarn into a ball-around-a-cake in order to end up with that same single long strand of yarn she'd started with. Sometimes she'd work on the yarn in the middle, loosening it enough that she could pass the growing ball through the massive tangle. She didn't want to leave the store until it was done, knowing it would tangle even worse in her bag on the walk home. Mrs. Prescott stayed with her until the end, and it took hours.

The chair said, "Lilah, did you have updates on the

business grant proposal?"

With Emerson's eyes on her, Lilah read straight off her notes. "We've been approved for a $250 grant from the Environmental Coalition to add planters and flowers to the traffic triangle at the corner of Washington and Main and the front entrance of town hall. Also, our grant application for $500 toward solar-powered flashing pedestrian crossing signs at the Main Street intersection has progressed to the final selection committee."

If the Historical Society was going to hate her, they might as well also hate her for solar-powered flashing lights.

That fuzzy pink yarn had broken Lilah's heart. She'd knitted her scarf, but the pattern itself mocked her. She'd reach one particular stitch in every repeat and remember how the snarled yarn was so tight the first time around that she couldn't finish the stitch. The finished project in her mind had been perfect, but the reality was, she'd ruined it for herself.

She'd ruined Emerson in the same way. The finished product of Emerson and Brooke had seemed perfect. But like an inexperienced knitter drawing an underspun cashmere from a center-pull ball, Lilah had created a disaster.

Afterward, other people had said the scarf was beautiful. Lilah always knew it was ugly.

The chair said, "Now, we'll take questions. If we call on you, you may speak for three minutes."

Michelle Hargrove from the Historical Society stood. "It's hardly fair to limit us to three minutes. Do you have to answer us in three minutes?"

Michelle was holding multiple typed pages. Lilah sighed.

The chair said, "If this involves a court case, then I'm afraid we can't answer your question at all, and the town of Brighthead will defer to the judgment of the court."

Lilah's eyebrows shot up. She hadn't expected that, but it sounded very legal.

With a huff, Michelle began reading off her paper. *We of*

*the Historical Society are concerned about the suggested use of the retired church building at 201 Main Street...*and on and on. It sounded nice and thoughtful, and they'd even attempted to tie it into economics.

At three minutes, the chair stood. "Thank you. Your time is up, and there was no question."

Michelle handed her paper to the person sitting beside her, who continued reading it.

Lilah looked at the chair. "Can they do that?"

The chair half-snorted. "Apparently so."

The second person kept reading.

Lilah raised her voice, "This involves a suit the Historical Society has already filed, meaning it can't be discussed here."

No change in the reading.

Lilah stood, trembling. The chair grabbed her wrist and tugged her back into her seat, then leaned closer. "This is grandstanding." It was just a whisper. "They're wasting our time and theirs, and they'll feel like they did something even though we're not listening."

Natalie was knitting, eyes riveted to the speaker. Lilah wished she'd been knitting through the meeting, too. Usually, she did. It had become a joke in previous months to include Lilah's current project in the minutes. Knitting through someone's tirade was an effective way of looking bored even as you paid close attention to every word.

Unfortunately, the Historical Society was being recorded for the local cable access channel. In effect, they were getting a chance to air their grievances without being censored. While they were being rude beyond belief to hijack the meeting, most people weren't going to care about procedure. They were going to hear about the iconoclasts who wanted to defile Brighthead's hallowed spaces, and nothing more.

The third person tried to hand off the paper to the fourth, and Brooke intercepted it. Lilah hadn't even seen her move toward them, but there she was. Brooke said, "I would like to ask the chair how it benefits the economy of

Brighthead to allow a historical building to stand abandoned."

Michelle snatched the papers from Brooke's hand. The chair said, "That's a lovely question. I can see no economic benefit to having an abandoned building at the town center."

Michelle handed the paper to the fourth person. From across the room, Natalie stood. "I have a question for the chair. Are there any town bylaws that regulate the type of work that can be performed inside a building, as long as it's legal work permitted by the state?"

The chair said, "I am aware of no such bylaw."

The sculptor stood. This had become a relay race. "I have a question for the entire committee. Is the sale of the old church building in any way under the authority of the Economic Development Board, or would lecturing the board about this matter constitute harassment?"

The chair was smirking. "I've already stated that the board has no say in the matter."

Brooke and Natalie were staring daggers at Emerson, but he didn't stand to say anything.

Michelle folded her arms. For goodness sakes, she might as well have stamped her foot. "The Historical Society has a legitimate question! We want answers about how the Economic Development Board can stand for this behavior by one of their own members."

"I stated before you began that this is not an Economic Development Board matter, and we do not police the private lives of our members." The chair gave a cold smile. "Moreover, since the Historical Society has already introduced litigation over the matter, we are unable to comment. You might as well have read your speech at the Coffee Palace drive-through, which—" and now the chair spoke louder because Michelle tried to interrupt, "—was exactly what we said at the start. If there are no other questions, we'll conclude our meeting."

Michelle said, "You're the Economic Development Board. We want an answer about how the destruction of a beloved part of Brighthead's history is of economic benefit of the town."

The chair replied, "Thank you for attending, and this meeting is adjourned."

The chair signaled the high schooler working the camera for volunteer hours, then signaled to Fred, the lone security guard, a skinny guy in his late sixties who'd be more likely to talk your ear off than shoot you.

Natalie and Brooke were facing down Emerson, but Lilah stayed seated. The chair said, "We'll walk you to your car to be sure you're safe."

Lilah huffed. "If they want to get me, they know where I live."

Everything felt so vulnerable all at once. Her barn. Her yarn shop. Her dyeing business. Her guild. There had been venom in Michelle's eyes and hurt in her cohorts' tones. Lilah needing an escort was madness.

Fred herded out the Historical Society members, who left without a fuss. They might hate art and might be rooted in the past, but they weren't likely to start a riot in a town hall meeting room.

Brooke stalked up to the table, and she leaned toward Lilah. "If Emerson hadn't already broken up with me, I'd have done it after tonight."

Lilah frowned. "He showed up for support."

"And he dropped the ball. We assigned him a question, too."

Lilah said, "Not a big deal that he froze. It worked."

"Yeah, and it would have worked better with him doing his part." Brooke glared across the room to where Natalie was talking to him. Natalie didn't look outraged, at least, and Emerson seemed uncomfortable. Again. The same way he'd looked when they'd taken him to task about giving up his exhibit.

Brooke said, "Natalie confronted him so I didn't have to."

Lilah shivered. With both of them here, Emerson wasn't going to do anything to her, that was for certain.

The chair approached, along with Fred. "Come on. We'll walk you outside."

Brooke called, "Nat!"

Somehow they ended up together in the hallway. Brooke pulled Lilah's trick from the camping trip, making sure she was on the opposite side of their party from Emerson.

Emerson said, "Do you think they're going to vandalize your car?"

The chair said, "I have no idea what to think. They're not idiots, but they're also not exactly rational."

Fred said, "They mean well. We'll just put Lilah in her car, and she'll be fine."

As predicted, the parking lot was empty. Lilah said, "So long as they didn't wire a car bomb."

Natalie shrugged. "Those are difficult to get right, so even if they did, it won't go off. You'll just carry it around until your next state inspection."

Brooke said, "As if. They all went home to sip fifty-year-old scotch while daydreaming about Manifest Destiny."

Lilah breathed into her cupped hands.

Emerson said, "You shouldn't be by yourself tonight."

The hair stood up on Lilah's neck. No. He was not suggesting—

Natalie said, "You're right. Emerson, were you able to grab dinner on the way out here?"

Lilah found her voice. "Guys..."

"The man needs to eat. And I need to know more about Adrian's sculpture that he sent a picture of to the group."

Brooke said, "Surely not Fruits de Mer. They're going to be booked solid."

"I'm thinking we grab a table at Sparrows." Natalie rested a hand on Lilah's arm, and Lilah tried not to flinch. "You did fine tonight, and they did nothing but put on a show."

Lilah glanced at Emerson and hoped he wouldn't also put on a show.

CHAPTER TWENTY-TWO

Lilah had been brilliant tonight. She'd held herself together, head high, while the Historical Society took a hammer to her dreams. Only her friends had been able to see how much it hurt her—and, even then, only afterward.

Emerson followed Lilah's car to Sparrows, a restaurant on Main Street with mid-priced diner-style food and a relaxed atmosphere. "At least it's not a Tuesday," Natalie said while the server passed out the menus. "Tuesdays, a running club meets here, and they get a little loud."

The server said, "I've heard everything about sneakers and hydration strategies, but they tip well."

Brooke hadn't come to the restaurant. "No offense," she'd said to Emerson. "It's not you I'm avoiding. After that meeting, I'm done dealing with people."

That opened things right up, then. No chance of hurting Brooke's feelings if Brooke wasn't even here. Natalie had even reassured Emerson over text to make sure he'd show up tonight. "Don't worry about Brooke. She can deal with you, and Lilah needs your support."

Lilah, needing his support. It felt right. It felt good, to make her feel stronger and safer just by being in the same building.

That left four of them at Sparrows: Natalie and Lilah, Emerson, and Adrian, a sculptor from Singapore. Natalie said to Adrian, "You have to show them your work in progress. It's amazing."

Adrian demurred, but when Natalie got out her phone to show them the photo he'd sent, Adrian backed down and passed around his own pictures. "It's very much a work in progress," he said when Lilah gasped.

Emerson's throat tightened as Lilah said, "Oh, but I can see the potential! I love your work."

Did she say that to everyone?

Adrian said, "You're too kind. Unfortunately for me, no one purchases potential, so I'll have to finish the piece."

Emerson said, "Is that why you let me store all those blank canvases in your barn? Because they're pure potential?"

Natalie said, "If you want pure potential, take a look at where she works. The potentiality in a yarn shop is endless, and if she requires even more potential, she can go home and create the colors she needs."

Lilah said, "All I need is a spinning wheel, and then I can make yarn."

Natalie added, "Because you require another hobby?"

"Clearly I ought to start dyeing fiber." Lilah leaned across the table to look again at Adrian's sculpture. "Where'd you get the idea?"

"The wind." Adrian grinned. "I wanted to sculpt the wind, and this is where I am."

The server returned to take their orders, and before they could turn the conversation back to Adrian, Emerson said, "What are the plans for the first night of exhibits at Fruits de Mer?"

Since that was necessarily limited to visual arts, Adrian would have nothing to say about that. Natalie, on the contrary, did have plenty to say about it, and she went over Colin's plans with great enthusiasm.

What was going on with Lilah? When she'd looked at his

paintings and identified the feelings, the themes, the tone —he'd thought she did that because she liked his work. For a minute, she'd seen *him*, and that was delicious and terrifying all at the same time. Emerson had rendered his feelings in visual cypher, and for years, no one had even recognized there was a code, let alone tried to decode it. Like Brooke, they'd said, "Oh, pretty," and moved along.

Lilah had looked at it and said, "You're touching on the loneliness of being misunderstood." Or she'd said, "There's a muted sadness in your painting that finds even the hint of new life to be a moment of mourning for the one that's passed."

He'd dared to think her soul was connecting with his— and Lilah was all soul. All thrill and vision and commitment.

Ever since kissing her in the barn, he'd hoped maybe after seeing his soul, she'd actually love him. Not immediately—not with Brooke's pain fresh in her mind. Now, though, with Brooke distant and the future before them both, all impediments aside—now, why was she turning that X-ray vision on someone else?

Lilah said, "I'm hoping we get a big turnout for the opening."

Natalie said, "Austin's sent press releases to every newspaper and newsletter he can find, trust me. We may be able to get the place packed for the first exhibit." She turned to Emerson and raised her eyebrows. "The pressure's off you, at least. You're batting second."

Lilah said, "We'll do the publicity routine for Emerson, too."

Natalie nodded. "But Emerson was worried it was all depending on him, and it's doesn't have to."

Lilah sighed. "No. It's all depending on me."

Adrian shook his head. "You hold yourself responsible for too many things. What has mattered all along is that you've provided the vision. It's not then on you to also make others carry out your vision."

Lilah looked up, eyes heavy with grief. "Everything I've

envisioned feels like it's going down the drain."

Emerson said, "That's not true."

Lilah met his eyes, and he could feel it again: her guilt that he'd fallen in love with her rather than Brooke.

He added, "None of what's happened is your fault."

"How can you say that?"

Natalie jumped in before Emerson could speak. "He can say that because it's true. It's not your fault the Historical Society decided to pitch a tantrum. It's not your fault if anyone's artwork isn't well-received or if two of the group members get into a fight."

Lilah snuck a look at Emerson. "What if it was my fault?"

"People are adults," said Adrian. "Adults don't make war on one another because a third party got in between. Even if you deliberately set out to pitch two members against one another, if they do, it's their responsibility and not yours."

Why did Adrian have to sound so level-headed and correct? Emerson said, "Those of us who are paying attention can see you've done everything right. That's why you're important to us."

She met his eyes.

Emerson said, "We see you. We see the value in what you're doing. And I'm a visual artist, so I need you to trust me in this."

Lilah's voice dropped to nearly a whisper. "I feel like you should hate me."

Emerson said, "Quite the opposite."

Adrian said, "We all admire you for everything you've done."

Natalie said, "Plus, you're a good person, even if the *Hysterical* Society can't see that."

Lilah gave a painful laugh. "Hysterical?"

"If they're running in circles screaming that we're going to profane a church that's got a congregation of mice and termites, that sounds like hysteria. They're not worried about moths, but artists?" Natalie shuddered. "Heavens to Betsy, have my lady's maid fetch my smelling salts!"

When Lilah managed to laugh, Emerson's heart lightened.

Adrian said, "They're worried about disrespect, but so far, they've behaved more disrespectfully than we have."

Natalie said, "Which I think we highlighted well at the meeting." She focused on Emerson, and he averted his eyes. "I wish you'd spoken up, though."

Emerson said, "I didn't need to. You made your point."

"It would have been better made if you'd finished out the tetraology of questions."

Lilah said, "It's okay. They wanted to rattle us, and they succeeded. I want to forget about it until the next time we have to deal with them."

The waitress returned with their drinks, so Emerson tried not to notice that Lilah had diverted Natalie from getting angry at him again. It was late, and they were all under strain right now.

Even so, Lilah was beautiful. She didn't realize how much power she gave off simply being there, being strong, looking her accusers dead in the eye. Lilah was amazing in ways Emerson was only just beginning to understand—and with Brooke not here, he could approach her. Maybe talk one-on-one with her. Maybe kiss her again.

Maybe kiss her lots of agains.

Trying to keep the nerves from his voice, Emerson said, "I'll make sure you don't deal with them tonight. I'll follow you home in my car, and then I can go into the barn first, like the Secret Service, to make sure it's safe."

Lilah half-rolled her eyes. "They're not going to follow me to my house."

Emerson forced a laugh. "I wanted to take the town green canvas home to work on. But if it makes you feel presidential to have a bodyguard, then I'm all for it."

Adrian laughed. "You're the guild president. That means Emerson can be the guild secret service."

Natalie shook her head. "Positions we never thought we'd need when we first started this thing."

Lilah met Emerson's eyes, and he rested a hand on his

heart. "At your service, my lady."

Her faint smile warmed him up. Maybe she was looking forward to a stolen kiss as well. "Thank you, officer."

Adrian swirled the ice in his glass. "You'll see. The Historical Society will back down because they have no real case against us, only ghosts and shadows. Then they'll get to know you, and they'll see you value many of the same things they do."

Emerson cut in, "And the way you work hard for the things and the people you believe in."

Lilah sighed. "I'm sorry, guys. You're fighting to make me feel better, but everything I look at, I see defeat."

It was so hard not to reach across the table for her, to take her hand and try to give her his strength the way she'd given him confidence so many times. "Everything that's happened, it's not defeat. It's just a detour that's making a better path for victory."

CHAPTER TWENTY-THREE

Lilah turned onto her driveway, and Emerson pulled up alongside her car when she parked.

Her legs were numb. She couldn't get out. Shouldn't.

Emerson approached her window. "I'll go in first and grab the canvas." Mouth dry, Lilah only nodded. Emerson added, "I'll check to make sure it's safe, but I don't expect it's not."

She handed him her keys.

No one would be waiting. All the lights were off. Other than the frogs and the crickets, everything was silent. When Lilah concentrated, she could hear bats. Above their darting forms were the stars, and she couldn't hear those. She got out of the car.

Emerson emerged from the elongated rectangle of light spilling from the barn door. "All clear." Holding his painting, he approached their cars. "I'm sorry everything's such a mess now."

Everything. Lilah said, "Thank you for driving here tonight."

Emerson gave an awkward smile. "Well, I needed my painting." That was a reasonable cover story, and Lilah didn't challenge it. "I'll text you tomorrow. We need to work out how we're going to do this."

Lilah said, "Do what?"

He put the canvas in the back seat of his car. "Me dealing with Brooke. Painting in your barn. The BCG."

He stepped forward so he could shut the door, and he was close enough that Lilah's skin tingled. "So, we negotiate?"

Emerson faced her, and Lilah flushed. He said, "Brooke's still irritated with me, but she says she isn't."

"Brooke's like that. She's calming down." Lilah's voice faltered. "She says that it was better it happened sooner than later. Of course, she also threatened to volunteer you to edit the BCG newsletter."

Emerson slapped a hand over his heart. "The cruelty!"

"She wants you attending every BCG meeting out of fear that we'll nominate you for something else." The light caught Emerson's eyes, and Lilah smiled. Even after all tonight's stress, he was relaxed. "You know she's a good person. If you didn't think that, you'd have waited until after the exhibit to break up with her."

Emerson stiffened. "Wait, did she try to get Fruits de Mer to pull the offer?"

"Of course not! That was my point." Lilah put a hand on his arm. "Calm down. She didn't threaten your profession. She said it would have been worse if you had waited."

Emerson's eyes were wide. "Is this going to cause a problem between her and Natalie?"

"As if. It's not even causing a problem between—"

Emerson froze, and Lilah couldn't hold back any longer. She stepped into his arms.

He wrapped around her without hesitation, crushing her against his chest and kissing her until it felt like her soul would float right out of her body to merge with his.

"I was so worried for you," Emerson murmured. He kissed her ear and then worked his way down her neck. Heat swirled through her. "Facing those people. You did so well, and they were so angry. I didn't know what to do."

Lilah ran her fingers into his locs, pulling his face closer to her mouth again so she could keep kissing him. "No enemies," she urged between kisses. "No fighting. Just you."

He pressed her back against her car, and she closed her eyes. The night air. The safety of being home. The man all around her.

The guilt inside.

The impossibility of resisting, and then the impossibility of continuing. Because here he was, the entire amazing person of Emerson, willing to stand in her world and become it, and Lilah wanted nothing more—but this wasn't right. It wasn't what it should have been. Wasn't fair to Brooke.

Wasn't meant to be.

He kissed her cheeks and tasted her tears, and he breathed, "Oh, sweetheart."

Lilah held him tighter because he was about to slip away. She shuddered back a sob, and he nuzzled her cheek.

How long was a respectable time to wait to date her best friend's boyfriend? The boyfriend she'd stolen? Could Lilah ever be comfortable with a stolen boyfriend? What if Brooke couldn't forgive her? What if Lilah couldn't forgive herself?

What if the taint of the beginning poisoned the rest of the relationship? Love could turn into resentment. Infatuation could turn into shame.

She relished Emerson's scent, warm and musky, comforting. His breath thrummed beneath her ear, and, still fainter, his heartbeat. This was both where she had always belonged and where she could never be.

It was time to tell him no. This could never happen. They couldn't be together because it wasn't right, not after their history. She looked up to speak, and then his mouth was once again on hers, and she was lost in his embrace.

"I'll protect you," he whispered.

When she recoiled, he let her go. Shaking her head, Lilah

flinched at her tears broke loose. "You don't understand."

He stepped toward her again, and Lilah didn't resist. "Help me understand."

She wanted him in her barn, cuddled on the couch beneath the fuzzy throw blanket, her head to his chest, all of him filling her senses. Needing to send him away but wanting him not to leave, she had nothing. No energy, no resolve, no perspective. Would it be so bad? He hadn't even kissed Brooke, and here he was, unable to stop kissing her.

Swallowing hard, she stepped back again, then one step further. "We can't do this."

Breathing hard, he said, "Why?"

"Because of Brooke. Because I ruined everything, and it's not fixable, and—"

"Of course it's fixable."

"I did it all wrong!" Her voice rose. "I told you. I will never let anyone hurt Brooke, and I can't hurt her myself."

Emerson said, "Never? Because I dated her first?"

"You and she were supposed to be together, and now you're here. How is that fair to her?" Lilah shook her head hoping he couldn't see her tears in the darkness. Even now, she still wanted to step forward again into his arms. Only then they'd kiss again, and the guilt, and the shame, and the rejection, followed by needing more comfort. Over and over—and it needed to stop. "We can't do this. I'm not for you."

Emerson's voice sharpened. "You seem like you're for me."

If only. If only. If only.

Emerson edged toward her, and Lilah's skin tingled. She could bolt like a startled rabbit. She could stay and let it happen again.

Emerson said, "I'm trying to look out for you. You stepped into the line of fire for me. You've been trying to do right by me from the start. You're generous and sweet and thoughtful—so don't be like this. Brooke will understand. You said yourself she's practically over it."

Lilah closed her eyes. *If only.* He was close enough again to touch her.

Emerson said, "Let me do for you what you did for me. Let me take the heat. Let me make things smooth for you. I'd never hurt Brooke, and I'll never hurt you, either. We don't have to tell her."

Clenching her hands, Lilah glared at him. "I'm not going to lie to her!"

"I didn't say we lie to her. We just don't tell her."

"I'm not twelve years old." Lilah glared into his face. They were inches apart. "I may not be a moral theologian, but I know it's not legitimate to say, 'I knew you'd have said no if I asked.'"

"You're not twelve, but Brooke also isn't your mother. We don't need her permission."

Lilah said, "I'm not asking her permission. I'm trying to be a good friend because I care about her, which apparently you never did."

Emerson's eyes flared. "I did date her for a month."

Lilah said, "Then you should care how she feels. Or is that why you broke up?"

Emerson recoiled. "You know why I broke up with her."

"That makes it worse!" Lilah exclaimed. "You're a smart guy! How are you not seeing this at all?"

Because he was selfish? Was he so self-absorbed that he could just discard Brooke for Lilah because he thought she was willing? If he could do that to Brooke, how long would it take for him to get bored of Lilah?

Except that wasn't him. Lilah would have staked everything on that. If she'd thought he was like that, she wouldn't have paired him with Brooke in the first place.

She folded her arms and leaned back on one leg, trying to get more space between them. His gravitational pull kept tugging her toward him, but she had to keep clear—had to keep her mind clear, her body clear—had to not end up once more in his arms because if that happened, she wasn't going to win free again.

"Didn't you just say she didn't want me wasting her

time?" Emerson's voice sharpened. "I was looking out for her best interests. I want to look out for yours, too. Let me protect you."

Then his hands were on her arms, and Lilah's skin was covered in goosebumps, and he was about to kiss her... and she couldn't go through with it.

"You're not going to protect me." Tears overspilled her eyes. "At the meeting, you couldn't even speak up for me."

She closed her eyes so she wouldn't see his face, wouldn't see how she'd hurt him. But she felt when he let go of her arms. She felt the chill around her as he stepped away, and she heard the ever-lengthening silence between them.

Her lips still tingled from his kisses, but she had to drive him away. None of this was fair. After this battle, everyone would walk away hurt.

Lilah's voice ticked up. "When you get vulnerable, you run. You ran from Brooke, and now you're trying to get me to hide you, too."

Emerson gestured toward the barn. "Yeah, you were hiding me by inviting me into your home, driving me around town, and going on vacation with me and my sister. Are all your plans that well-thought-out? The way it never occurred to you that Brooke and I had exactly nothing in common? Or the way it never occurred to you that some people might object to their historic church turning into an art studio?"

"You're a coward." Lilah clenched her fists to stop her hands from shaking. "You wanted to back out of the art show because you didn't want anyone to see who you really are. They're going to do the same thing I did and look at your paintings, and they're going to see exactly who you are—and you can't deal with that."

Heart pounding, she glared at him. "You know why I'm not going to get into a relationship I have to hide? Because I don't do things I'm ashamed of. If people look at me, I want them to see me. All of me. How are you going to protect me, or even stand at my side, if you don't want to be seen?"

She felt the moment his heart broke, the moment her rage crackled against his shock and shattered him. Either he was going to argue with her or he was going to leave, but really, she just wanted him to leave. Leave before she pulled the next truth out of his heart and held it up before him like a prize fish reeled out of a lake.

He shouldn't have followed her home tonight. He shouldn't have been here at all, considering that he couldn't speak up for her at the meeting.

Even the crickets seemed to have silenced, and nothing was moving. No cars on the main road. No sounds from the landlord's house. Not even a clink from Lilah's wind chimes. Just the trapezoid of light splashed across the gravel driveway, the hanging lights twinkling in the barn, and her and Emerson standing face to face, heart to heart.

When it emerged, Emerson's voice was thin. "You win." Gravel crunched as he walked around the car. "Should I get the rest of my paintings from your barn, then?"

"You can leave them until the exhibit." Lilah's voice was no steadier than her hands or her vision. "I'm not going to damage them."

"No, you'd never damage *artwork*." Emerson snorted. "It wouldn't be in the spirit of the guild."

Lilah's chest tightened. "I'm sorry."

"You're not sorry." Emerson opened his door. "Not in any way that's meaningful."

He slammed the door and started the engine, and then he was backing out of her driveway.

It was better this way. Lilah knew it, and still it hurt.

CHAPTER TWENTY-FOUR

So he was a coward, was he?

Emerson drove home with a half-completed painting and only half a heart, and more than his fair share of confusion.

A coward? Why? Because he was looking out for Brooke's best interests? Because he didn't speak up at a meeting when everyone else had it well in hand? He'd shown up to give Lilah support, and he'd done just fine at it until the minute she decided to punish him for—for what? For letting her kiss him when she'd thrown herself at him? Or was she punishing him because she was attracted to him?

The next morning, he drove to work with all the confusion but also some of the anger, and then he had to deal with his irritating boss as well. He was still getting down his second coffee when she dropped a file on his desk. "Behold, I have a gift for you."

Emerson fought irritation and nausea. "Of course you do."

Ellen said, "As long as we're both getting paychecks, we're both getting gifts from the director on a regular basis. Funny how that works."

Only then she didn't leave. Emerson wondered how to figure out what she wanted next, when she said, "I heard a rumor, backed up by the local newspaper and, as it turns out, your own website. You're a painter?"

Emerson's skin crawled. Ellen was looking right at him. The receptionist was paying attention, too, although she made it appear as if she were entranced by whatever was on her screen. Probably that aforementioned website.

Emerson forced a smile. "Who would make up a rumor like that?"

"Seems like you made up the rumor yourself. Surely there aren't two Emerson Charleses working in Acadia." She raised her eyebrows. "I wish you'd told me. I'd have arranged an outreach program for local artists to come paint in the woods."

Emerson would rather arrange having his appendix removed with a hedge trimmer. "I can't do that."

"I don't see why not." Ellen looked bright-eyed and excited for the first time since he'd arrived. "You've seen how many artists come here with backpack easels and canvases. You'd be uniquely skilled to talk to them about the logistics of landscape painting in real life."

Emerson shook his head. "It's really not like that."

"Then what is it like? Haven't you gone out there with a paintbrush to work your magic? At the very least, a camera?" She raised her eyebrows. "I saw a few familiar locations on your website. This is an opportunity for all of us: for visiting painters, for the park, and for you."

Emerson recoiled. "How for me?"

"Let's get your work out there. You don't need to have exhibits in *Brighthead*." She shrugged. "The park can't officially promote your work, but we can feature you as an artist who gives tours."

"This isn't a discussion," Emerson snapped. "Unless this is an order that came down from the director—and I can't see that it's any of the director's business—then it's not up for discussion."

Ellen looked hurt. "Think of the other artists you could help."

Why did it always come down to that? Helping other artists should be a pleasure, not a club to beat everyone into submission. "I can't see that I owe it to anyone to show them how to climb a mountain and figure out what to paint."

She said, "But you're part of a crafters guild."

Ellen must have spent her entire night stalking him online. "That's how I help other artists. Not by leading a hiking tour into the woods."

She fell silent.

He said, "Is there anything else I need to get done today?"

She said, "No, but I would like to see your paintings. And I was going to ask for a quote so I could send a press release about an Acadia employee having an art exhibit."

"No, thank you." He gestured to the folder she'd dropped on his desk. "If there's nothing else, I'll get to work on this gift you left me."

Ellen raised her eyebrows, more startled than irritated. "Enjoy. I have a meeting with the budget department."

The receptionist still hadn't resumed typing, and Emerson didn't miss the way she watched Ellen return to her office.

His paintings had nothing to do with his job. He'd kept a fence between the two. Blast Lilah for insisting he take the exhibit. Blast the restaurant for sending out press releases. Blast it all. He could have backed out.

He still could. Lilah said he was a coward, so, fine. Maybe he should own the cowardice and hide everything after all. The restaurant would be okay with their generic wall-hangings for the two weeks his stuff should have been on display. That's what would have been up there anyhow if Lilah had stayed in her lane and spent her days dyeing yarn and working at Bright Stitches.

He'd call Austin during lunch. (Austin would be thrilled to get a phone call during their busy time—really, Emerson ought to call sooner.) But he didn't have time to call now, and certainly not with the receptionist listening.

Instead, Emerson looked through the folder his boss had dropped on his desk. It was a proposal for an educational program to head into the Maine schools next autumn, along with pamphlets from similar programs so he could get a sense of how other organizations handled it.

See, this was what he should be doing. Introducing school children to the concept of the National Parks Service, and making sure everyone knew Acadia was important for more reasons than bringing tourism dollars to the state of Maine. The public needed to learn about conservation. They needed to learn about wildlife. They didn't need to learn about canvases and paints and different types of brushes.

This was worthy work. Painting was a hobby. It wasn't life. Life was the stuff you did to make your hobbies possible.

He texted Sonia. "I'm going to back out of the restaurant exhibit."

She texted back, "If you do that, I'm going to kill you. And then I'll take all your paintings and put them on display anyhow."

He huffed.

She texted, "Are you having imposter syndrome, or what?"

He replied, "I'm not going to show off. I don't need the attention, and it's just making trouble."

Only awful things happened when you drew attention to yourself. You got followed in stores by security. You got people calling the cops because a Black man was walking through the neighborhood after dark. You got random folks watching you when you laughed louder than they did because you were starting trouble.

And yes, he'd been a good park ranger because when you did that job, you were supposed to draw attention. "Attention, visitors!" you'd call, and they'd snap to look at you because it wasn't Emerson getting their attention—it was the role getting the attention. It was the uniform they were noticing. It was the scripted explanations.

Painting led to the wrong kind of attention. It led to people thinking he'd yank out his soul and hang it on the wall of a restaurant for diners to criticize. Or his boss to analyze in her office. Or local amateur painters to come to the park to listen to another amateur painter talk about how to carry an easel up the side of a mountain and use acrylics because they dried faster.

As for deliberately bringing his paintings somewhere and hanging them up—he'd burn them first.

Sitting at his desk, his chest tightened, and he closed his eyes.

He couldn't imagine life without painting. He loved those paintings. He spent hours on each of those paintings —dozens of hours, maybe hundreds on some. It wasn't fair. He only wanted to create them. Keep them. Save them. Why had he let Lilah talk him into showing them off?

Sonia texted, "You're making a mistake."

Sonia knew nothing about his mistakes. Nothing at all.

She added, "This is about Lilah and Brooke, isn't it."

He replied, "Brooke is doing fine. I saw her last night at a meeting, and she had nothing bad to say."

"So it's Lilah?" Sonia texted.

Lilah, desperate and warm in his arms, and then angry as she glared into his face, saying everything she knew would hurt the worst. And she knew it would hurt because she knew him. She'd paid attention all the times he hadn't been aware she was doing so. She'd been in love with him for a while, and she'd taken aim and fired with the strength of all that information she'd gathered. She knew his soul.

No one else should see that. The minute those paintings went up, it was indecent exposure of the worst kind, so much worse than being naked. Naked, they only saw your skin.

Sonia added, "What happened with her?"

Emerson replied, "Nothing's going to happen with her."

Sonia texted, "But something did."

He didn't answer. He was supposed to have a hard line between his work life and his personal life, and instead he was texting his sister about painting and Lilah while he was on the clock.

The nature programs for the schools were a great idea. They could bring kids into the park, and they could send rangers into the schools. One of the suggested programs would allow their wildlife rehab people to bring animals so the kids could see the effect humans had on the environment, and also see the ways humans could help the environment when it needed a little nudge in the right direction.

That was what mattered. Not painting the fragile intersection between humanity and nature.

It was time to pull out of the restaurant exhibit. He'd call Austin at lunch.

Natalie's text to Emerson was just, "No."

He drummed his fingers on the table. She couldn't just say no. He was the one who had his paintings. They couldn't hold the show without him.

She went on: "You don't understand how much Colin and Austin have already put into this. Not to mention what the entire BCG has put into this. We've sent press releases. They have people scheduled to show up."

He replied to her, "Reschedule someone else. Tell everyone I dropped dead. For that matter, if I did drop dead, the BCG and the restaurant wouldn't be ruined."

"It's way too late to pull out just because you're getting cold feet."

He texted back, "I got cold feet six weeks ago. Lilah and Brooke should have listened."

He should be eating lunch, but he hadn't touched it. The call to Austin had gone quickly and simply. Emerson had put his baked potato in the office microwave and waited for the fallout.

Before that potato was up to room temperature, Austin had unleashed Hurricane Natalie, and that left Emerson staring at his loaded baked potato without the slightest interest in a second forkful.

Natalie texted, "That would have been the time to hold your ground if you didn't want to do it. Since you caved, you're committed."

She wasn't exactly calling him a coward. That was Lilah's gig.

Natalie continued, "You don't have to show up. Those paintings do need to be there."

Emerson snorted, and he texted back, "You're saying I'm not important."

"You're the one saying you're not important. I'm the one saying everyone spent time and money on the assumption that you were a man of your word."

Had Lilah given her lessons at hitting below the belt? How did Colin deal with her? Although based on something Brooke had said, in the beginning, Natalie had taken him out at the knees, too. Apparently with good cause.

Natalie sent, "We can hold the show with the six paintings already in Lilah's barn."

He said, "So I should drive there tonight and pick up my paintings."

She sent, "You should take a seat and tell me why you want to pull out. We'll figure out a workaround."

"I don't want a workaround."

Natalie didn't reply, leaving him with his baked potato.

Ellen entered the break room. "Smells good. I should start doing that." She shook her head. "I apologize for upsetting you, but I'm still not sure what I did wrong."

He tried not to sound bitter. "Forget it. Just treat me the way you always do, as Emerson the not-painter."

"It seems like such an amazing skill. I can't even draw a stick figure." She put her container into the microwave, probably leftovers. Emerson didn't ask. "All these images came out of your head and hands. I've always admired the artists who climb a mountain with a sketch pad and a charcoal pencil. Six hours later, they climb back down again with the landscape made permanent. It's magic."

Emerson mixed up the inside of the potato with his fork. "A magician never reveals his secrets."

"I wish you would. Taking an art class is on my bucket list." Ellen shrugged. "It's your choice, but I do wish you'd change your mind."

Natalie still hadn't replied to his final statement. Over at Bright Stitches, she would be ranting at Lilah that Emerson was an insufferable flake, and Lilah would be reiterating yesterday's verdict: he wasn't a flake so much as a coward.

Cowards don't stand their ground. She shouldn't have asked for what she didn't want.

Ellen retrieved her meal from the microwave, stirred it up, and stuck it back in for another thirty seconds. "Can you recommend any other guild artists who'd like to do this? You could lead the hike, but they give the talk." Her eyes narrowed as she stared off through the wall. "Come to think of it, maybe we could go the other way: we send someone to your guild to talk up Acadia. Things like natural crafting."

Emerson said, "I know at least ten artists who would kill for space in your gift shops."

Ellen laughed. "I know at least one park director who doesn't want to be involved in a homicide investigation!" The microwave beeped, and as her food came out, she said, "Would you mind if I join you? I've never gotten to know you. You're always a mystery, which is why I was curious when I saw your name in the events section."

When he shrugged, she sat across the table. "Your artwork aside, I was intrigued by the crafters guild. The restaurant is impressive. It looks like there's going to be an exhibit before yours, someone who does mosaics?" When

Emerson nodded, she said, "So it's all kinds of artists?"

"Anyone who considers themselves as doing crafts." He tilted his head. "The owner of that restaurant is also a member."

"They do call it culinary arts." Ellen raised her forkful of reheated something—it looked like chicken casserole. "Which, you'll notice, I wouldn't qualify for, either."

Emerson said, "You must do something."

"Watching TV and reading aren't hobbies that end up in museums. People's eyebrows don't go up when they hear you're an avid consumer of art, rather than a producer of art."

Emerson said, "So what hobbies do you have?"

She said, "I collect antiques."

"We have an antique restoration dude."

She laughed. "Yes, that would be artistic. I know what they're worth and buy them and then re-sell them. Oh, and antique books. I have several boxes of signed antique books."

Emerson said, "You also do hiking and camping."

She nodded. "It's not that I have no hobbies."

The phone buzzed, and Emerson looked down to see Natalie had texted. "You need to come to the premiere exhibit so you'll see it's not as harrowing as you're making it out to be."

Had she cogitated so long and only come up with that?

A second later, this appeared: "At the very least, you have to come to show your support."

If one man's presence was going to make or break the exhibit, then how well did they expect this to do in the first place?

Ellen was watching his face. "Someone made you angry?"

"I'm trying to get out of doing the exhibit." Emerson sighed. "Your reaction told me what I needed to know."

She frowned. "My reaction? Thinking you did great work?"

"I don't want the attention."

She ate slowly, eyes still narrowed. Then, "From a

program director's perspective? I think you have to."

He rolled his eyes.

"We're hosting that event for the Girl Scouts in two weeks. Imagine the havoc if the Girl Scouts called today and said all their presenters weren't going to come."

Emerson said, "That's different. Think about how many people are involved."

"It's a smaller scale. We have ten presenters on the schedule. We have Scouts looking forward to attending. We've made multiple phone calls and done a lot of behind-the-scenes work to make it happen. Scale down Acadia to the size of a restaurant, and that's one presenter but nearly the same amount of behind-the-scenes work. If our event were to get cancelled, think about how irritated you'd be. How empty."

Emerson turned aside.

"Remember the falconry exhibit? You were upset about that getting cancelled, and you'd only been with us a few weeks."

Emerson looked up at Ellen, puzzled. He'd tried not to seem upset. He'd listened and commiserated with the other staff, but he hadn't stormed about.

She'd been paying attention. Like Lilah: she'd seen the things he didn't want seen. He was the new man in the department and had tried not to draw attention, especially when it wasn't him who had been devalued. But that just went to show: Emerson took up more space than others. His ordinary actions got noticed as extraordinary.

Ellen said, "Now think about how angry we would have been if they hadn't pulled out due to a surgery. If they'd just changed their minds."

Emerson muttered, "I get it."

He dug back into his potato. He ought to get back to work. Get to the point where he could clock out and not have to talk to anyone.

"At any rate," he said, "the BCG's event liaison is trying to make me go to the premiere. To see it's not scary—as if I'm a nervous three-year-old."

The director nodded. "Go. Once someone else has led the way, even if it's not quite right, you'll have a better sense of what you need."

CHAPTER TWENTY-FIVE

The BCG members didn't throw Lilah out of Fruits de Mer, so she counted that as a win. Or at least, she counted that as no one having realized she was poison.

The first exhibit ("world premiere," as Austin wrote on all his press releases) featured Marjorie Tempest, who created mosaics out of "found objects" from the beach: sea shells, sand, stones, driftwood, and sea glass. From a marketing perspective, it was perfect for selling to tourists, and Lilah had reason to believe Marjorie cleaned up every tourist season: first cleaning up the beaches, and secondly cleaning up cash-wise.

Across the room, Emerson had shown, but he had the common sense to stay away from Lilah. Still, she kept an eye on him to make sure he wasn't getting too close. Instead, he and Adrian were talking to a Brighthead resident who worked in textile restoration—something Lilah wouldn't have considered an art form until the woman had joined their forum.

Lilah took time to peruse all the images, and they were wonderful. Lighthouses and rocky shores and a seagull standing on the sand. Such talent, and such marketing smarts.

Not all of the visitors were BCG members, and that was a relief. There were a couple of local reporters taking pictures, and quite a few tourists who'd shown up for a Thursday afternoon before their last day at their timeshares. Marjorie stepped into the spotlight, talking as though made for the attention.

How about that?, Lilah thought in Emerson's general direction. *Someone who isn't afraid we're going to notice her.*

That had been the theme all day. Lilah was wearing her brightest colors and had done her nails in an entire rainbow. If anyone wanted to be noticed, Lilah had transformed herself into a study of the same.

"I'm so honored to be taking a place in Brighthead's finest restaurant," Marjorie gushed during a brief speech, accompanied to perfection a few minutes later by Colin reading a speech where he said, "We're honored to be featuring one of Maine's finest artists."

Natalie stood tense at Lilah's side. "He was worried about the speech. I thought for a while he was going to have Austin put on a suit and pretend to be him."

Lilah choked on a laugh. "Is he ashamed to be here?"

Natalie said, "No, of course not!"

Motion caught Lilah's eye, and she realized Emerson was standing within earshot, and he was glaring at her.

Glaring, or, well, just staring.

Brooke came up to Emerson, holding a tiny plate with hors d'oeuvres. "Have you tried these? They remind me of the lunch we got at the Renaissance Faire."

He turned toward her, moderately confused, but he took a bite.

Lilah tried to rewind the conversation in her head. She'd asked if Austin was ashamed to be here—and the last thing she'd said to Emerson was that he was ashamed to have people see him.

Natalie went on, "Colin would rather be in the kitchen feeding everyone. Austin's the outgoing one. It's why they work so well together."

Austin swept up to them. "Are you bragging about me?" He put his arm around Natalie's shoulders. "Go right ahead. I can take it."

Natalie side-eyed him. "I was talking about your brother, the love of my life."

Austin rested a hand on his heart. "Alas, I cannot compete." Then, smiling, he turned to Lilah. "This has been an excellent turnout. The publicity machine worked well. Any developments with the church building?"

"More posturing and threats." She sighed. "We don't even get to court for another three weeks."

Emerson had called Lilah an idiot for not realizing people would get upset about repurposing an old church. Austin didn't say, "Well, naturally," but then again, he was the tactful twin.

"I invited the Historical Society tonight," Austin added, "so they could see you guys face-to-face. I figured once they're looking at the art, it will become obvious you're not iconoclasts. But I don't know if any of them came."

Natalie said, "I haven't seen their ringleader, but maybe she sent her minions."

Austin rubbed his chin. "I can take them. I'm Colin's minion."

Lilah said, "And I'm Natalie's minion. That has to be good for something."

Austin pointed at her and beamed. "Okay, so given that we have a quorum of minions, and I'm the charming twin...?" He turned. "Emerson! Get over here."

Talking with Brooke, Emerson seemed startled, and then his eyes narrowed when he saw Lilah alongside Austin.

By contrast, Brooke seemed relaxed in a way that unnerved Lilah. Normally Brooke would be uneasy in a crowd of this size, at least until she found her bearings.

But that was it, wasn't it? How had she found her bearings at the first two BCG meetings? By attaching to Emerson.

Lilah turned away, fighting tears. Everything had been a

misunderstanding. Brooke had anchored herself to Emerson not because she was attracted to him but because she always did that. In fifth grade, she'd anchored to Lilah and let Lilah lead the way socially. At the first BCG meeting, she'd latched onto Emerson because he was easy to talk to—and then she'd modeled her behavior on his. That mirroring was just what Brooke did. Only, Lilah hadn't bothered to look at it from Brooke's perspective. She'd looked at it from her own: she liked Emerson, and therefore Brooke must be behaving that way because she liked Emerson, too.

Natalie put a hand on Lilah's shoulder while Emerson and Brooke made their way over to them. "Brooke's okay. I have every reason to believe she's over him."

Lilah muttered, "Apparently there wasn't much to get over."

"Yeah, they never became more than friends, so it's best just to leave it at that."

When Emerson got close, Austin shook his hand. "Thanks for coming out here. I was hoping once you saw how well we treated our guest artist, you'd let us host you after all."

Emerson sighed. "I've been over this."

"With Natalie, but not with me." Austin raised his eyebrows. "Your exhibit is important to us, so how can we make it more comfortable for you?"

Lilah shifted a little further from Emerson, trying not to meet his eyes. He still felt like lightning to her—his presence, his voice, and even the way he carried himself. It was harder now that she knew how he felt to hold, to kiss. She shouldn't be in the same room.

Even so, she had to give credit to Austin: he'd slipped right into his managerial role, only instead of talking down an irate customer to keep him as a patron, he was de-escalating Emerson to keep him as an exhibitor.

Emerson folded his arms. "You aren't going to let this go, are you? It's not something you did wrong."

"Then what can we do right?" Austin gestured to the

walls. "I loved what I saw of your artwork, and I'd be honored to feature you. Natalie told me about some of your recent pieces, too, and everything I heard convinced me you'd be an excellent fit."

Emerson said, "I'm not at all convinced of that, and—"

Austin said, "But you have pictures of Brighthead Bay now, right? And the lighthouse? You've been working for weeks on these. It would be a shame not to show them off."

Emerson glanced away from Austin and ended up catching Lilah's eye. She tensed, and he looked away from her.

Brooke said, "I saw how hard you worked on those six. Even if you don't show the rest of them, I'm sure you could display those."

Austin nodded. "We'd be pleased with only the six. There's no requirement to fill every wall."

Emerson glared away.

Austin said, "Plus, we can make your opening less of a to-do than tonight. You won't have to make a speech."

Natalie snickered. "Marjorie wanted to make a speech, but I think that's because she usually sells these at town fairs, so she's comfortable with her sales pitch."

Brooke said, "I've seen her on the forums. She's very comfortable *talking.*" When Natalie chuckled, Brooke turned to Emerson. "That's fine for her, but you should do what's best for you."

Austin opened his hands. "Say the word, and we'll accommodate however you need because we want what's best for you, too."

This was the artistic equivalent of comping the meal and giving a ten percent off coupon.

When Emerson looked at Lilah, her mouth went dry. Anything she said was going to cement his refusal.

Brooke, on the other hand, said, "Don't you trust us? We all think you should do this, and all of us have done right by you so far."

Emerson's gaze trained on Lilah like a laser. Brooke

might have just shot down the entire effort with that one well-intentioned line.

Lilah hadn't done right by Emerson. Of everyone in the room, Lilah was the one who'd failed him the most.

Brooke put a hand on Emerson's arm. "How about me? Have I ever steered you wrong?"

Emerson turned to Brooke, and Lilah tensed, but Emerson only said, "Really?"

Brooke nodded. "Really. I want this for you."

He sighed. "Fine. But just the six paintings I made for here."

Brooke beamed, and Natalie pumped her fists. Austin shook Emerson's hand. "Thank you, man. It means a lot to us to have the honor of hosting your first exhibit."

Even after getting what he wanted, Austin was still closing the sale. Lilah should have half that kind of marketing expertise.

Natalie flagged over one of the servers. "To celebrate, you have to try one of these. Colin kept testing them out on me last week, and I think he nailed it."

Emerson took one. "Does Colin consider it selling out when he modifies the food to suit the clientele?"

Natalie laughed loud. "What?"

Emerson gestured at the tidbit. "Lilah and I had a discussion last week about tailoring one's work to the tastes of the audience. If someone does that, Lilah thinks they're hiding."

The hair stood on Lilah's neck. "That's not what I said. Of course a restaurant has to cater to the diners."

Emerson said, "And why would that be different than a painter changing his subject matter to cater to the viewers?"

Brooke drew closer. "I was there when we convinced you to paint new paintings. Lilah was in favor of it, not critical." She studied Emerson. "Lilah's the last person who would criticize you for changing your art."

He looked her dead in the eye, and Lilah stood taller because her only other option was cringing. She wasn't going to run. Not from him. "You're mischaracterizing the conversation. I dye different yarns when it's tourist season."

Natalie said, "She can barely keep the souvenir yarns on the hook, so yeah. You must have misheard her."

Emerson didn't remove his gaze from her. "I heard her loud and clear."

Natalie turned to Lilah. "What did you actually mean?"

Whatever that last hors d'oeuvre was, it had turned to an oil slick in Lilah's mouth. She'd said anything to Emerson—anything at all—trying to get him away from her. It wasn't fair to confront her like this, not when the whole point had been to keep Brooke from finding out. Hadn't he suggested keeping it a secret from Brooke? So why was he pushing her to divulge it right in front of Brooke?

Or had he not been trustworthy from the start? "I don't know." Lilah glanced away and back at the shell collages. "Apparently I don't know anything, anymore."

Barefoot, Lilah wandered the barn without looking at Emerson's paint area. She'd been half afraid he'd stop by to pick them up, in which case her plan had been to give Natalie the keys because of unavoidable BCG business that needed to be straightened out with Austin at the restaurant. Immediately. What business that was, Lilah still hadn't determined. She'd have come up with something, and it would have been unavoidable.

Here she was, instead: free, and shaken by how close he'd been, and how ready to reveal everything he'd been saying he wanted to hide.

A buzz from the phone. Brooke. "That was a lot less awkward than I was afraid it would be."

With Emerson's ire focused entirely on Lilah, there'd been none left for Brooke. Lilah replied, "I hoped he'd be okay."

"I wasn't even worried about him. I didn't know what I'd say when I saw him again, but it turns out, it was fine. We talked like nothing had happened, so I guess he was right. Nothing did happen."

Pragmatic and practical, Brooke was rolling with the punches a lot better than Lilah. "I'm sorry," she texted.

"There's nothing to be sorry about. You had a good idea, but it fizzled. It happens."

A minute later, Brooke texted again. "At least you got curly hair from the bargain. Also business ideas from Sonia."

Lilah replied, "The hair makes it not a total loss. I haven't done anything with Sonia's advice."

Brooke replied, "Well, get on it."

Lilah shot back, "Tonight?"

Brooke texted, "Tonight. I adjure you to have made your first million by morning."

Lilah replied, "Good night, Brooke."

Brooke returned a laughing emoji.

Lilah changed out of her nice clothes into comfortable shorts and a T-shirt. Sonia did have good advice, especially about turning customers into fans. There'd been so little time between Sonia leaving and Emerson breaking up with Brooke and then Emerson and Lilah... Well, Emerson and Lilah being together. And then being apart. There'd been the fight with the Historical Society and then the Economic Development Board meeting.

It's a job, Lilah could hear Sonia saying to her. *You've got to get up and do your job whether or not you feel like it.*

"Maybe that's true if you're making coq au vin," Lilah muttered to herself, glancing at her curly hair in the mirror. "Art is different."

Selling out. Hiding yourself. Catering your work to the customer's expectations.

It wasn't wrong. Emerson had the right to show some

paintings to only his family, the same way Lilah had the right to tell some secrets only to Brooke. From that perspective, maybe she could just get up and go do her job without feeling like it. It didn't take emotional effort to make "green."

She flipped on the work lights over the dyeing station, then turned on the electric burners. Well, then, what to do?

It didn't take emotional effort to make green, but it did take emotional effort to come up with combinations. Think about *Pride and Prejudice*. Right after Lizzie realizes she loves Darcy but will never have another chance with him, would Lizzie be able to pick up her embroidery and design a pillow?

No, not unless it was a very grey and blue pillow, like rainfall.

Although after that nasty woman came and scolded Lizzy for potentially being engaged to Darcy—those would be orange and yellow, like sparks.

Lilah stopped in front of her dyeing station, then glanced at her TV. She had at least fifteen minutes before that water boiled. And she had a *Pride and Prejudice* DVD.

Standing with the water boiling before her and the TV image frozen at her back, Lilah stood with a notepad in her hand, listing moments from the six-episode *Pride and Prejudice* miniseries—one from each episode—and the colors that went with them.

And then, she began.

She noted every step of her process, each test skein a snapshot of Lizzy and Darcy as they started apart, came together, came apart, and finally came back together again. She skipped from scene to scene, choosing colors and rendering emotions into visual form. "Tolerable, I Suppose," she named the first skein, and she divided it sharply between Darcy's black and steel and Lizzy's gold and cream. She popped that into the steamer and then began the next, calling it "Wickham" and hand-painting red all over it before layering more colors.

By the time those two skeins were set, Lilah had an

announcement ready to go on her website.

—

By subscription only!
Six Pride and Prejudice-*themed colorways,*
Every month, a new skein of Pride and Prejudice *yarn will arrive in your mailbox!*

—

She photographed a couple of teaser pictures, but she didn't set up the product page on her website.

This was scary. This was selling out. This was hiding herself, wasn't it? Instead of baring her soul the way she usually did in her work, she was ducking behind Jane Austen's soul for cover.

This was the same as the Brighthead colorways, though. She'd done it before.

Turn customers into fans, Sonia said. To become someone's fan, you needed to connect with that person. That meant showing herself to her customers.

Emerson was afraid to step out and show his soul. Lilah would have to do that. She could show her soul in how she connected with *Pride and Prejudice.* She could show her soul in the way she interpreted it and went vulnerable before the thing she loved. She could interact with the thing she loved. She could—

Well, she could just put herself out there the way she'd told Emerson to do, and if no one wanted to join her subscription service, well, that was what vulnerability was about. About putting yourself out there to be rejected.

Emerson didn't want to be rejected, so he never took chances. Lilah was going to step right out and do it.

But not now. Not right now.

CHAPTER TWENTY-SIX

Ellen stuck her head into Emerson's office with a smile. "How was the premiere?"

Emerson said, "I have photos."

"Exciting!" She took his camera and paged through. "Wait, these are shell mosaics?"

"And beach glass, and stones. Oh, and some driftwood, too."

"I want her contact information. Imagine if we could get her to do an Acadia series? Mosaics made with found objects at the park." Ellen handed back his phone. "Sorry, I can't turn off my program-director mind. I'm sure we could secure a grant for something along those lines."

Emerson said, "If the BCG takes off, they may be the ones paying you the grants."

"Or a local university. I've got connections." She opened her hands. "And? What have you decided?"

Emerson sighed. "I'm going to let them have the six paintings I made of Brighthead, the ones I designed specifically to go into the exhibit." He gave a half roll of his eyes when Ellen nodded excitedly. "Don't be like that. You're right about how much work went into everything.

They won't do a gala. I won't show up as the Guest of Honor. They'll hang my paintings on the wall, the ones most likely to sell, and that will be the end of it."

"So, nothing from your website? I'd like to see those in person."

Emerson scrolled back through his photos and opened the folder with the Brighthead paintings. "It's just the local landmarks. The bay, the lighthouse, the statue."

Ellen said, "Who's sitting on the rocks?"

Emerson fought the urge to snatch back his phone as she zoomed in on the pair of figures. She added, "I can almost hear what they're talking about."

Emerson muttered, "They're probably talking about what a jerk I am."

"That sounds exciting." She stepped into his office. "I'm learning a lot more about you than I figured you'd ever tell. Is one of them your sister who visited?"

Ellen knew just about nothing about him—only that she'd approved his vacation. "They're two members of the guild. The founder, and a woman who works at the yarn shop with her."

Ellen gave a sly smile. "And were you dating one of them?"

Emerson snatched back the phone, and Ellen said, "Really? You were?" And then, when he scowled, she said, "Were you dating both of them?"

"Not at the same time. Actually, not at all."

Ellen shut his office door and leaned against it. "Okay, back up. Which one did you date?"

"The woman who co-owns the yarn shop, the one with the long hair. The BCG founder set me up with her because they're best friends, and she thought we'd go well together." Ellen nodded, so Emerson said, "The thing is, we had no chemistry."

Ellen said, "You're saying the founder set you up with her best friend, but she should have set you up with herself."

"Now she's claiming 'girl code' means she can't date me

because it would hurt her best friend's feelings."

Ellen frowned. "Did you and the friend have a bad breakup?"

Emerson laughed. "She didn't even love me. There was nothing there. I'd take her places, or we'd go for walks, and it was okay. My sister said, 'Do you want to just be okay?'"

"Your sister has a point."

"Exactly! Whereas Lilah—she's the founder—she's funny and interesting and smart, and she's so alive. She lives in a barn full of string lights, and she dyes her own yarns as a business."

Ellen sat on the corner of the credenza. "Go on."

"She's amazing, and the thing is, she had feelings for me, too, but she never said a word because she would never cheat and would never want to betray her friend. When I broke up with Brooke, I figured, the field is wide-open. She and I could get together and nothing was stopping us—except for the 'girl code' thing."

Ellen sighed. "No wonder you wanted to back out of the show. So much drama."

Emerson shook his head. "That's not why I wanted to back out. I told you—I don't want the attention."

She waved a hand. "You're an artist. Of course you want the attention. You just don't want the wrath of a bitter ex and a reluctant girlfriend."

Emerson frowned. "None of that is right. Brook is five miles from bitter. Lilah isn't reluctant at all. She's actually enthusiastic when she lets her guard down." Emerson's cheeks warmed when he thought about how enthusiastic Lilah had been. "It's more like—"

Ellen sat on the corner of his desk. "More like what?"

He shook his head.

"You want to fade into the background. That's why you're in an office rather than climbing mountains. Yes, yes, I know, you like the stability of a well-paying job." She waved it off as though Sonia wouldn't have killed for exactly that. "But there's something that keeps you from taking the spotlight no matter how much you deserve it. You won't even take other painters on a hike to show them how to paint in a national park."

Emerson put his elbows on his desk and rubbed his temples.

Ellen said, "Let's revisit the enthusiastic founder with feelings for you. She sounds like a good and loyal person. She loves her friend. She seems to love you. She loves art. So what's stopping you?"

Emerson said, "She is."

"Then you need to get her out of her own way so she can see what she's missing. And for that," Ellen added with a wink, "you need to show up."

It wasn't about showing up. Emerson had been showing up all the time.

He'd shown up every day to his job, and his boss had never thawed to him because she'd never gotten to know him. Well, not until now.

He'd shown up at Lilah's barn to make paintings. He'd shown up to dates with Brooke and a vacation with his sister. He'd been showing up. What he didn't want to do was show off.

Keep your head down, and do good work. That had been advice from his grandmother and advice from his mother and advice from his father. Promise to do the work, and then do it. People will notice you that way, but otherwise? Letting them see you meant...

Well, what did it get Sonia? Sonia with her striking hair and her distinct clothing, her height and her volume—had getting noticed gotten her a job? Although she did say it got her good tips. Which was what he'd always been told: do your work well because people noticed that, and they appreciated it.

"That's the point," Emerson said over the song on the radio as he drove home. "Do your job and don't show off."

He passed an exit, then said, "Except you're supposed to get noticed for doing your good job."

Huh.

So...say that his job was painting. It wasn't, but say it was. Then all he had to do was pour images onto the canvas, and do it well. Notice should follow afterward. He kept saying he didn't want an exhibit because that was showing off—but what if the exhibit wasn't "showing off" as much as it was "hard work that got noticed." The reason he'd gotten the exhibit in the first place was that first Lilah and later Colin had noticed his hard work.

Emerson felt as if his soul were splayed out on those canvases, and to Lilah they certainly were. But would Ellen have noticed? Brooke never had. He'd taken art interpretation classes, and whenever they studied, he knew in some respect he was touching the soul of the painter in the way the painter revealed it through his or her choices. Why paint this and not that? Why emphasize this feature rather than that other? All the decisions led to a final outcome, and yes, the soul was revealed in the decision-making process...but most people weren't going to look that deeply.

Moreover, Emerson didn't need to be ashamed of who he was.

He was a park ranger and a painter and a failed boyfriend to Brooke. He was a would-be boyfriend to Lilah, and that was fine. Lilah wanted him, too, so now Emerson had to ask himself how far he wanted to go in pursuing her. How much he was willing to risk.

"Everything," he whispered in the car. "Everything."

If Lilah was worth everything, and Lilah thought his soul worth admiring, then that meant Emerson didn't have to hide it. Hiding it would only lose the things he wanted. So now, for this, he needed to bare everything. He needed to open wide and let the light flood in.

He pulled up in front of his apartment and didn't even leave the car. He hit the button on his phone, and when Austin took the call, Emerson said, "We need to talk again about the exhibit."

CHAPTER TWENTY-SEVEN

Emerson entered Bright Stitches while Brooke was checking out a customer. Although she looked up when the door jangled, she didn't seem startled. Instead she and the customer kept up their chat about patterns and needle sizes, and then Brooke handed over a receipt as well as an urgent imprecation that Brooke must—must—see the finished product.

"Of course you'll see it." The customer tucked her wallet back in her purse. "I'm planning to bring it here for the blocking class."

Brooke brightened. "That will be great! Give me two weeks' notice if you want me to preorder your pins and boards."

When the customer left, Brooke looked Emerson in the eyes—no anger, no confusion, no nothing. She really hadn't been into him, had she? "Did I forget you were coming? No one reminded me, but I don't think—"

He raised his hands. "I'm here on the spur-of-the-moment. I wanted to talk to you, but I thought it was better to do it in person than over the phone."

"This sounds serious." She glanced at the clock over her

shoulder. "Hang on." A minute later, she had the front door locked and the sign flipped to "closed" even though technically she had five minutes. "If you don't mind me cleaning up while you talk, what's going on? Is it about the exhibit?"

Emerson followed her to the register where she started straightening up. "Partly."

"Please don't pull out again." Brooke's brow furrowed. "I don't understand what's going on, but I promise you, it's going to be fine."

"I need to make sure it's going to be fine."

She walked three skeins of yarn to a cubby. The shop was neat, bright and clean-looking, and she went unerringly to the correct rainbow to stash these in their right place. "Do you want me to call Lilah and Natalie so we can brainstorm?"

"I'm brainstormed out at this point. I need to get myself together, and you're level-headed." Emerson braced himself. "Would you mind if I brought you out to dinner, one more time, as a friend? For planning purposes?"

Brooke turned to him, one skein still in her hand. "Sure, but the full brain trust includes Natalie and Lilah."

Emerson said, "For this, I only want your opinion."

Brooke said, "Give me time to shut down, and we can go to the burger place on Main Street."

He took her in his car, since she had ridden her bicycle to work. She seemed upbeat, although Emerson could hear the strain in her voice. "Have you heard from Sonia? I hope she's doing better with her job search than we are with the church on Main Street. It's not looking good, even without the court battle."

Emerson frowned. "How's that?"

"Because no one wants to irritate the Historical Society, and everyone feels free to irritate the Crafters Guild. I have no idea what's going to happen, but I figure however it goes, it ends with us in another building."

Emerson sighed as he pulled into a spot on Main. "I honestly don't understand people."

"If you tell people a church is just a pretty building, they'll scold you that no, a church is made of the people who come worship together. Then all of a sudden, when there's no people worshipping in the pretty building, suddenly a church is a building." She unbuckled. "I admit to wondering if you weren't pulling out of the expo because you didn't want to deal with them."

Emerson said, "I didn't want them to notice me, and that's why I need to talk to you."

They ordered at the counter and then took a number to a table to wait for their food. Brooke poked the number-holder. "I never trust this kind of setup. I think they're going to forget to bring my food, or that they won't find my number." She gestured to the establishment's twelve tables. "Not that this is a rational fear. I just feel like I should walk away from the counter with more than a paper number."

Emerson chuckled. "I promise, I won't let them forget you."

Brooke said, "Well, you paid for it. But seriously, what's so important that it not only involved me, but it also justified you paying for dinner?"

Emerson said, "You've got a good head on your shoulders, and I want your unvarnished opinion."

Brooke's brow furrowed again. That wasn't displeasure, he realized with a start. Her frowning meant she was thinking. In all this time, he hadn't decoded her facial expressions, whereas he could read Lilah's mind with a glance.

He said, "What do you think this art show is supposed to accomplish?"

Brooke leaned forward. "I strongly suspect that what this art show was supposed to accomplish, as far as Colin was concerned, was cementing himself in the mind of Natalie as a generous guy whom she would love to date."

Emerson laughed loudly, and Brooke grinned. Emerson said, "It did!"

"I blame Austin for that. Austin could sell sand in the

Sahara, and this has his fingerprints all over it." She arched her eyebrows. "From that perspective, rest assured, your sacrifice will have the salutary effect of buttressing the bond between Natalie and Colin."

Emerson mimed wiping sweat from his brow. "That's a lot of vocabulary for one sentence."

"As befits the context." She cocked her head. "Now, as far as the BCG is concerned, these shows are supposed to create name recognition in the community. We get our group name out there and at the same time benefit individual members, which over the long haul benefits every one of us because of the 'rising tide lifts all boats' phenomenon."

The server arrived with their tray, and Brooke brightened. "Thank you!" she said as their hamburgers and fries landed on the table, and then she passed back the wire stand with its paper number.

Emerson said, "Do you feel better now?"

"With the food in front of me? Yes, now I feel much more certain that they won't forget to deliver it." Her eyes sparkled, but she still hadn't let go of the conversation topic. "Okay, next we have Fruits de Mer's perspective, which is that hosting a local artist in their venue confirms their framing as a fine dining establishment that deserves to attract the very classiest of individuals and charge the very classiest of prices."

Emerson wrinkled his nose. "That, I can't get behind."

"While it's crass, food is only ten percent of what you're paying for at a high-end restaurant. Everything else is the service and the ambiance." She glanced around. "This place, the food is likely fifty percent of what we're paying. You're paying," she corrected, again smirking. "That covers three of the four participants, leaving us with you."

Emerson's eyes narrowed. "Therefore, let's talk about me. What is this art show supposed to accomplish for me?"

Brooke frowned again. "Shouldn't you know that already?"

Emerson sighed. "I'm second-guessing everything. My vision, my purpose, why I'm painting in the first place."

Brooke winked at him. "Well, in that case, why don't you eat your hamburger while I psychoanalyze you with all the talents I've honed over the course of three years running a yarn shop?"

"Sounds like you have a lot of talent."

"I'd better," she muttered. "I certainly haven't got any skill."

Emerson shook his head. "Brooke, Brooke, Brooke."

"You did me the favor of being honest, so to the best of my ability, I'll return the favor." She ate some of her hamburger, then looked him briefly in the eyes. "I think you do have a vision and a purpose, but they're highly private to you. Why you're painting in the first place—that's a different question, so you answer me. Why did you start?"

That was easy. "I took a required art class in high school, and I was good at it."

Brooke said, "Always a good reason to stick with something. Plus, I'm betting you saw the world differently from everyone else you knew, and you wanted to show that world to them."

Emerson drew up short. "Really?"

"Really. You were probably the kid everyone knew would win all the poster contests in grammar school. But when you're doing more than making designs for fire safety month, the messages are more hidden."

Emerson pointed at her with a French fry. "Exactly! And they become more personal than remembering to change the smoke detector batteries."

She said, "But you kept doing it for reasons other than you were good at it. Why?"

Emerson said, "You tell me."

Brooke frowned again, this time for almost a minute, and when she spoke, she didn't look up. "Taking a stab at it, I'm guessing you paint your heart out and have encoded messages in your art which are obvious to you and not to anyone else. Then, suddenly, you get an offer to have people look at your art for real. And that's terrifying."

Emerson sat back. "I wouldn't say terrifying."

She stared at her tray. "I would say it's terrifying. When I create a pattern, I have to put it out there—but now let me tell you a secret about pattern creation: most people aren't going to buy my patterns. Some people are going to look at the finished object and say, 'Who would knit that?' but even the people who like it, most aren't going to buy it. For every thousand people who look at my patterns, I figure two or three purchase, and the rest move on. Some will stick the pattern on a maybe-someday list, but even so." She shrugged. "That's a lot of rejection."

Emerson said, "Do you encode your soul in your patterns?"

Brooke sighed. "My soul is mathy and awkward. It doesn't fit right—don't object, you know it's true—whereas I try to make my patterns beautiful and well-fitting. In a way, my patterns are an attempt to make something that's not me. It's entirely different from what you're doing."

Emerson sat back. "And if your patterns are the opposite of you, when they get rejected, it must feel easier because it's not you being rejected."

She raised her eyebrows. "To the contrary, what it means is that even when I try to fit in, I can't do it."

He flinched.

She sat taller. "You've got a lot less experience of your work being rejected, and that's to be expected. You haven't tried to show off your paintings yet. Someone may buy one, but most likely all six of those paintings will come back home at the end of the exhibit. You need a goal, though, so let me offer one: your goal is to learn to exhibit your work. Your goal is not to be afraid of what some critic in a forgettable newspaper says about your vision, your technique, or your subject matter."

Emerson looked aside.

Brooke added, "For all that you seem to think your paintings reveal something about you, I would say this:

you have nothing to be ashamed of."

Emerson said, "All my life, people told me not to attract attention."

Brooke nodded. "Me, too. First I had to not divert attention from my brother, and then I needed to not pester my grandmother. I needed not to stand out in school because kids are jackals who'd swoop in for the kill. I've worked hard to fit in well, only to discover most people don't have to work that hard to fit in. Regardless, I think you should show yourself off. Get that attention. Stride out there and be yourself."

Emerson shuddered.

Brooke said, "It works for Lilah. She walks in and owns the place. Then she makes room for other people to join her."

Well, people other than Emerson. He pulled out his phone. "I know I said just the six paintings, but if I were to show any of the others—?"

Brooke raised her hands. "I don't have the kind of artistic sense to give good advice about what paintings you should display. You know your best work. Show that, and don't hold back."

He swallowed. "But, when we're talking about commercial appeal—"

"You've got six paintings full of commercial appeal." She picked up her burger. "Make the rest of the wall space count by displaying the best."

Brooke was just as friendly through the rest of the meal as she'd been while they were dating. At the end of dinner, as they were cleaning off the table, Emerson apologized for the way he'd let her down. She said, "You know I'm fussy and stand on ceremony. And speaking of rejection, none of us likes it. Even if I'm getting rejected nine hundred and ninety-eight times a day."

He stacked all the napkins back on the tray. "Do you consider everything well and truly over between us?"

She tilted her head. "This wasn't an attempt to get back together, was it? I have a personal rule about never dating exes."

He shook his head. "This was explicitly an attempt to talk to you about what I should do with the art show."

She raised her eyebrows. "Good. Everything is well and truly over on both sides. Thank you for being sure to prevent any misunderstanding."

He said, "And would you say we're both free to go about our lives?"

Her eyes lit up. "Have you found someone? Go for it!"

He faced her, open-mouthed. "You won't feel like I rebounded off you?"

"Why would I? If you have a chance to be happy, seize it! Life is short." Brooke grinned. "Does your crush love art? Any chance you can arrange for us to meet at the exhibit?" Her smile turned sly. "Or is this mysterious crush why you changed your mind about exhibiting...?"

Emerson raised his hands. "I changed my mind because you guys harassed me into changing it."

"Entirely in your best interests," she exclaimed. "And now you have a place to show off to your crush—the good kind of showing off. The kind where you do something amazing, and they get to be amazed."

As they walked back out to his car, Brooke rubbed her hands together. "Is it someone from your job? Someone else from the BCG? Someone Sonia set you up with? Introduce us, and I can spill all the beans about you and everything about you."

Emerson laughed. "Now that's a threat! Get in. I'll drive you home."

"Just back to the shop, if you don't mind." She buckled in and tucked her backpack between her feet. "I biked to work today, and while I could drive in tomorrow and throw the bike in the back seat, I'd rather just stick to the routine."

"Should you be biking in the dark?"

"It's dusk. It'll be fine if we go now."

He started the engine. "Well, then, the shop it is."

They headed back down Main Street. Brooke said, "You

diverted the conversation from your crush. Is it mutual? Have you told them you're available?"

Emerson's hands tightened on the wheel. "I'm going to keep that a secret for now, just in case."

"That's not even slightly fair. I asked nicely." She winked at him. "Do elbow me in the ribs if they come to the opening, that way, I can spend my time guessing who it is."

Emerson's voice ticked up. "You have to keep that a secret, too."

Brooke sighed. "Yeah, Lilah might take it hard if you find someone so quickly. She feels awful for setting us up because things didn't work out."

Emerson shook his head and glanced aside.

Brooke huffed. "The thing is, it did work out. It got you painting again, and I got to see a Renn Faire and climb a mountain and go on a camping trip. Neither of us is filled with animosity. We walked away with what I think is a decent friendship. And look—you're not even stuck trying to get over me. That looks like a success."

Emerson turned to her. "How do we prove that to Lilah?"

Brooke snorted. "I've known Lilah since fifth grade, and she may think I'm stubborn, but I *know* she's stubborn. Once she's got an idea, she takes it to the bank. That's why she's so locked into the church building."

Emerson's heart dropped.

"She'll always feel a little bad, like she wasted our time." Brooke gathered the straps of her backpack. "She's taking it harder than I expected, though. That, plus it looking like we'll lose the church, is a lot for her. So from that perspective, it's good you agreed to do the exhibit."

Emerson gathered himself as they pulled up in front of Bright Stitches. "Do you know what she did with the skeins she dyed—the experimental ones?"

"The *Pride and Prejudice* line? She's debating putting them up for order. I think she should. But it was something Sonia said that gave her the idea, so I suspect she's a bit hesitant to put it into practice. She's already got the gorgeous hair because of you. Benefitting even more by having die-hard fans would make her feel even worse."

Emerson turned back to Brooke, who hadn't spoken to him this much even on any of their dates. "You take an idea and run with it, too. But no. I mean the skeins she did to match my paintings."

Brooke's eyes widened. "I hadn't seen those! I bet they're gorgeous! Will she bring them to the exhibit? I'll need to pester her."

Why had she hidden them from Brooke? What was going on? "Don't. She wasn't happy with them."

Wasn't happy with *Emerson,* but he'd leave out that part.

The small lie stopped Brooke in her tracks. "Oh. Maybe she overdyed them. It happens. Or maybe she's just going to sell them as one-offs."

He said, "Can I come inside? I might recognize them if I saw them hanging on the stand."

She glanced overhead. "Not for long, though. I don't have my light-up gear."

She brought him under the jangling bells of the shop door, flipping on the lights as she entered. They'd positioned Lilah's display at the front, and Brooke poked through quickly. All the yarns were twisted up in hanks, not hanging free the way they'd been in the barn, but they didn't seem familiar. Emerson looked through the Brighthead Colorways, but they all looked like one another, and they weren't speckled or uneven the way he remembered the copycat skeins.

"These are all standards, not one-of-a-kinds." Brooke stepped back while Emerson fought disappointment. And confusion. And nausea. What had she done with them? Surely she wouldn't throw them away. Even if they were hateful, they were sellable stock.

Stock. Or was it artwork? Had she put her soul into those skeins the same way he put his soul into his paintings? In that way, had she made a little bit of her soul visible to Emerson?

Brooke teased, "If they'd been here, would you learn to knit?"

Emerson said, "Maybe I'd turn them into paintings, too."

"Oh, like the game you play with Google Translate, where you put in a Robert Frost poem and translate it into Romanian and then translate the Romanian back into English." Her eyes crinkled as she smiled. "I should stop by her barn and see if they're still over there."

He said, "You'd knit one up?"

She shook her head. "Some yarns look good in the skein, but they have to stay skeins or else they lose their beauty. Which is kind of a shame—all that unspent potential."

Yeah. Except losing Lilah would be more than kind of a shame. More than unspent potential. He and Lilah had a connection. Lilah had used the word "soulmate." What did that mean for her soul if they never got together? Would they always be split in two, always waiting, always incomplete?

Brooke hesitated. "Don't look sad. It's okay if the yarn stays unknit. Some things never find a way to be beautiful."

Emerson stepped forward and lowered his voice. "Stop it. You're hinting about yourself, and that's wrong."

Brooke looked way. "I'm not angry at you."

"I know you aren't, but you sound down on yourself."

She said, "You're the expert on people being down on themselves."

"I am, and I'm telling you, there's no cause. You're beautiful. We just didn't have any chemistry."

She said, "Like yarns that aren't right for the pattern. And it's okay if some skeins stay unknit." She shrugged. "One of my friends from school is like that. He's becoming a priest, so he's also like a skein of yarn that will never have a pattern, and he says that's more than fine because it's a divine calling."

As she picked up her backpack, Emerson said, "How do you know the yarn is being called to a pattern?"

"How do you know an image is right for a painting? It's by feel." She frowned as she looked off to the side. "After enough experience, I could tell how the colors will begin stacking up on themselves and whether the colorway will swamp the texture, or whether the color repeat is too long for the rounds. You'll look at a pattern and know, this needs a solid, or you'll know this will show off speckles."

As she went to wheel out her bicycle, Emerson looked at the rack of Lilah's yarns.

He had two skeins of her yarn at home, tucked into his shirt drawer. The first was the sock blank painted like the Irises, but the second was the sun-dyed skein where she'd had him sprinkle drink mix powder on the yarn and let the acid and the heat bond the color into the wool.

In a way, that's what they'd done to one another: the acid and the heat had blended them, and now they'd left an indelible mark on one another. Lilah was wrong to say "soulmates." More like soul imprints. Before he'd met her, he'd never felt incomplete. But now that he had, now he had to be with her.

The Kool-Aid colors wouldn't make a good painting, though. He stepped forward to the rack and examined her other skeins. Not the solids or the tonals. But the variegateds—some of those sparked ideas. He pulled three off the rack, then one at a time released them from their twists to dangle free in his hands.

Brooke wheeled her bicycle to the front and started buckling on her helmet. "Is it the same with art? If you look at a group of colors, do they give you an idea of what they should become?"

"They do." He turned to her. "Can I buy these? But don't tell Lilah."

Brooke glanced out the door. It had become full dark.

Emerson said, "Let me buy these, and then I'll drive you and your bike home." When she still looked uncertain, he said, "You've helped me a lot. Let me make sure you get home safely and put at least one skein back in its stash."

CHAPTER TWENTY-EIGHT

Three more variegated yarns sold last night. Lilah made a note to dye a few more of the Lake Nights colorway, but there were still plenty of the Sorrel Woods. She'd wait on those.

The hours dragged at the shop. When Brooke and Hal had split up, Brooke had said working was the best way to deal with the heartbreak, but Lilah couldn't make it click for her. When customers came, they were annoying. During times with no customers, she tried to think of what nail polishes she hadn't used lately (did she still have black?) but instead kept thinking of Emerson. Worse, sometimes she'd think about the BCG and the fight over the church. Or about how they'd strong-armed Emerson into showing work he didn't want shown.

She'd called him a coward, and here he was, fully employed in proving himself a coward. He'd hated what she said to him, but even so, he wasn't doing anything to dissuade her.

Brooke arrived at work while Sit and Stitch was still going on. She gushed appropriately about everyone's projects. Lilah had told her early on to show interest in what people were working on, and Brooke had immediately made sure to do this. Still, she wasn't just showing interest: she gushed. *Oh, that's the cutest stuffed animal! I love that lace pattern! You matched the yarn and the pattern so well.*

Fortunately, that meant Lilah didn't have to muster up emotions she didn't have available.

Annoyingly, Brooke was so blasted cheerful.

Natalie walked away from the table after helping a customer figure out a treble crochet, and she approached Brooke. "Any reason you're here early?"

"How could I stay away? Plus, I wanted to work on my own socks." She pulled out a forty-eight-inch circular needle with two half-socks dangling from the flexible cable. "I love how these are coming, and it's nice hearing the community talking."

One of the women said, "Are those for the young man you were out with last night?"

Lilah's head shot up. Brooke gave a nervous laugh. "Actually, they're for my large feet. I'm thinking boot socks."

Natalie's eyebrows were practically in orbit. "Who did you see last night?"

Uneasy, Brooke avoided looking at Lilah. "Emerson wanted to talk about the exhibit. He turned up when I was closing the shop, so we went for dinner." She forced a smile. "I should have known everyone would know everything in this tiny town."

The woman replied, "I thought he was sweet on you."

Brooke said, "He's definitely sweet, but he's only a friend. You'll have to find someone else to marry me off to."

Lilah edged toward the table. "What about the exhibit?"

Natalie said, "Please tell me he's not backing out again."

"On the contrary, he was willing to let me talk him into showing a few other pieces. Maybe. He hadn't decided." She waved them off. "There will be an exhibit, and his paintings will be in it."

Lilah said, "Then what did he want to talk to you about?"

Brooke fell silent. Natalie said, "Ooh! Is he starting things up again with you?"

Lilah's stomach churned. She wanted nothing more than to escape. It was just, to stand up and walk out now, when it was obvious Brooke didn't want to tell her what she'd done with Emerson last night, would reveal everything Lilah wanted to hide.

Brooke tried to sound breezy. "There was nothing to start back up. He had some questions."

Questions he couldn't have asked via text? Or posted to the BCG online forums?

The only reason for Emerson to have driven an hour to Brighthead—when he didn't even know for sure Brooke would be there—was to rekindle things with Brooke. Having lost his bid to get Lilah, he might as well have someone.

Natalie said, "You could have tapped me and Lilah to join you."

Brooke shook her head. "I asked. He wanted just one opinion, not three."

Any live body would do. It didn't matter which one. He had a willing partner in Brooke, and that was it. It wasn't fair.

Brooke looked at Lilah, and her face changed. "Oh, don't worry. I wouldn't have gone if I hadn't felt safe. He was a gentleman. He even drove me home."

Emerson had been willing to keep his relationship with Lilah a secret from Brooke. So—had he now conned Brooke into keeping a renewed relationship secret from Lilah?

Brooke said, "Also, we talked a bit about the church building."

One of the women snapped up her head. "You're never going to get that. They're trying to make everyone as offended as they are over at the Historical Society."

Brooke said, "It makes no sense. The building is empty."

The woman raised her hands. "You don't need to

convince me. But they're out on the street trying to terrify everyone about the scary artists planning to defile an ancient holy site."

Lilah shook her head.

"Maybe they're right," said another customer, this one a crocheter. "Maybe a church isn't the best place to be creating art."

Lilah snapped, "The Bible begins with God creating stuff. I'm going out on a limb and guessing God doesn't mind if humans create things, too."

Brooke said, "I'm beginning to think we should give up, though. I don't like feeling as if everyone's branding us as iconoclasts who want to spit in the town's face."

Natalie said, "Not to get too deep into the hyperbole, or anything."

Brooke's mouth twitched. "I hate fighting."

Lilah sighed. "There's still the court case, and there's the town planning board meeting next week. The Historical Society twisted some arms and got us on the docket."

"Which night?" Natalie said.

"Wednesday, of course. The same night the exhibit opens."

Brooke sighed. "I want to tell them to stay classy, but they'd take offense to that, too."

One of the woman laughed and then smothered it.

Lilah said, "It's okay. I'll skip the opening."

Brooke said, "No! You're Emerson's biggest cheerleader."

Natalie said, "We'll figure out something. Maybe we can delay things."

Lilah said, "He's not giving a speech, so there's no reason I have to be present when it opens. After the Historical Society flays me alive, maybe then I can put in an appearance." She took the chance to walk back to her yarn display. "It's not as if I haven't seen all the paintings before."

Brooke sing-songed, "What if he brings some new ones?"

Lilah pivoted. "Really?"

What, was Emerson hiding even deeper, slapping

together something else he could say wasn't his own work?

Brooke shrugged. "He wasn't sure what else he'd display, but when we got my bicycle, he was looked at the yarn and got inspired about color combinations."

Lilah's mouth trembled. "He said he wasn't going to paint anything else for the exhibit."

Brooke shrugged. "What can I say? He did some soul-searching, and he changed his mind about a number of things."

Changed his mind about Brooke...?

It wasn't fair. It wasn't fair that Lilah rejected Emerson in order to protect Brooke, and then Emerson boomeranged right back to Brooke, either because she was available or because maybe Emerson blamed Brooke for them not getting together. By hurting Brooke, Emerson could hurt Lilah, too.

That wasn't like him. Emerson had never been like that —but maybe he was one of those guys who was nice until the moment you said no.

Why else would Brooke be unwilling to talk about her date with Emerson, except that they'd resumed their relationship?

Lilah's heart ached, and she pulled out her phone to double-check what of her inventory needed to be replaced. Brooke had forgotten which customers bought those last few skeins, and that wasn't like her, either. After Natalie and Lilah had taught Brooke how to make small talk with customers, she'd gotten into the habit of storing whatever details she learned. "So, do you have plans for these skeins?" and then she'd remember, even weeks later. "Did you get to make that Multnomah shawl?" Was she starry-eyed and distracted in love?

Three variegated skeins had sold—to the same person? Lilah recreated the colors in her mind, and they wouldn't play nicely if they were all in the same project. Maybe a mom was making identical-but-different scarves for three of her kids?

Everything was a disaster. Lilah never should have gotten involved—except if she hadn't, Marjorie Tempest wouldn't have had her first exhibit. Lilah wouldn't have curly hair. Yes, these were little things, but maybe Lilah could scavenge a few tiny victories out of the bad.

She went back to the table. "I'm starting a new line of yarns," she blurted out before she could second-guess herself. Time to commit. "By subscription," she added as the knitters and crocheters expressed their curiosity. "Six yarns, one theme, one a month."

Brooke beamed. "These are going to be terrific. You know I want in on these."

"When can we see them?" said one of the women.

Lilah smiled. "This time? It's hidden. I'm only going to dye as many as I have subscribers."

Natalie said, "I was hoping you'd decide soon."

Lilah tried to loosen the tightness in her shoulder. "Well, I've made up my mind. Even if it's a mistake, I'm going to make it—in public."

CHAPTER TWENTY-NINE

The Historical Society members sat together toward the front of the room, but they'd strategically left empty seats so they could look like more people than they actually were.

Not that they needed to. The fact that the planning board meeting was taking place at the same time as Emerson's opening meant the BCG faction was split. Given the choice between viewing art at a French restaurant while nibbling hors d'oeuvres versus attending a boring and possibly contentious meeting, most of the artists wouldn't choose the meeting.

Even so, Lilah had Natalie at her side. She'd sent Brooke to the exhibit. This morning, she'd left the barn unlocked so Brooke could enter with Emerson to frame his paintings, then load them into the restaurant van.

"You could have the morning off," Brooke offered, but Lilah didn't want it. Didn't want to see Emerson in her space. Didn't want to witness the moment he finished divesting himself from her life. Plus, it was better to give Brooke time with Emerson, especially if they were together again.

Which hurt. But over the past ten days, with Emerson eerily silent and Brooke generally cheerful, Lilah had made peace with them getting back together. It was what she'd wanted in the first place. If Emerson never said anything to Brooke about him and Lilah kissing outrageously over at her barn—well, that just meant he considered it a mistake, best never mentioned or thought about again.

Meanwhile, Brooke had been thrilled: *He's inspired. He's painting a lot.*

That was good. Whatever inspired Emerson, it was good.

Except...it should be Lilah inspiring Emerson. In a perfect world, Lilah would have realized he belonged with her right from the start, and she should have been the one standing out by his car that first night, asking him to go hiking with her. Emerson should look at Lilah and be inspired—at Lilah sitting on the rocks, or Lilah on the town green, or Lilah's home, or Lilah's creations. When something made him smile, Lilah wanted it to be her that prompted the smile and she who smiled in return.

The planning board began their meeting, which Lilah knit through because the agenda held nothing of interest. She had a pair of socks on the needles—plain vanilla socks in a gradient she'd hand-dyed last week when her heart had been hurting and her eyes stinging and her phone silent. Gradients took a lot of time, but she loved the effect. This one started out yellow-gold and meandered through three color stages until it ended with a midnight purple.

That felt right, for now. Begin with the brilliant promise of sunrise and end with something that's very nearly the color of mourning. But at every stage, you don't realize the change until it's too late to stop the progression.

She'd dyed these intending to make a fraternal pair of socks (one yellow at the toes and ending in purple at the cuff, the other beginning in purple and ending in yellow) but then she inverted it so she'd have yellow toes on both sides. She could knit all the way up the leg to the sadness, and the brightness would be hidden beneath her shoes, that way no one would ever see the original hope.

Two socks, knit on the same needle at the same time. A good way to ensure an identical pair. Soulmates or sole-mates, who knew any longer? Warm hands, warm hearts, warm toes. A perfect fit.

Natalie set aside her crochet project to double-check the agenda. One more item until they'd open the floor for discussion items.

This had to happen. Acquiring the church building should have been a slam-dunk. Anyone who saw what Lilah saw should have wanted it to work just as much as she did. Standing in that abandoned church for the first time, Emerson had immediately grasped her vision in his hands.

Natalie sent a text, then murmured, "Things are going well at Fruits de Mer."

Lilah said, "If they could send that energy this way, I'd appreciate it."

Natalie chuckled. "Hold that thought."

Streamers of good vibes and wishes would be filling the sky like variegated strands of yarn, each one cast out from the heart of an artist or an art enthusiast who wanted a future for the BCG. Then, in a band of color, each of those sweet impulses would wind together and prove to the Historical Society that it was time to agree this was a continuation of the church's existence rather than its destruction.

Five minutes later, the final agenda item closed, and Lilah steeled herself. The chair said, "Michelle Hargrove of the Historical Society."

Michelle not only stood, but she walked to the front. "I would like to thank the town planning board for allowing me this opportunity to address you about a matter of great concern to the community. I must object to any plans to sell the Main Street Community Church building to the Brighthead Crafters Guild."

Lilah took notes as Michelle spoke. She didn't write down that Michelle was an excellent speaker, nor that she occasionally glared at Lilah and Natalie, nor that she would turn sometimes toward her cadre of Historical Society people and get them to make agreeing noises.

Natalie checked her phone again. "Keep on talking," Natalie murmured. "Not long, just until everyone dies of boredom."

Lilah leaned toward her. "I don't want them on the brink of dying right before I start speaking."

Natalie huffed. "If they die, they can't vote on anything."

Michelle glared at them, and Lilah smirked at her.

Just because the building was originally meant to be a church—the fact that it was actually used as a church—didn't mean it couldn't transform into something else. The building had a purpose, true, but it could have a second purpose. The building didn't have to collapse just because the first dream had died.

When Michelle finally ended, Natalie told Lilah, "Go first, and talk as long as you like. I'll follow afterward."

Lilah whispered, "What's up?"

"We have reinforcements coming."

Would it matter, though? More voices didn't mean the planning board would be amenable. If anything, they already looked annoyed.

Lilah raised her hand, and the chair called on her. Gathering herself, she stepped into the aisle. "Thank you," she said to the chair. "I'm Lilah Marcille. I'm an independent yarn dyer, as well as an employee at the Bright Stitches yarn shop, and I'm also the founder and current president of the Brighthead Crafters Guild, an interdisciplinary collaboration of artists committed to mutual support and networking."

When the committee members nodded, she tried not to feel defeated by their blank expressions. They'd remained blank for Michelle, too, and Lilah had experience remaining impassive from the opposite side of the desk. Now, though, it ached. The war was lost before they'd begun.

"We at the Brighthead Crafters Guild understand Ms.

Hargrove's concerns about the church building," Lilah said, making sure to use Michelle's name rather than invoke the entire Historical Society. "We've already spoken with her about how we intend to handle the situations she's worried about, and how rather than working against the building's beginnings, we as artists will be trying to enhance the founders' aims and fulfill the building's goals."

She'd practiced her speech while dyeing yarn and while loading wet yarn into the spin dryer. She'd rehearsed and refined parts of it in the car. She needed them to see— needed them to feel the way art could breathe life into an empty building. Its original congregation had abandoned it, but the artists could nurture it back into a vital force, not only for Main Street but for the town and later for the region. Lilah presented the statistics she had from the Economic Planning Board just in case the planning board needed numbers rather than visions.

When Lilah finished, Michelle stepped forward. "They're giving us promises, but those promises aren't enforceable. Once the building is theirs, they can do whatever they want inside the walls. They can defile the building and pervert its original intentions."

Lilah said, "For that matter, even if you find another church denomination to take over the building, once they have it, they can teach any doctrine they want and worship any way they see fit. Unless you propose knocking down the building, there's no way to guarantee future owners won't cross your particular vision of what that structure should be for."

Michelle said, "Artists live for shock value and drama. You may have a vision, but so does every other artist, and like you, they're going to be uncompromising."

Lilah said, "To the contrary, I have compromised with you several times through this ridiculous ordeal. From where I stand, it's the Historical Society that's being uncompromising."

Michelle said, "We have been very tolerant."

Lilah said, "No, you have been very driven to preserve the past at the expense of the future. That's not tolerance. If there's no future, then what's the point of preserving the past? Why should we know where we came from, unless it's to better understand where we're going?"

From behind her came, "Excuse me, but with the board's permission, I would like to share something."

Lilah whirled and found herself facing Emerson. Emerson, who was holding a large canvas.

Brooke stepped forward from behind Emerson. "Emerson Charles is one of the painters from the Brighthead Crafters Guild. His first exhibit opened tonight at the Fruits de Mer restaurant, but he's joining us in order to show the planning board a visual representation of what we have in mind."

Brooke and Emerson propped the canvas at the front so everyone could see, both the planning board and the audience members, and not coincidentally the camera broadcasting to the local channel.

Emerson had painted the church's interior. He'd painted it from the vantage of the choir loft as the viewer gazed on the nave. The stained-glass windows streamed with light, and their myriad colors splayed out over the floor of the church where artists worked.

Emerson had painted figures in motion—a painter to the side, a woman with a spinning wheel, and a musician with a violin beneath his chin. He'd placed paintings on the walls in various points, and three individuals standing before one in heated discussion. Toward the front stood a woman at a lectern speaking to several seated members.

In short, he'd drawn the church alive—reborn to shelter a new community with a new purpose.

This was Lilah's vision. Now everyone could see it.

Blinking hard, she fought to keep from crying. Emerson had done this? Was that an artist on the ground floor with a skein of yarn spread between her hands? And the pictures—were those Marjorie's shell mosaics? And the wooden statues from their driftwood artist? And beadwork?

Emerson stepped forward. "This is the community we are poised to form—a heart that can beat right at the center of Brighthead. The church used to serve this purpose when the church was a thriving community. It's been five years that this building stands abandoned. Brighthead deserves something living at its heart, not just an empty space where something used to be."

Lilah approached the painting. "This is Susie and her beadwork." She traced her fingers in the air over the canvas. "Marjorie and her shell mosaics. Edgar and his weaving. That's Horace's painting of Mount Washington."

Brooke said, "Emerson painted one of his own paintings into here, too. It's a recursive painting."

Emerson laughed.

Lilah waved over the planning board. "Come see this. Come up close."

Instead, Emerson carried it to them, and Lilah kept talking about the new things she found in the painting. Emerson must have worked for the entire two weeks—and here it was, her dream, brilliant and visible for everyone to see. Lilah turned to Michelle. "You come see it, too. This is what we want everyone to have."

Michelle stepped forward, but her frown didn't uncrease.

"Community. Creation. Outreach." Lilah's hands clenched. "This is what the Brighthead Crafters Guild is about."

Michelle turned to the board. "You can see they'll stop at nothing to manipulate you into letting the town give them this building."

"Sell," Lilah said. "The town is selling an abandoned building. If anyone's been manipulative, it's been you when you're misrepresenting every aspect of this transaction to anyone who will listen."

The chairman said, "Thank you, both. If you'll return to your seats...?"

Emerson left the painting at the front, but he and

Brooke joined Lilah and Natalie. Brooke nipped around to the far end with Natalie, and Lilah found Emerson sitting beside her.

He should be with Brooke, shouldn't he? She trembled at his nearness, but she wouldn't take her eyes off that painting.

The woman holding the yarn—was that herself? With the curly hair?

The chair began with, "While this item wasn't originally on the agenda, it does fall under our jurisdiction," and Lilah tried to read her mind to learn which way the wind was about to blow. The BCG needed the planning board's approval to get the town to sell the building. Of the five members, one was a friend of Michelle Hargrove, so Lilah knew how he'd vote. They needed to carry three of the four remaining members.

The friend of the Historical Society interrupted the chair. "Doesn't it make more sense for us to take a preliminary vote, rather than all five take time to speak? If we're all in agreement, we won't need to waste everyone's time."

Tension clenched Lilah's stomach, and she tightened her fists. Emerson put his hand on hers, but she pulled away.

He had no right to touch her. She had no right to take comfort in his touch.

Annoyed, the chair looked at the others. "Do the rest of you agree?"

Some mumbling, but eventually they decided to vote, so from one end of the table to the other, they began: No.

No.

No.

No.

Lilah couldn't even raise her eyes as it got back to the chair.

The chair said, "I'm sorry, Lilah, but while I think your plan has merit, I'm not going against the majority. The church has a lot of emotional meaning to the town."

Art had emotional meaning, too.

Art they'd never get a chance to see now that they'd scuttled her dream.

Emerson had his hand around hers. She couldn't bear to pull away.

The chair said, "I'm going to say no even though I would love to say yes. Mostly because I don't think the town needs a lengthy lawsuit, and the Historical Society has threatened to take both the BCG and the town to court to prevent the sale."

Cowards. They had the spine of a jellyfish and the bravery of a mole rat.

From the other side of the row, Brooke said, "If I may ask a follow-up question, what plan does the town have for the building, instead?"

The chair said, "At the moment, we have no plans."

Michelle from the Historical Society said, "I'd like to state for the record that if the Brighthead Crafters Guild attempts to purchase any other landmark building, or a building of historical significance, we'll file a motion against that, too."

Emerson turned to face her. "Thank you for going on record to say it was never about the church in the first place. It's artists you hate." He lowered his voice. "Specifically, artists who look like me."

Lilah looked over her shoulder at Michelle, who'd puckered her mouth as if she'd bitten into a head of garlic.

The chair said, "I believe this matter is ended. If anyone else has any questions, please raise your hand."

No one did. The board adjourned the meeting.

CHAPTER THIRTY

Lilah looked devastated.

Emerson could feel it, too—the sensation of freefall as the bottom dropped out of the paper cup into which she'd poured her dreams, paused in the moment between letting go and splashing down. He wrapped his arms around her, and she collapsed into his embrace with her face in his shoulder. He couldn't tell if she was crying. He couldn't tell if he was about to.

Lilah believed in the magic of his paintings, so he'd tried to pour out magic for her. He could grasp her vision in his fingers and then spread it out in the form of acrylic and pigment. He'd recalled every instance when she'd gushed her dreams for that empty church, and he'd taken those photos of that same church and invested them with her love. The vibrancy she'd held in her heart, he'd spilled it onto the canvas. He'd captured that potential energy by suspending the viewer in midair above the choir loft, gazing down on a community it would be so easy to fall into and be surrounded by forever.

How could art capture art itself in all its forms? But he'd attempted to.

Instead, he'd painted a dream that died before ever cracking its shell into the world, and Lilah huddled in his arms.

Natalie stood. "I'm going to intercept Michelle if she attempts to talk to Lilah."

Brooke joined her. "I'm in the mood for a night in the lockup, aren't you? Let's retrieve Emerson's painting and draw her away from here."

Emerson kept Lilah at his side while Natalie and Brooke secured his canvas. He glared at the chair (who wouldn't look in their direction) and willed the universe to bend in such a way that the Historical Society members could never again come near Lilah.

She'd so wanted a guild space. A shared studio. An apartment for artists-in-residence. That final shot wasn't called-for. Why shouldn't the BCG buy its own permanent space? They didn't have the money, though. They'd secured a grant to buy the church specifically because they'd be restoring an historic site. No significant site meant no money. No money meant no building. Plus, after this, who'd even rent to them, knowing the Historical Society was just as likely to file an injunction against the landlord of the 1989-era 93 South Main Street, Suite 2?

Brooke and Natalie had the painting, and Natalie was glaring daggers at someone just beyond Emerson's line of vision.

Taking Lilah's hand, Emerson helped her to a stand. "Let's get going."

Lilah pulled back. "You need to get back to the exhibit."

Emerson guided Lilah past the Historical Society members, hoping one of them tried to touch her so he could knock them back in self-defense. They all had the common sense to get out of her way. More's the pity.

In the parking lot, Emerson clicked the button for his car, and Brooke put his painting in the back seat.

Lilah whispered, "Thank you for painting that. Brooke said something inspired you, but I didn't realize that was it."

Emerson said, "You inspired me."

"Please, don't." Her voice broke. "I poison everything I touch. Go, and be happy, and be inspired, and that's enough for me to be happy, too."

Emerson said, "I made the painting for you. I felt your vision, and I wanted to embody it. I needed you to see how first and foremost, I understood you. Not just a building or a gathering space, and not just the things you want. I understood you. And I wanted you."

Lilah looked up into his eyes, and she was sad. So sad. Emerson put his hands on her shoulders and drew her forward, but instead of stepping into his arms, she stepped back.

His heart fell.

She swallowed hard. "I can't respond to the death of a dream by killing someone else's dream. I won't react to the destruction of one community by destroying a different community."

Emerson said, "Nothing's been destroyed."

She flung out her arm. "Everyone's been destroyed! Don't you see? They threatened to stop anything we try."

Emerson said, "So move the guild out of Brighthead. Move it to Hartwell. Move it to Juniper or Bar Harbor. Michelle Hargrove may be a big fish here, but ten miles away, she's not even a plankton. We're going to have our names in lights and our art on pedestals. While she's busy enshrining the past, we're forging the future. And not just art's future. Our future, too. Just say yes, Lilah."

Lilah's mouth trembled. She started to step forward, but then she stopped and looked at Brooke, still standing by Emerson's car with Natalie. Brooke, her best friend.

Her mouth contorted into a frown.

Emerson knew then the same sensation Lilah had shown in the meeting, hearing five nos one after the next after the next—the bottom dropping out of the paper cup. The liquid, en route to the pavement.

She whispered, "There's no future for us." And she walked toward her car.

Natalie and Brooke both looked at Lilah in retreat.

Emerson called, "Please come to the exhibit."

Lilah hunched her shoulders. "You know I can't."

Emerson turned to Brooke, "Go with her."

Brooke sprinted across the parking lot.

That was final. Even when everything was clear—even when Emerson had proven he wasn't a coward—Lilah wouldn't get past her own reservations.

She'd never been his. Even though it was perfect—even though she thought them soulmates—that didn't matter to her. The only things that mattered were her pre-existing visions of how the world ought to work. She wanted the BCG in the old church. She wanted Brooke and Emerson together, even if they didn't want to be with each other. She wanted a champion and a defender—or rather, a defender who wasn't Emerson.

At least he'd tried. At least he'd shown her how much effort he could put in and how he was unafraid to do it in public. Lilah, who claimed she could see his heart through the acrylic and varnish, somehow couldn't see how despite everything, he still loved her.

Natalie called, "I'll see you at the restaurant." Then she walked over to Emerson. "What are you going to do now?"

Emerson said, "What else is there? I'm going back to my work."

CHAPTER THIRTY-ONE

Brooke caught up to Lilah at her car. Lilah said, "You need to go back with Emerson or Natalie."

"I need to be with you." She went to the passenger side. "My car is back at Fruits de Mer, so you need to drive me there."

Lilah called, "Nat? Brooke needs a ride!"

Brooke followed that up with, "And Lilah's going to give it to me!"

"Fine." Lilah unlocked the car. "I'm not getting out. I'll drop you off and go home."

Brooke buckled herself into the passenger seat. "Absolutely not. Yes, we just got trounced by the myopic planning board, but there's a beautiful victory waiting for you in our fine French restaurant, and you deserve to see it."

Lilah huffed.

"Wasn't that painting amazing?"

A shiver went through Lilah. "I couldn't believe it."

Brooke chuckled. "He didn't even want to show it to me, but I made him send me pictures of some parts. The woman holding the yarn is you. I know you didn't get a lot of time to look, but it's definitely you."

Lilah's brow contracted. "Why would he do that?"

"Because dreams require a dreamer. Even I know that." Brooke shook her head. "We'll get your dream off the ground. There are other buildings, even if the Historical Society people have sawdust where their brains ought to be."

Lilah pulled out of the lot. "They've apparently declared their souls to be a historical site with the state, and therefore no improvements can be made without submitting them to a committee."

Brooke said, "Their committee has a hundred-year backlog, so if your ideas aren't historical when you start, they will be by the time they make the decision."

Lilah sputtered a laugh, and it sounded bitter. "Also, could we find some kind of historical flagpole so we can insert it where the planning board committee members spines should be?"

Brooke said, "I'm going to introduce a measure at the annual Town Meeting to have them renamed the Invertebrate Board."

Now Lilah did laugh without bitterness. Brooke's voice flattened out further. "The weathervane on top of your barn has more conviction than they did. *Sorry, Lilah, but even though we know you're right, we don't want Michelle making a frowny face.*"

"Right?" Lilah slammed a fist against the dashboard. "Why does no one see this? You don't compromise everything you believe in just because it's difficult. Otherwise it's a whim, not a conviction."

Brooke said, "That one guy was clearly Michelle's friend."

"Does she have friends? Or does she have sycophants?" Lilah huffed. "People like that wouldn't know friendship if it hit them in the face. Friendship demands sacrifice. It also requires you to stand up to your friend when your friend is acting like a bonehead. Did they do that? No. They flattened like a house of cards."

Brooke sighed. "My plan is this: we'll sulk about it tonight and make a lot of nasty remarks at the Historical Society's expense. Then, tomorrow, we'll start looking for another way to have our studio space and our artist-in-residency program."

Lilah muttered, "Which Michelle will then attempt to scuttle."

"Now that we know we have a nemesis, we'll play it smarter." Brooke shrugged. "Look, if nothing else, Michelle's about thirty years older than us. She's going to die eventually."

Lilah spit out a laugh she hadn't expected. "Brooke!"

"Do you think her ghost will haunt the hallways of our new studio space?" Brooke tried to hide her grin by looking out the window, but she didn't quite succeed. "Think of how many artists will apply to work with us once they hear they get to stay in a haunted workspace. Good grief, we'll be fighting them off with a stick."

Lilah said, "The next time there's a knot in the yarn, don't get mad—just assume it's the ghost."

"Emerson might not want to paint with a ghost looking over his shoulder, but he doesn't need to be our artist-in-residence."

Again the bitter taste returned. "Unless he marries you and you're both in residence."

Brooke huffed. "Please leave that alone. He's not going to marry me."

Lilah said, "You inspired that painting. You said yourself, he was truly inspired after you went out to dinner with him again."

Brooke shook her head. "Not me! He has a crush on someone else, but he won't say who."

Lilah stiffened. "What?"

"I know, right? I kept teasing him, but it's a state secret. I'm not even supposed to be telling you, but maybe you can figure it out. All week, I've been hoping his beloved would show up tonight to the exhibit, but then—" Brooke stopped abruptly. "Why didn't you go out with him?"

Lilah went cold. "Did he say that?"

"I've wondered that from the start. You set him up with me because you pitied me after the unceremonious loss of Hal, but I didn't get why you didn't try to get with him yourself."

Lilah furrowed her brow. "I don't pity you."

"Oh, please. You've been looking out for me since I was ten years old and didn't know anyone in the entire town of Brighthead. I know when you get all, *Oh Poor Brooke,* but this one has me puzzled."

Lilah blinked hard. "Don't do this to me. You're my friend because I like you, and I thought you liked me. If you think I'm your friend as an act of philanthropy, then that means you're only my friend because you think you can't do better."

Brooke huffed. "We're actual real friends, but the friendship started because you felt sorry for the new girl sitting alone at the lunch table. Then you fixed me up with Emerson, and it was nice. But it was only nice, not electrifying. I think over time, he'll become just as good a friend as you are, but that's all we're supposed to be. He's a good listener, and I think he's smart, but it's not a match."

Lilah ventured, "If he has a crush on someone, you're not upset?"

Brooke shrugged. "If anything, I'm happy for him. Whoever it is kickstarted him into doing three new paintings. And—"

She cut herself off.

As Fruits de Mer came into view, Lilah could hear Brooke's brain click all the puzzle pieces into place. Lilah slowed to pull into the lot, and Brooke said, "It's you. Emerson is crushing on you."

Brooke's voice ticked up. That was genuine excitement. "Lilah, you have to go in there! You have to see the new paintings—and then you have to go to him and thank him, and see if it really is you."

"No! Brooke, no!" Lilah pulled into the first spot she

could, even though it was far from the entrance. She wasn't even between the lines. "I can't!"

"But you think he's amazing—I mean, I think he's amazing, too, but you're even more excited about him! He's an artist, and he gets you and the way you think in color! Your interests and his dovetail so well. His sister even likes you!" Brooke turned to her, light in her eyes. "I bet it's you he's gushing about!"

Lilah shut off the engine and the headlights. "I know he's gushing about me. That's why I can't go in!"

Brooke recoiled. "Why?"

"Because I'm never going to hurt you. If I steal your boyfriend, how can I call myself your friend?"

Brooke opened her hands. "Do I have a boyfriend? No. Ergo, you cannot steal him. March yourself in there and look at Emerson's paintings, and take his hand, and kiss him. See what happens."

Lilah faced Brooke. "He *was* your boyfriend. I can't take him. Your happiness means more to me because you're my friend."

Brooke shot back, "And I'm *your* friend. That means I want you to be happy."

Lilah clenched her hands. "It's not right. The plan was for you and him to be together."

"Yes, and the plan was for the Main Street Church to have worship services every Sunday for the next thousand years. Did that happen? No. And should everyone now pivot to deal with the new reality and take the very amazing chance we're offering to breathe life back into a town monument? Yes. But are they? No. Yet you're not celebrating *their* stubborn adherence to plan."

Lilah's mouth trembled.

"Neither will I admire your stubborn adherence to plan." Brooke unbuckled her seat belt. "You just said friends are supposed to speak up if you're being boneheaded, and you're being boneheaded. You're my friend, but you're forgetting I'm your friend, too. I appreciate that you don't want to hurt my feelings. Nothing you could possibly do right now would hurt my feelings *except* if you make both yourself and Emerson miserable on my account, as if I'm a fragile eggshell that needs to be encased in cotton." She looked Lilah in the eye. "I'm not telling you what to do, but you're doing yourself and Emerson a disservice if you don't come inside and see the exhibit."

Brooke slammed the car door, and she stalked across the lot to the restaurant without looking back.

Emerson's car pulled in, followed by Natalie's. Lilah sat in her seat, lights out and eyes watering. Emerson glanced around the lot, but she was parked far enough back that he didn't see her. Even so, she stayed totally still, just in case her movement drew his attention.

Brooke was straightforward. If she said that, she meant it.

The BCG was suffering because someone else wouldn't let go of the past. And here was Lilah, mummified in a past idea.

Emerson paused until Natalie joined him, and they both went inside. Lilah sat in the parking lot, alone.

Buildings can change. Lilah had pinned her hopes on that.

Painting styles can change. Emerson had shown her that.

Relationships can change. Brooke had shown her that.

Could ideas change? That had to be Lilah's call, and now was the time to make it.

Muffled sound permeated the exterior of Fruits de Mer as Lilah approached, and she edged open the door to a simultaneous increase in volume. Inside were lights and noise and motion, and she stepped to the side because grand entrances shouldn't follow a grand failure.

A decent crowd had turned up. The white-and-black-clad

servers of Fruits de Mer were canvassing the lobby plus half the dining area with trays of nibbles. Turning down an offer of hors d'oeuvres, Lilah scanned the room looking for Emerson.

He had crossed the dining area to Brooke. Natalie had gone with him. One of the BCG members (a quilter) seized Lilah by the arm and gushed about how lovely everything was, but Lilah didn't do more than smile and nod. The quilter guided her to the first of the paintings.

This was the Myth Brightman statue, and it matched the light and ambiance. Emerson had selected a frame that went with the wall, carpet, and furniture colors. Lilah had guessed right about the commercial aspect, but she'd missed that the restaurant already had a vibrant personality. Emerson hadn't.

Next she found a painting of the town green, and her heart twinged when she saw the corner of the church in the background. Nothing for that, though.

The quilter was chattering while Lilah craved silence, but silence wasn't going to happen. Not here, not tonight. The quilter asked what had gone down at the meeting, and Lilah only said, "We lost. I don't want to talk about it."

She moved to the next painting, and her heart stalled out.

This painting didn't coordinate to the walls. She'd never seen it before, and yet she saw it every day—her kitchen window, alive with her salvaged plants, the thriving field behind, her handknit dish towel thrown over the faucet, a light catcher dangling in the sun. She looked at the placard alongside, and the title was, "Life," and beneath that, "Not for sale."

She blinked hard. When had he done this? Why hadn't he said anything?

The quilter said, "I can't believe they turned us down. They're not getting another buyer."

Ignoring her, Lilah moved to the next painting, which was just Brighthead Harbor—but there on the rocks sat the two figures Brooke had immediately picked up as herself and Lilah. Then, the next one.

Three smaller paintings all inhabited the same wall space. Alongside each was a loose skein of Lilah's hand-dyed yarn.

She touched the yarn. This was the Sorrel Woods colorway. This— All three were the colorways sold the night Emerson and Brooke had gone out to dinner, the night Emerson had confessed to Brooke that there was someone special. This was one of the things Brooke had kept a secret.

Emerson had designed each painting with the canvas lengthwise, and her skeins were arranged so the colors of the yarn and the colors on the canvas were a pair with one another, the same way she'd made yarns that mimicked Emerson's paintings. He'd reversed the process, and he'd found a picture—no, an entire story—in three of her loosened skeins.

He'd called the series "Invitations," and the paintings each had a caption beneath. The first painting worked with the Sorrel Woods colorway, and had an Impressionist feel, but Lilah thought it was her, her hair wild in the wind, her head tilted. The second panel was the Lake Nights colorway, and here Lilah followed the dreamer to a lake at night. Maybe not Emerson's most inspired leap of creativity, but it was amazing. It was the lake they'd visited, their campsite laid out before them, the moon half-covered by clouds.

He'd based the third painting on the Emerald Mist colorway, which was mostly green and grey. He'd turned that into an image of her barn with Brooke's bicycle leaning against the rolled-open door, and the forest making up the green in the background.

Her hands tightened. Her question to him had been where he was in these paintings, and why he was hiding himself. She could see it now. He was in her position, standing as the viewer. She was in the place of the painter, seeing her life, seeing herself and the moments when he'd interacted with her, only now she could observe her world from a distance. She saw him being part of it but wanting to be invited closer.

Like the plants, straining toward the sun and growing because that was what life demanded. Like her, laughing and inviting him closer. Like her barn door, open and waiting for him to enter her life.

This was where he was in his paintings. This was his heart, here on display for everyone who cared to imagine it.

She felt eyes on her, and in the next second, Austin said, "Natalie told me what they did. I was afraid you wouldn't show up."

Fighting a frown, Lilah nodded.

"I'm sorry." Austin called over one of the servers. "Food doesn't fix everything, but it's the only thing I have."

Lilah took a smoked salmon and cream cheese crostata just to keep Austin happy. "You set this up nice."

"I'm glad you convinced him to go through with it. He called last week to ask how many paintings he could bring after all, so I was scrambling between lunch and dinner with a tape measure trying to get all the walls." He laughed. "He gave me a number and then called back and told me to make room for three more, but they're small, and—" Austin shook his head. "What can I say? I'm used to demands to add three people to a reservation, so I made it work."

"You did a great job." She shifted her weight. "Thank you. You've done a lot for the BCG."

Austin said, "I just wish the Historical Society were here because there's a lot more I wish I could do."

Lilah grabbed his arm before he could walk away. "You've been talking to Brooke. Does she seem okay to you? Like, when she's with Emerson, is she all right?"

Austin nodded. "She's fine with him. Natalie was worried how they'd get along, but Brooke's completely relaxed. I'd never have realized they had a history."

Brooke might pretend in front of Lilah, but she'd see no reason to pretend in front of Austin.

Austin said, "They're right over there if you want to talk to them."

"I'm going to stay a few more minutes and then sneak out." Lilah sighed. "It's been a long day."

"Gotcha." Austin nodded. "Thank you for putting in an appearance."

She moved to the next painting.

He and Brooke must have spent the whole afternoon assembling frames in the barn before bringing them here. That must have cost a mint, too. A few of these paintings had better sell, otherwise he'd be in the hole for it all.

This was too much. The pressure, the loss, the revelations. Brooke's anger. Emerson's earnestness. It was so much to process, and the only person Lilah could maybe talk about it with was Natalie, who'd be with Emerson. Natalie knew all the players. Natalie would have a good perspective.

Lilah decided to slip out the door, but then a beader intercepted her to express outrage about the Historical Society. Lilah had nearly escaped her when the first quilter returned and had a number of unattractive things to say about Michelle.

A third person (a wood burner) joined with his own tales about the Historical Society. "Two years from now, the town can try to collect rent from the rats that moved in when no one else was allowed to." He laughed. "Do they think some other five-hundred-year-old denomination is going to have a resurgence in Brighthead?"

"Maybe a convent will move in," said the quilter, "except Michelle won't want them either because their nuns wear brown habits instead of black ones."

The beader added, "And, *oh my stars,* what if they ring the church bells?" She laid a hand over her heart. "No, don't take down the bells. But don't ring them, either! It will destroy the character of the neighborhood."

Lilah said, "What if you half-ring them, enough to keep them functional but not enough to disturb Michelle while she's meditating on their historical significance?" and the other three laughed.

The wood burner said, "Just for that, we're going to find somewhere else to build."

"I've got a tent," said the quilter. "I'll pull a permit so we can set up on the town green."

Maybe it wasn't so bad to be among friends tonight. The BCG members weren't blaming Lilah after all. They also weren't saying what Emerson had, that it had been a failed venture from the start. Instead it was just right: her and friends and a common goal. For tonight, a common enemy. Then, tomorrow, they could look for another place to grow.

Lilah glanced over her shoulder to see if Natalie was still with Emerson—and she wasn't. Good. Emerson was... across the dining area with his family. Sonia still had her amazing ombre hair, so that was good, and she was laughing with a tiny, trim woman who might be Emerson's boss. Again, good. With Emerson occupied, Lilah headed toward Natalie.

Natalie's eyes lit up, and she rushed over. "Isn't it amazing what Emerson did with your yarn? He said you inspired him first by making colorways based on his paintings, so I want to see those, too."

Lilah said, "I need to—" but then from behind, Austin started talking into the mic.

"Everyone, I want to thank you again for being here tonight."

Lilah turned toward Austin at the hostess stand, and alongside him stood Emerson. She stepped backward, but Natalie stopped her with a hand on her arm. She whispered, "I thought not giving a speech was one of his criteria."

Lilah's mouth went dry. "I suspect every one of his criteria has changed."

Natalie chuckled. "Well, yes, considering there are a lot more than six paintings."

Austin gave a couple of unremarkable remarks crafted to pave the way for Emerson to make more memorable ones, and then Emerson took the mic.

He began, "As Austin said, thank you all attending my first exhibit," then had to pause while the audience clapped. "I've been more unnerved than I should have been. You've all been supportive and constructive."

He looked across the room and set eyes on Lilah, and then he smiled. At Lilah's side, Natalie's hand tightened on Lilah's arm.

"Above all, I need to thank the original founders of the Brighthead Crafters Guild, all three of whom collaborated with me specially to make tonight happen. Natalie Prescott, Brooke Evart, and Lilah Marcille."

More applause, and people turned toward them. Lilah waved, hoping she'd hidden the tremble that ricocheted through her.

Emerson said, "I didn't want to show off my artwork for any number of reasons. I've always attracted unwanted attention, so I learned to disappear from public view. Putting my artwork out there for anyone else required a leap of faith, only I had no faith in myself."

Brooke slipped up alongside Lilah and Natalie. "Glad you came inside," she breathed into Lilah's ear.

Emerson still had his eyes on the women. "Fortunately, our trio of founders had faith in me, and they let me lean on theirs. They opened their hearts and in some cases their homes, and they helped me get back in touch with my own art. They reintroduced me to nature and to storytelling, and they showed me how art comes in many forms. It comes in the way we nurture one another, and by doing that, we nurture one another's talents. Even little bits of life, like the top of an onion, begin to grow under that nurturing."

Lilah's breath quickened.

Emerson said, "While I was afraid even to inhabit my own world, Lilah was stepping out and trying to bring our guild to an even greater part of the world. I wanted to hide in the shadows, but she wanted a prominent place on Main Street. I wanted to keep my work hidden, and she wanted to display our group's work front and center. Then it looked like my first instinct was right, because Lilah did get attention. She got bad attention from people who couldn't break out of their mold and understand that growth is good, and change is necessary. Ultimately we lost that fight, but in watching her fight, I realized hers is the better way—the braver way. Lilah isn't afraid to show the world who she is or what she believes."

He paused to let the others applaud again. Lilah smiled at him.

He met her eyes, and then he smiled back.

He said, "Lilah, will you join me?"

Brooke nudged her, but she was already moving, crossing the dining room toward the hostess stand at the lobby. Austin sidled out of her way, and Emerson stood next to her at the mic, facing her.

She met his eyes, and despite it all, he was still welcoming. Still waiting for her. Still standing here, ready to be her everything.

And now, she could be his. There was nothing in their way. Their misunderstandings, their expectations and hurt feelings—all those faded as she stood before him, her soul trembling in his presence.

Emerson took her hand. "What the BCG did for me that I didn't understand was it created both a community and a safety net. Lilah understood from the start that artists thrive when we have one another. She tried to plug me into the community when I thought I wouldn't fit. She eased the way for me to make new friends, and by doing that, she gave me the opportunity to see through new people's eyes. Over and over again, I've seen her doing this with other artists—identifying their best and brightest potential and then encouraging them to reach it. In the end, that's what these exhibits are for. Not just for exposure and potential sales and good food—which really is good," Emerson added sidewise to Austin, who opened his hands with a grin. "Lilah arranged all this so we can thrive, and I wouldn't be here today without her help."

Emerson drew Lilah closer to the mic. "This evening would not have been possible without Lilah. Lilah gave me space in her barn to paint, and she gave me the benefit of the doubt when she had no reason to. Lilah gave me access to her friends and access to her creativity." He turned to her. "Lilah, please, do me the honor of giving me your heart."

She stepped into his arms, and he kissed her.

There were general awws, and a few people clapped. Emerson kept his arm around her shoulders. Natalie looked shocked, but Brooke was giving them a double thumbs-up.

Emerson kept his arm around Lilah's shoulder. "Thank you for being here with me tonight," he said. "Thank you for the beginning of my new artistic family."

CHAPTER THIRTY-TWO

"Knock knock!" Emerson called from the barn door. "Is it safe?"

Lilah didn't look away from the water she was pouring into a squeeze bottle. That plus the goggles and the respirator mask were all the clues Emerson needed as to the relative safety of crossing the room and giving her a kiss.

He'd risk death for Lilah if he had to—but he didn't have to.

Still, he had news, and now the news had to wait.

Lilah kept adding and stirring, and the blue in the bottle started diluting. At the end, she added the final bit of water and swirled it to make sure all the dye powder had dissolved.

She looked over at him. "I've got two more to do. Is that okay?"

The respirator muffled her voice. Emerson gave her a thumbs-up.

"I can hear you just fine." She snickered. "It's speaking that's a problem."

While she resumed mixing, (a purple) Emerson examined

the painting he'd left on Lilah's easel last weekend. On a smaller canvas, he'd begun painting the interior of the yarn shop—skeins and shelves together, plus a pair of knitting needles crossed on a wooden table.

This was less a commercial painting than something he'd felt catch his heart the last time he'd stood in Bright Stitches. Among the color combinations, Emerson had become hyper-aware of all the possibilities inherent in the yarns: the solids, the tonals, the variegateds. The stripes. The hand-painteds. The gradients. He could combine all those possibilities with the different yarn weights and the different fiber types. He could factor in the different crafts one could use to work up any yarn. And then he could add in all the possible intended finished objects.

From the doorway of Bright Stitches, Emerson had beheld infinity. No wonder Lilah had first conceived the BCG in that universe of color. With everything possible, she'd grasped the impossible and decided to render it in real life.

With everything possible, Emerson wanted to explore it all with Lilah. Meanwhile, here she was, creating the building blocks for more infinite possibilities.

Lilah saw nothing but potential. Now she was seeing potential with him.

Emerson got back to work on his Bright Stitches painting, struggling to create the feeling of a high-twist laceweight skein (another of the infinite factors: how high a twist in the yarn, and if it had a corona). Outside the open barn door, a wren landed on the dirt, poked at the base of a weed, then darted off again.

Fingertips rested on Emerson's shoulders, followed by hands, followed by a massage of his muscles. He sighed, letting out the tension. Lilah waited until he'd set down his brush to kiss his neck. Shivers ran through him.

"Your painting inspired me to dye more yarn." She sounded amused. "It's recursive inspiration, since the yarn inspired you to make the painting."

He swiveled his chair to face her. She half-sat across his

lap (a swivel stool wasn't the best place to try balancing them both, they'd discovered) and he kissed her for real, soft and slow.

With her forearms on his shoulders, she fingered the edges of his locs. "You said you had news?"

"Sonia has a job."

Lilah's eyes lit up. "Awesome! What'd she get?"

"A flower shop just opened two extra branches, and now that they're a chain, they need a better system than the owner stuffing receipts into a manila folder before cutting the employees personal checks every Friday." When Lilah shuddered, Emerson shook his head. "My sister was never the floral type, but she says you don't need to know a thing about flowers to know what they cost—and better yet, she says with all those flowers hanging around, she's not the most eye-catching thing in any of the shops. She'll take over their accounting, plus she's also going to manage things like their delivery service."

"Savage!" Lilah hugged him. "I'm so glad she branched out into other kinds of applications!"

"She's over the moon. She said thank you for the encouragement, and for giving her a break to stay here for a week."

Lilah shook her head so her curls bounced out. "Thank her for my hair, then. That's what collaborations are for."

Emerson said, "For trading favors?"

Lilah traced her fingers over his neck, and warmth shot through him. "For putting people together."

She looked closer at the painting, and he swiveled the seat so he faced it, too. "I love what you did with the ball winder and the swift. And—" She hesitated. "You made the yarn hank look like an infinity sign."

Emerson smiled. "I did."

"Eternity, cast in yarn. Or is it cast in acrylic paint?"

He reached up to her arms around his chest and squeezed her closer to him while she rested her chin on his shoulder. "How about a forever full of both?"

"Inspiration and colors and yarn. I like it." She tilted her head against his. "That's the real purpose of art. To show us truth. To reveal potential. To enable us to touch eternity."

She leaned around to kiss him, and when her lips met his, he knew: this was art. This was the way to touch eternity.

Epilogue: Brooke

Brooke and Lilah both looked up with a smile when Emerson came through the Bright Stitches doorway, but Brooke stayed at the table while Lilah darted across the shop to hug him.

They were so cute together. Brooke loved Lilah, and finding out Lilah wanted to cut off her own happiness at the knees...? Fortunately for them all, Lilah had come to her senses without Brooke having to shake her. Emerson had never looked this delighted, and Lilah spent her days emitting a tangible cloud of happiness pheromones.

Emerson kissed Lilah. "Did you hear from Austin? Another painting sold!"

Lilah cheered, and Brooke applauded for him. "I'm waiting to hear again how correct we were...?" Brooke teased, at which Lilah rolled her eyes and Emerson nodded.

"You were very correct."

Brooke chuckled as she returned to her knitting chart. This motif wasn't behaving. She'd wanted for a while to set up a pattern of a leafy vine against a mesh background, but it wasn't working the way it did when superimposed over reverse stockinette. How irritating.

She mocked up what the next row ought to look like, then knitted it (one correction already halfway through the first pass—that didn't bode well) and then she looked at the result. Nope. She tinked back the whole row, then erased the markings on the graph paper and tried again.

And again, it didn't work. She might have to rip this back to the beginning of the chart just to make it behave. Sometimes patterns were like that: set it up wrong, and you couldn't recover afterward. What she was looking to do might not even be possible.

"Hello? Brooke?"

Brooke looked up to find Lilah in front of her, backpack on her shoulder, Emerson at her side. "I know you're in the Charting Zone, but Emerson and I are leaving."

Oh. Brooke looked around, but no one else was in the shop. "Thanks. I'll try not to get lost in the charts again."

Three to four o'clock was a relative dead hour, so Brooke would have sixty minutes to develop her pattern. Natalie got a steady trickle of customers in the mornings, but Brooke had her influx between five and seven, when yarnies got out of work and needed to nip in for a replacement needle or just a little fiber love.

In the meantime, Brooke cleaned up after the day's Sit and Stitch, reloaded the coffee machine for tomorrow's customers, opened the boxes dumped by the UPS guy, and all the while kept mentally correcting her errant shawl pattern.

The Bright Stitches door jingled open. Brooke turned with a smile to greet the customer, only to gasp when it was Jonathan Levesque.

"Hey!" He was back from seminary already? She rushed across the store. "I didn't realize you were in town for the summer."

Even as the words gushed from her, she realized they were all wrong. Jonathan didn't look like a man pleased to be home, or even pleased to be setting foot in the store. He averted his eyes, and Brooke stopped just short of standing in front of him. "So, um..." What was the right greeting for someone unhappy to be here? "How are you doing?"

"Fine. It's good to be back." He didn't sound convinced of his own words. "My mother said you guys were selling local crafts. She suggested I show you what I've been making."

At the Sit and Stitch table, Jonathan pulled a hand-turned wooden bowl from his backpack. "Oh!" Brooke cradled it in her palms, a smile emerging unbidden. "I love it!" She carried it to the Crafters Guild display. "This would work beautifully in our craft area, and if you have a bunch to sell, I'll put out the word with the rest of the guild so they can sell your bowls, too."

Even so, he still looked...? Looked like what?

During high school, Lilah had helped Brooke create a labelled graph of fifty different facial expressions to study. This wasn't angry. Not even unhappy. Resigned, maybe?

Jonathan shoved his hands in his pockets. "They can't be used for food because of the finish, but they're good for decoration."

"Absolutely! If you have a few, I'll write you up a consignment form, and we'll get them out on the shelves." She grabbed the paperwork from the register. "How long do you plan to be in town?"

Silence stretched long and broad between them, and Jonathan shifted his weight. "I'm not certain."

Back when Jonathan had entered seminary, a bunch of friends had thrown him a fun sendoff—in effect, a "bachelor party" for a pre-priest. They'd taken over the function area at the back of Sparrows and hung out eating and talking and playing board games until the manager got annoyed. Brooke had joined Jonathan in a game that involved all the landmarks of the United States.

"Where do you think you'll end up?" one of the guys had asked.

Jonathan had replied, "I have no control over that. The bishop sends priests wherever he thinks they're needed."

The guy had replied, "You mean you could get a message that on Tuesday, you're needed in Milford, and Monday night you've got to pack?"

Nodding, Jonathan said, "I'm told that's the hardest part of the priesthood."

"Even harder than celibacy?" the guy exclaimed, and there'd been more good-natured ribbing.

As uneasy as Jonathan seemed right now, the bishop must be deciding where he'd be assigned. The last year of formation was supposed to involve serving as a deacon at a large parish. Any day, Jonathan might be getting the call: *Pack your bags; you're going to Guilford.*

Looking at Jonathan's defeated stance, Brooke said,

"I'm sorry."

Jonathan's head raised. "Sorry about what?"

"The uncertainty. You said the bishop sending you anywhere was the hardest part." She handed him the form. "Since you don't know how long you'll be here, when your bowls sell, I can send the check to your mother, or we could arrange for an electronic payment."

Jonathan's eyes were wide. "It's actually different than that. I'm not certain how long I'll be here—because I'm not going back."

Brooke's mouth went dry. "You're not?"

He shook his head. "It's a long story, but I'm not going back to seminary. I've got a job now doing carpentry, and I'm talking to Father Tim about maybe taking over the youth group or religious education, but yeah. Until I figure things out, I'm in Brighthead. So if anyone actually wanted to buy something made by me, you could just hand me the cash."

Brooke's stomach was so tight she felt nauseated. "I don't understand. The priesthood was your dream ever since I met you."

Again, an emotion ghosted through Jonathan's eyes, but he turned aside. "You don't need to tell me."

"Sorry." Brooke picked up the wood-turned bowl again and ran her fingers over the rough edges where the bark remained. "How much do you want to charge?"

"I have no idea." He pursed his lips. "I don't want to price myself out of the market, but they take time to make."

"Spoken like a true crafter. Let me test a price point, and if they're not moving, I'll see about lowering it." A smile teased at her lips. "Not for the people who ask for a discount. The key is to suss out the ones who are close to buying and then see if a discount convinces them. We'll get these sold." She flipped over the bowl. "You need to wood-burn your name and the date onto the bottom."

Jonathan didn't look up from his form. "As if anyone cares."

"Begin as you mean to go on." Brooke immediately

kicked herself for that because Jonathan had begun with a purpose and now wasn't going on with it. "It's better to have your name on your work." She handed him a black sharpie. "At least sign and date these."

He signed all three bowls, looking robotic. She said, "You should be proud. They're beautiful."

He half-rolled his eyes. She added, "Why'd you change your mind?"

He still wouldn't look at her directly. "I didn't change my mind. And no, they didn't kick me out. It just wasn't right, and now I'm here." He looked up again, his mouth tight. "Thank you for selling these. It's not the money. My mother's getting tired of my bowls filling the garage, and we ran out of relatives to foist them on."

Brooke laughed, and for the first time, Jonathan smiled.

At least he hadn't lost his ability to smile. "Welcome to the world of hand crafts: eventually, you have to do something with the things you create." She set his bowls on the craft display, and he came up behind her.

"You think they belong there?" He sounded uncertain.

"Absolutely." She laid a hand on his arm. "They're as well-made as anything else in the display. Can't you see that?"

Jonathan sighed. "I'm not sure of anything anymore."

Brooke hugged him. "It sounds like you're going through a lot, but if you can't be sure of yourself, then let me be sure for you. This is where they belong, and for the time being, Brighthead is where you belong, too."

THANK YOU!

Thank you so much for reading about Emerson and Lilah! I hope you enjoyed the ride.

I'd like to say thank you to several people who helped with this book. All my early readers, Charity Horinek my editor, and Once Upon a Cover for designing a fabulous cover.

I grew up in a family of painters, so I was constantly surrounded by oil paintings in various stages of creation, a living room half-covered in plastic sheeting, and the smell of turpentine. (I'm sure that's totally healthy.) My stepfather painted, his mother painted, and later on, his son painted. Emerson's paintings (and even his style) aren't based on any of theirs.

I want to thank Rebecca Brown from Chemknits for putting together a whole video series about yarn dyeing. I watched everything I could, and her series was invaluable.

Please join me for Maddie Mondays, where you'll hear more about the backgrounds of these stories, as well as a little bit about my weird life. For example, if you're already there, you might remember my version of Natalie's overnight shawl. I also recommend books I've enjoyed, sales, and interesting craft projects. You can sign up for that here: https://stats.sender.net/forms/erBXBe/view

Don't worry about Brooke. She gets her story next, and that's the one I'm most excited about.

Up Next!

Brooke! She's such an interesting character. She's deeply perceptive but also misses so many things that are obvious to everyone else. She's ruthlessly competent and at the same time doubts herself. She's self-critical but radically accepting of everybody else.

And of course, she's about to end up in a situation where all of that is going to come to bear. Please join us for the final story in our yarn shop trilogy, **Love by Design**.

Love doesn't come with an instruction manual.

Brooke never fits in. Relationships are confusing, and there aren't mathematical theorems for relating to people. Instead, solo, she spends her days designing knitwear patterns and selling yarn, as well as volunteering with the still-homeless Brighthead Crafters Guild.

Brooke's childhood friend, Jonathan Levesque, has slunk back to Brighthead in defeat. He's longed to be a Catholic priest for as long as Brooke's known him, but instead he "discerned out" of seminary. Even worse, his amazing great aunt has tried to sabotage his priesthood by leaving him her home in her will—under the condition that he gets married.

A furious Jonathan has the solution: marry Brooke on paper, then divorce and give her the house. She can donate it to the Crafters Guild, and the guild will finally have its headquarters.

These terms are clear, and finally Brooke has a place she fits. At least, it works until Jonathan starts stepping outside the carefully-planned limits, and once again, Brooke finds herself creating her life without a pattern.

Love by Design is available in paperback and for Kindle. Pick up your copy today to complete the series!